BROTHER

A Novel

ANIA AHLBORN

G
Gallery Books
New York   London   Toronto   Sydney   New Delhi

G

Gallery Books
An Imprint of Simon & Schuster, Inc.
1230 Avenue of the Americas
New York, NY 10020

First Gallery Books trade paperback edition September 2015

GALLERY BOOKS and colophon are registered trademarks of Simon & Schuster, Inc.

For information about special discounts for bulk purchases, please contact Simon & Schuster Special Sales at 1-866-506-1949 or business@simonandschuster.com.

The Simon & Schuster Speakers Bureau can bring authors to your live event. For more information or to book an event contact the Simon & Schuster Speakers Bureau at 1-866-248-3049 or visit our website at www.simonspeakers.com.

Interior design by Robert E. Ettlin
Cover design by Anna Dorfman
Cover photograph © Hans-Peter Merten/Stockbyte/Getty Images

Manufactured in the United States of America

19 20   18

Library of Congress Cataloging-in-Publication Data is available.

ISBN 978-1-4767-8373-4
ISBN 978-1-4767-8378-9 (ebook)

Children begin by loving their parents; as they grow older they judge them; sometimes they forgive them.

—Oscar Wilde

BROTHER

Praise for bestselling author
ANIA AHLBORN and *WITHIN THESE WALLS*

"Terrifyingly sad. . . . *Within These Walls* creeps under your skin, and stays there. It's insidious. . . . The book's atmosphere is distinctly damp, clammy, overcast, and it isn't all the Washington weather: its characters' souls are gray, dimmed by failure. Ahlborn is awfully good on the insecurities that plague both aging writers . . . and oversensitive young girls . . . which leave them vulnerable to those who . . . know how to get into their heads. So grim."

—*The New York Times Book Review*

"Cruel, bone-chilling, and destined to become a classic, *Within These Walls* is worth the sleep it will cost you. Some of the most promising horror I've encountered in years."

—Seanan McGuire, *New York Times* bestselling author

"A monstrous Russian nesting doll of a book, holding secrets within secrets; the plot barrels headlong towards one of the most shocking climaxes you're ever likely to read. This one's going to wreck you."

—Nick Cutter, national bestselling author of
The Troop and *The Deep*

"Ania Ahlborn is a great storyteller who spins an atmosphere of dread literally from the first page, increasing the mental pressure all the way through to the terrifying, chilling ending."

—Jeff Somers, acclaimed author of
The Electric Church and *We Are Not Good People*

"Ever-mounting terror and a foreboding setting make for pure storytelling alchemy. . . . Ania Ahlborn goes for the gut with surprise twists that will stay with you for days. Not a book, or an author, that you'll soon forget."

—Vicki Pettersson, *New York Times* bestselling author

1

MICHAEL TWISTED IN his bed, the threadbare blanket he'd used all his life tangled around his legs. A girl was screaming bloody murder outside.

People used that saying all the time, *bloody murder*, despite never having heard anyone being murdered before. Reb called it an analogy. When Michael asked what that was, Reb said they were things people used when they didn't know what they were talking about. Nobody in town had ever heard someone scream bloody murder before, at least not really, but they kept on saying it like they had. *That baby's yellin' its head off, screamin' bloody murder in the cereal aisle.* Reb said that if they wanted to hear a baby scream bloody murder, all they had to do was ask.

Michael craned his neck and cast a glance toward his bedroom window. The glass was dirty from years of sideways dirt and rain. The glow of the porch light below his room shined like a flashlight through a cloud of dust. Those girls usually went quiet fast. They'd yell so hard they ended up making themselves hoarse. *Them's the perks of livin' out in the wilderness,* Momma had once said. *You scream and scream and ain't nobody around to hear.*

Michael stared up at his bedroom ceiling, old wood boards warped from various leaks the farmhouse had taken on over the years. He waited for the girl to lose her voice. That screaming bothered him, though he'd never admit it. It gave him nightmares, but he never complained. He only wished Momma would kill them while the sun was shining rather than waiting 'til dark. If it didn't matter how hard they screamed, Michael didn't get what the difference would be. Day or night, dead was dead. At least during the day he wasn't trying to sleep.

The girl eventually went silent and Michael let himself relax. Each muscle uncoiled, limb by limb, and he imagined himself on a beach he assumed was real, though he couldn't be sure. He had a picture postcard from a place called Honolulu. He didn't know where that was, only that the sand was white and the water was impossibly blue. In that postcard, people lounged beneath colorful umbrellas while a cotton candy–pink hotel stood in the background. He had found it in a backpack belonging to one of Momma's girls. Reb said it wasn't stealing if they weren't alive anymore.

The comfortable silence was short lived. Another blood-curdling shriek crashed over him. It pierced the still-dark hours of the morning, forcing Michael back into the present. There was commotion beyond his window. Shadows cut across his bedroom wall as figures moved on the back lawn. Michael rolled onto his side, let his bare feet sweep the rough planks of the floor. He pushed the ragged window curtain aside, his free hand trapping his hair in a circle of fingers at the nape of his neck. It was long now, sweeping his back a good three inches below the shoulder. His sister, Misty Dawn, was enamored with the likes of Jim Morrison. She had encouraged him to grow it out; Reb was thrilled when Michael took her advice.

You know why Jim Morrison killed himself, don't you? Because he got tired of looking like a chick.

Misty Dawn always came to Michael's defense with a jab at Reb's high-waisted jeans and green leather jacket. She liked to insist that he was as handsome as the guys from one of her favorite bands—one that Reb loathed with all his might. Misty Dawn comparing Reb to Benny Andersson and Björn Ulvaeus was usually enough to have him jumping into his Delta 88 and spraying the side of the house with gravel.

The screaming girl stumbled across the backyard.

On cue, the muffled chords of an ABBA song sounded through the wall separating Michael's room from Misty Dawn's. Misty didn't like the screaming either, but she absolutely loved Swedish pop.

On the lawn, strips of silver tape clung to the girl's ankles just above her bare feet, but her hands were still secured in front of her by the wrists. She was shaking her head, her mouth working on words Michael couldn't make out. It almost looked like she was trying to sing along with Misty's music, the upbeat tempo a striking contrast to the horrified expression she wore on her face.

Wade stood not more than ten feet from her, his hands shoved deep in the pockets of his dirty jeans. He tipped his chin up toward the second-story windows, his attention drawn by Misty's music. Wade and Michael locked eyes through the grimy glass. They held each other's attention for two bass beats before Wade looked back to the girl, who was begging for her life. Wade had been an army man, a Vietnam volunteer in the early sixties, years before college kids marched into DC wielding crudely painted protest signs. He wore his standard brooding expression, as though the girl's screams were transporting him back to the rice paddies, to a hail of gunfire and the *thwap-thwap-thwap* of helicopter blades.

Rebel was down in the yard as well. He circled the girl like a hungry wolf, poking at her with a long tree branch the way a mean-spirited kid would tease an insect. Reb's name was actually Ray, but Michael never called him that. Ray had asked the family to call him Rebel years before, back when he was eleven or twelve, but all he got was a few chuckles and multiple eye-rolls. Michael had been the only one to comply with Reb's request, partly because he wanted to make his brother happy, and also because Michael was scared of what would be done to him if he ignored the demand.

Momma was outside too, though all Michael could see of her was the long shadow that drew across the ground from the back porch. He imagined her cast in silhouette, the porch light shining bright behind her head like a halo, her tall, slender frame giving her a praying mantis look.

Only Michael and Misty Dawn remained inside—Michael standing at the window, Misty more than likely twirling in the center of her room, the frilly bottom of her nightgown riding light upon the air as her bare feet danced across the floor. Michael transferred the rubber band he wore around his wrist to his hair, pulling unruly brown waves from his face. Putting the window to his back, he slid down the wall and reached for his boots—a sock stuffed into each one. It wouldn't be long now. Maybe a few more minutes of screaming before the yelling would become nothing but a wet choking sound. After that, it would be Michael's turn. Time to go to work.

The creak of floorboards pulled his attention to the door. The music grew louder as it gently swung inward, and Misty wavered just beyond the threshold. Her hair was a soft tangle of strawberry blond, the exact same hue as Reb's and Momma's. It was the same color Wade's had been too, before it had faded to a muted shadow of its former self. Misty was twenty-one—two years older than Michael—but her meekness lent her a strange sort of youth. Standing there in her pale pink nightgown, her cheeks ruddy with a post-dancing flush, she now looked fifteen or sixteen at best. She raised a single shoulder to her ear and stared at him with doleful eyes.

Misty kept as much distance between herself and Momma's "hobby" as she could, but it didn't keep her from partaking in the spoils. She hated the screaming and all the blood, but she loved the shiny things the girls left behind—rings and bracelets, necklaces and earrings. She had a whole collection of artifacts hoarded in her top dresser drawer. Michael smuggled the jewelry into Misty Dawn's pockets when Momma wasn't watching, and in exchange, Misty let him use her record player whenever he wanted.

"Don't worry, I ain't gonna forget," Michael told her. He put on his socks, shoved his feet into his boots, and pulled the laces tight—ribbons of worn cotton cord that were stiff and black where they looped into bows.

"Thanks," she said, flashing him a wide smile despite the screaming coming from outside. She was ready to pivot on the balls of her feet and pad back to her room when she stopped short. They stared at each other as Momma's voice cut through the crisp morning air.

"Michael!"

His name coiled through the farmhouse's framework and glass with an undeniable sense of urgency. It tainted the upbeat melody that had filled the upstairs hallway. Momma wasn't one for emoting, but this time she punctuated her call with what sounded like panic.

Michael bolted up from the floor, stood to his full six-foot-two height, and shoved the drapery aside. Momma, who Reb called Claudine, had descended the porch stairs. She was looking up at Michael's window, searching for his face, waiting for it to appear. Michael's gaze darted from Momma to Reb, who was running across the backyard toward the trees.

It took Michael half a second to process what was happening.

It took even less time to conclude that his brother would never catch the girl.

Michael rushed out of his room before Misty could move. She staggered backward and caught herself on the hallway wall as he launched down the stairs. He raced through a kitchen that held little more than a stove and a scar-topped table and sprang off the covered back porch. A flying leap propelled him

6

off the steps and onto the ground. He blew past Reb within seconds.

Michael was fast. His height gave him a distinct advantage over his brother. Rebel was only five foot eight and had stopped to catch his breath at the mouth of the woods, either because he was winded or because he didn't feel like continuing the chase. Rebel wasn't exactly known for making an effort when Michael was there to do the work.

The girl was a decent runner. Michael caught a glimpse of her dirty white T-shirt as she weaved through the trees. She held her bound arms out in front of her, her bare feet stomping a forest floor blanketed in last year's leaves. She veered left. Michael broke away from her, going right instead. He knew these woods as well as the interior of the house; right was faster than left. He'd cut her off at Misty's favorite spot—a hill that overlooked the Great Appalachian Valley, trees as far as the eye could see. He splashed across a small creek and circled around to where he knew she'd end up. Left would take her to a steep embankment covered in birch and aspen trees. Right would take Michael around the hill to a gentler grade, allowing him to outrun her and wait for her at the crest of the slope.

When he got to the top of the hill, he could already hear her strangled, struggling breaths. She scrambled up to what she hoped was escape, crying and trying to pray while she gasped for air, muttering something about "God" and "help." Ducking behind the trunk of an oak, he watched her climb the hill. She spun around and looked down at the valley below her, empty of any pursuer, but also devoid of any roads or houses or clues of which way she should run. But that didn't seem to matter. The terror on her face blossomed into hope. She had outrun her attackers; she had saved herself. Soon, she'd be a face on the news, giving interviews about how some charming guy in a brown Oldsmobile had picked her up while she'd been hitching along State Road 10. That was when her abductor had grabbed her by the back of the head and slammed her face into the dash. The car was a '68 coupe; the dashboard was a solid slab of steel. It was a wonder Reb hadn't killed her. When she had fallen back against the passenger seat, unconscious, Michael was surprised her nose hadn't been shoved right up into her brain.

Michael hated chasing down the ones who managed to break away, hated how he extinguished the flash of dogged optimism that sparked in their eyes. He couldn't stand the way they looked at him, as though he'd walked in on a private moment. He despised the way their eyes grew to twice their original size and their mouths worked the air, as though chewing invisible food. He liked it better when they died in the yard, where all he had to deal with was an unblinking stare and a slashed throat. People were much easier to deal with when they were dead.

He gritted his teeth and stepped out from behind the tree.

The girl saw him, her reaction just as he had predicted—terror, disbelief. Her eyes bulged out of her head, the skin beneath them purple half-moons of blood. When her mouth fell open, Michael saw that Reb's little move in the car had broken one of her front teeth in half. She began to gobble the air, backing away, struggling for breath, her bound hands held out in front of her to fend him off.

Michael squeezed his eyes shut and moved in.

Once upon a time, he had convinced himself that chasing girls would get easier, that he'd get used to it and these moments wouldn't affect him. He was waiting for autopilot, a way to disconnect himself from his emotions, a way to make his eyes glaze over like Wade's seemed to. He was tired of seeing the shock, the fear, the dread. But it had been years at this point. Autopilot had yet to come.

His eyes snapped open when he heard her run again. But instead of bolting after her, Michael wondered whether the Morrows really would disown him if he returned empty-handed. For a good five seconds, he considered letting her go. The girl staggered away from him, her bare feet bloody, dead leaves clinging to the sticky bottoms like makeshift shoes. But the sixth second brought clarity. If he let her escape, he was sealing his own fate. She'd come back with the police. The cops would arrest the Morrows like they had those guys Rebel had read about in the paper and idolized so much—Mr. Bundy and that Gacy fellow, John Wayne.

He fell into a sprint.

She screamed.

He caught her by the right shoulder and spun her around in mid-run, her legs folding beneath her. She hit the ground hard, crying out in pain. But she didn't give up—she kicked her legs to propel herself away from him, performing an armless crabwalk across the forest floor. Michael reached down to catch her by the wrists, but she coiled up and shoved her feet hard against his chest. He stumbled, surprised by the force of her kick. He reached for her again, but she pulled the same move, leaving him stunned as she shrieked for help that both of them knew wouldn't come.

"*Get away from me!*" she wailed. "*Get away, you fucking freak!*"

She rolled onto her side and scrambled to her feet, but she was in agony. As soon as she stood, Michael noticed her right arm hanging limp at her side, looking broken. Whimpering with every step, which was now little more than a desperate jog, she looked like a runner at the twentieth mile of a marathon. She was exhausted but determined to keep going, pulled forward by the promise of a finish line. Except this finish line was at the foot of the Morrow's back porch steps.

Michael followed her easily, walking behind her as though the two of them were taking an early morning stroll. She shot a glance at him over her shoulder, looked away, and began to sob. It was a distinct cry, hopeless and empty, torn from the chest of the walking dead.

He wanted to place his hand on her shoulder, to tell her that it would be okay, that Momma usually made it quick. But he doubted the girl wanted such reassurance. Lost in his thoughts, he hardly noticed when she slowed, paid no mind to the fact that he had cut the distance between them in half. She swung around to face him, threw her bound arms over his head, and opened her mouth as wide as she could, ready to tear his throat out with her teeth. Michael jumped back, but she moved with him. He grabbed her by the elbows and gave her a shove, feeling the duct tape pull hard against the back of his neck before tearing free. The girl fell, stared at her now-free arms, and, despite her dislocated shoulder, began to scramble again. Michael jumped on top of her, no longer in the mood to draw things out. The girl released a garbled scream, whipping her good arm in his face, her fingers bent into a claw. She slashed his cheek with her nails. Kicked her legs beneath him as hard as she could. Michael managed to pin down the girl's arms and render her helpless, fascinated by how much fight she still had.

There was no way to get her back to the house like this, not with her thrashing around the way she was. He moved his knees one at a time, crushing her fighting hand into the damp earth, and caught sight of a stone within arm's reach. He grabbed for it, sunk his fingers into the ground, and unearthed a three-pound monster, grubs and worms squirming in the pale indigo light of the morning.

Someone yelled in the not-so-far distance, though Michael couldn't make out the words over the girl's constant wail.

When he hefted the rock up over his head, she stopped fighting, as if suddenly coming to terms with her fate. He was caught off guard by her stillness. Her face was red and puffy with tears, the bags beneath her eyes now horrible black bruises, her teeth smeared with blood. And yet somehow, at that very moment, she struck him as angelic—a beautiful girl who probably looked a lot like Momma had when she had been that young. The girl stared up at Michael with a look that left him dumbfounded, as though she was seeing God.

"Why are you doing this?" she whimpered.

Michael's chest constricted. His fingers tightened around the stone. He wanted to explain that it wasn't him, that he had no choice. But all he could manage was: "Because I've got to."

And then he brought the rock down against her head.

Wade and Rebel crested the hill just as the stone rolled from Michael's grasp and onto the ground.

"Shit!" Reb spit out, charging forward. "What're you tryin' to do, kill her?" He shoved Michael away from the girl with an impatient hand, leaned down, and pressed two fingers against her neck to feel for a pulse. A moment later, he shot Michael an aggravated look. "You're lucky," he murmured. "You think you let her run far enough?"

Wade's hand fell onto Michael's shoulder. That distant look was still in his eyes, but three words rolled smoothly off his tongue: "Good job, son." He patted Michael on the shoulder, then turned to make his way back to the house.

Michael watched him go before casting a look at his brother. When their gazes met, Reb rolled his eyes at their old man's back.

"Goddamn loon," Reb muttered. "Bring her back." He stepped away from the unconscious girl. "And you better hope Claudine don't care you're bringin' her back half-dead neither. I ain't taking blame for this." He sidestepped Michael to follow their father, murmuring beneath his breath.

Michael looked back at the girl splayed out on the forest

floor. Her breathing was shallow but steady. He had knocked her out pretty good, but there was no telling how long she'd stay under.

"I'm sorry," he told her, then he hefted her onto his shoulders.

The next time he'd be alone with her they'd be down in the cellar.

The next time he'd see her, she'd be undeniably dead.

2

———

MICHAEL WAS SPRAYING down the cellar floor with a garden hose when Reb appeared at the top of the stairs. Diverting his attention from the spirals of watery red that circled a rusty drain in the floor, Michael looked up at his older brother. The narrow stairwell that flanked the sagging wooden steps shadowed Reb's hard, angular features. Michael had never said so before, but Reb looked a lot like a bird—the kind that used their hooked beaks to pick apart roadkill. A vulture, especially when he glared, and that was something Reb did a lot.

Rebel crossed his arms over his chest. His stance reeked of impatience, as if to suggest that Michael was taking way too long with this girl—first with the rundown, and now the disposal.

"Are you done or what?" he asked.

Michael gave the floor a final once-over with the hose and hung it on a metal hook jutting out of the wall, the spray attachment dripping onto a concrete floor.

"Pretty much," Michael said. "What's goin' on?"

"We're goin' on a run," Reb told him. "Hurry up." He was trying to sound casual, but Michael picked it up in his tone.

They hadn't gone on a booze run in nearly a week. Reb was drying out.

"Gimme a minute," Michael told him. "Just gotta lock up." He wiped his cold, wet hands on the front of his jeans and stomped his boots against the floor to shake off some of the water that had soaked into the leather. Reb ducked out of the storm cellar without offering any help . . . something he didn't do for anyone. Sometimes Michael got the feeling that Rebel only spent time with him because he was fast enough to outrun any gas station clerk in West Virginia. Because when it came to true friendship, Michael had caught his brother rolling his eyes a hundred thousand times, as though Michael was the stupidest, most annoying person in the whole entire world. Misty called it sibling rivalry, and while Michael didn't know exactly what that was, he sure didn't like how it felt.

Climbing the creaky wooden staircase, Michael surfaced from underground. He needed to change out of his wet clothes. Crunching leaves beneath his boots, he let the propped-open storm doors fall shut with a crash, then slid the deadbolt into place. He hooked a padlock through a metal loop to secure the room below, then turned to go inside. The hose water had made his hands so cold that his fingers ached. But the blast of a car horn stopped him short before he could make it inside. Rebel hung out the window of the Delta. His left arm swept across the ugly metallic-brown paint while his right clung to the steering wheel. Reb had spotted the car at a junkyard near Lewisburg the year before. He and Michael had stolen it right off the lot, towed it out of there with Wade's old pickup truck.

A bloodhound barked at them to stop, but the old boy never did make a move to protect his master's property. That dog was smart. It hadn't been willing to put in the effort it would take to defend little more than four bald tires and a pile of scrap. The Morrow boys had spent the rest of the night scratching VIN numbers off of body panels with chisels and screwdrivers. And while the Delta was in sorry shape at the time, Reb thought that it was a real find. A jewel among junk. All it needed was a little polish to make it shine.

"Where you goin'?" Rebel called out.

"To change," Michael shot back, hooking a thumb toward the farmhouse behind him.

"Man, you couldn't change if your life depended on it. Let's go."

Michael grimaced, but rather than arguing that his socks were squishing between his toes, he changed direction and wandered toward the car instead. Settling into the passenger seat, he sighed. They'd have to drive a good twenty miles one way to get to a suitable hit. As Rebel liked to say, you don't shit where you sleep.

· · ·

The gas station sign read MOE'S, written across a metal awning that hung over two lonely pumps. A sign out front advertised 1.15REG for a gallon of gas and ICE COLD DRINKS in capital letters, some of them crooked and ready to fall off the marquee. Reb made a couple of passes before pulling around the side of the building. It was a small, middle-of-nowhere stop that serviced maybe a dozen customers per day—tired, wayward strangers in need of a frosty TaB and a Hostess CupCake.

Michael slid out of the car, grabbing an old sweatshirt out of the backseat as he went. Pulling it on, he zipped it up and pushed his hands into the pockets across his stomach. He was trying to look casual as he took the corner and stepped across the bank of windows at the front of the store. A little bell chimed overhead when he pulled open the door.

The guy behind the cash register regarded him with disinterest. A *Flash Gordon* rerun playing on his rabbit-eared television kept him distracted from what was more than likely his first customer of the day. The cashier looked to be in his late thirties or early forties, though it was hard to tell with that bushy Paul Bunyan beard. He hunched his square shoulders forward as he sat on his stool, peering at the TV so intently that it looked more like he was studying the show than watching it for fun.

Michael avoided eye contact as he wandered down the center aisle. Chips and pretzels were to his right. Cans of motor oil and replacement fan belts to his left. He veered right when he reached the wall cooler at the back of the store. The hard liquor was on an end cap across from the Pabst and Schlitz. There wasn't much to choose from, but Reb didn't care what it was as long as it got him drunk. In shitkicker stores like this one, it didn't pay to be picky.

Michael cast a wary look back at the cashier, his right hand catching a bottle of Jim Beam by its neck. He turned his back to the register and made like he was considering which beer to buy while he slid the bottle beneath his baggy sweatshirt. Michael was rail thin; at six two, he weighed less than 175 pounds. The bottle-in-the-sweatshirt trick usually paid off because it left him ample room to work with. A bigger guy would have looked like he had grown a block-shaped stomach tumor since entering the place. But on Michael, it looked like nothing more than a lot of fabric on a long-haired yokel in a backwoods store.

He started to make his way to the front, his heart pounding in his throat despite the fact that he'd done the exact same thing dozens of times before. An old guy had once pulled a gun on him. When Michael made a break for it, he found the double barrel of a shotgun pointed right at his chest. He still didn't understand how he had made it out of there alive. The guy could have shot him in the back as Michael ran across the parking lot with Reb's liberated bottle of scotch clamped in his fist, but the old guy had spared him, maybe because he'd caught a glimpse of his reluctance, or maybe because he didn't want to deal with a dead body that day. Parked just a few yards from the front plate-glass windows, Reb had seen everything. As soon as Michael had leapt into the car, Reb slammed his foot on the gas and they flew down the highway. They had both sat in stunned silence for a good half mile before Reb burst into a fit of maniacal laughter. Michael hadn't been able to help himself; he joined in too, despite having nearly lost his life over a bottle of Johnnie Walker Red.

The cashier looked up from *Flash Gordon* and straightened his shoulders, readying himself for a ring-up, but Michael's hands were empty. Michael slowed his steps, tried for a smile.

"Sorry," he said. "You ain't got what I need."

"Oh no?" The cashier tipped his head to the side, his gaze only wavering when the chocolate brown Olds slowly rolled past one of the gas pumps. Reb's head turned a full ninety degrees to see what was happening inside. That's when a flash of realization crossed the cashier's face.

Michael should have made his break right then, but something made him hesitate. They locked eyes. Michael tried his damnedest to look innocent as the cashier's gaze wandered along the faded cotton of his sweatshirt.

"Bit warm for that, ya think?" he asked.

"Depends on where you're from," Michael countered. A sweatshirt in the dead of a West Virginian summer wasn't a big deal when you lived in hell.

The cashier tipped his head to the right, as if confused by Michael's response. That split second of befuddlement gave Michael the chance he was waiting for. He lunged toward the door. But the cashier was quicker than he looked. He launched himself off his stool and bolted around the counter as Michael neared the exit. The cashier was fast, but his stocky build left him clumsy. He clipped a display of plastic travel mugs—a dozen of them went clattering to the floor—and then pulled a Wile E. Coyote, his legs pumping like a cartoon beneath him as he stumbled, trying not to break his own neck. Michael used the man's momentary loss of footing to his advantage. He darted out of the building, the bottle of whiskey now in full view.

Reb had rolled the Olds to the far end of the lot and

parked alongside the road that would take them away from the scene of the crime. Michael scrambled for the car, his arms pumping hard, the sweatshirt feeling like it was made out of lead. The amber liquid in the bottle caught the sunlight, its shadow giving the illusion of him wielding a crystal club. The car began to roll again, slowly at first, ready for him to jump in, *Dukes of Hazzard*–style. After so many runs, he had perfected the move. All he needed was an open window. In and out, nice and easy.

He wasn't more than five yards from escape when he began to relax. His racing heartbeat started to settle despite his full-on sprint. The cashier was in pursuit, but a good fifty feet behind him. No doubt he'd be left to shake his fist in the air as the two punk thieves disappeared down the road, Reb hooting and wailing with his head jutting out the driver-side window.

Except the closer Michael got to the Delta, the faster it rolled. What was supposed to be an easy five-mile-per-hour head start was suddenly double that, then triple. Still at a full sprint, he watched the car blast down the road without him, leaving him to choke on a cloud of road dust. Stunned, Michael slowed his run. He forgot that the cashier was still behind him until the guy crashed into his shoulder, linebacker style. Michael stumbled, and for a terrifying moment, the cashier had him by the sleeve. Michael jerked his arm out of the cashier's grasp and swung the bottle of Jim Beam, clipping the guy's jaw. The guy stumbled backward in surprise. He let go of Michael's shirt and nearly tripped over his own feet as he pressed his hand to his face, momentarily dazzled by pain. In that fleeting moment of freedom, Michael turned and booked it down the side of the road like an Olympic long-distance runner. He only hoped to God the guy didn't jump in his car and try to track him down.

Michael ran for about a quarter mile before he saw the Delta on the side of the highway. The parking lights were on, and the tailpipe rattled in time with the engine. Michael looked behind him as he gulped in air. The cashier had either given up or was getting his car. Regardless, he was out of sight, and Michael was confident enough to slow to a jog.

The closer he got to the Oldsmobile, the angrier he was. He could see Rebel through the rear window, sitting behind the wheel as casual as ever, puffing on a Lucky Strike. Michael clenched his jaw as he stepped around the car, peeled his sweatshirt off, and opened the passenger door. He retook his seat. But before he could gather up the courage to lay into his brother for the shit he just pulled, Reb smirked at his indignant expression.

"Sorry," he said, breathing out a chest full of smoke. "I guess my foot slipped." Reb reached over and grabbed the bottle by its neck, yanking it out of Michael's grasp. "But good job," he told him, his eyes going dark. "*Son.*"

Michael looked away, staring out the window into the trees that flanked the quiet highway. He resisted temptation, didn't dare give Rebel the satisfaction of standing up for himself. It would only give him more ammunition. They'd get home, and he'd spout off about how Michael had spoken out of turn, how he was forgetting his place. Michael wouldn't be able to sleep for days, terrified of his bedroom door swinging open in the middle of the night, afraid that Rebel would fill the doorway with his silhouette, demanding that Michael get up so they could take a little field trip into the woods.

"Oh, *what*?" Reb asked sharply. "Suddenly you can't take a goddamn joke?"

Michael refused to respond, waiting for the car to start rolling. He was on the verge of protesting their stillness, ready to insist that the guy back at the gas station could pull onto the highway and roll up next to them within a minute or two. Maybe then he'd cock a sawed-off shotgun and blow them both away with a single trigger pull. But Michael didn't say that either. He was too distracted by his own imagination, black thoughts flooding in. It would have been nice to see a spark of true emotion upon his brother's face for once. It would have been novel to see a spark of terror light up his eyes—the same kind of terror he so often forced Michael to see on the faces of all those nameless girls. Maybe it wouldn't be so bad, getting his head blown off, as long as Rebel would be just as dead as him.

"Whatever," Reb mumbled, shifting the car into drive and slamming his foot against the gas. The Delta fishtailed onto the asphalt. "Not like Daddy wouldn't bail your ass out if you *did* get caught."

Michael bit the inside of his bottom lip to keep quiet. The idea of Wade springing him out of jail gave him a jolt of satisfaction. He knew that if it were Rebel, Wade would let him stew in the pen for at least a day or two. Michael hoped he *was*

Wade's favorite, if only to get back at Reb for being so damn unappreciative.

. . .

Rebel caught Michael by the arm just after pulling the emergency brake into place. Michael's door was already open. He was desperate for some space. But Reb's fingers clamped hard around his wrist and his eyes narrowed into that vulture glare.

"I feel like I shouldn't have to remind you," he said, "but I will since you're so fuckin' retarded. You talk and you're dead."

Michael twisted his arm out of his brother's grasp, but he remained inside the car, his eyes fixed on his hands. Whether he was Wade's favorite or not, Michael belonged to Rebel. Nobody would so much as bat an eyelash at Reb's decision regarding Michael's future, or the lack thereof.

Reb snorted, as though miffed by his brother's lack of response, then grabbed his bottle of Jim Beam and shoved his way out of the car. When Michael failed to move, Reb ducked his head back into the vehicle and spit out: "Get outta my ride, dipshit."

Michael slid out of the passenger seat, grabbed his sweatshirt, and walked toward the house. His feet were cold, his socks still damp from the basement cleanup. He fingered a gold loop inside his pocket. He had forgotten all about it until he shoved his hands into his jeans. The girl hadn't had much jewelry, just a single ring around the middle finger of her right hand.

Wade and Misty Dawn were sitting at the kitchen table while Momma seared meat on the stove. They all turned to look at Michael when he stepped into the house, then they turned back to their respective tasks. Momma's kitchen knives glinted in the musty light. Wade had laid them out in a straight line, arranged from largest to smallest upon a stained tea towel. Wade drew one of the blades across the surface of the whetstone he held in his left hand. The hiss of metal against rock mingled with the sizzle of frying food. Misty was working on a new macramé project. Currently, she was wild about making plant hangers and wall decorations. She'd knotted together a belt to wear with her various hippie skirts and had recently completed a hobo bag with tassels so long they nearly swept the ground when she walked. Michael approached the table, pulled the ring from his pocket, and covertly dropped it into Misty's lap. Her eyes lit up, but she said nothing. Rather, she moved her macramé over it and continued to work.

Rebel stepped inside the house a minute later, the bottle of Jim Beam already missing its cap. He took a swig before advancing further inside, then slid the bottle across the table prior to collapsing into his seat. He slouched, kicked up his dirty shoes, and regarded his family with a bemused look. He was like a king looking down upon his peasants, watching them toil away at the mundane.

"Makin' another ugly belt?" he asked, raising an eyebrow at his sister.

"It's a halter top," she murmured beneath her breath. "Don't see no reason for you bein' rude, neither."

Michael stared down at his feet. He made a move to exit the room, wanting nothing more than to pull off his soggy boots.

But he stopped when Wade posed a question: "You went out like that?"

Michael turned to face the Morrows. Wade sounded as though he was directing his query at Reb, but he was surprised to see Wade staring at *him* instead.

"You have blood on them boots," Wade said. "Probably have blood all over, but you went out anyway. Into town, right?"

"Not into town," Rebel cut in, defensive. "Just a goddamn gas station. No big fuckin' deal."

"You think that's smart, Michael?" Wade asked, ignoring Reb's interjection.

Michael's stomach twisted. He had made a mistake, and mistakes weren't taken lightly in this house. He should have stood up to Rebel, should have insisted he had to change before they went anywhere. This stuff was a matter of staying safe or getting caught. He had put the entire family at risk.

"Are you gonna answer me, or are you gonna stand there lookin' stupid?" Wade asked.

Michael's jaw tensed.

Rebel rolled his eyes and grabbed the bottle, holding it just shy of his lips.

"I'm sorry," Michael murmured, afraid to meet his father's gaze.

Reb laughed, then took another swig.

Wade's movement was sudden. He shoved his chair away from the table, stepped across the kitchen, and slapped the bottle out of Reb's grubby hand. It thunked against the hardwood and slid across the floor, spilling precious amber liquid onto the planks. Reb made a move to grab it, an exasperated, almost childlike yelp escaping his throat, but Wade gave him a shove back into his chair.

"You mean to tell me that goin' to the gas station was *Michael's* idea?" Wade asked. "You tryin' to lie to me about that?"

Reb bared his teeth at his father and pushed him aside, snatching the bottle off the floor. He stared at it, wild-eyed. Only a fourth of the way full now. "Son of a bitch!" Rebel slammed the bottle onto the table. Michael flinched at the noise. Misty jumped, but her eyes sparkled at the exchange. Misty loved drama. Next to her records, it was all that she had. "I had to drive forty miles round trip for that shit!" Reb roared at his dad.

"Might be cheaper to save on gas and pay for it in town, don't you think?" Wade asked.

Misty breathed a soft giggle, prompting Momma to twist away from the stove and grab her by the hair. She gave it a vicious pull.

"You best shut up, girl," she hissed into Misty's face. "You ain't part of this." Releasing her, Momma shoved her daughter's head down toward the surface of the table, as though trying to slam Misty's face into the wood.

Michael swallowed against the lump in his throat. He pressed himself flush against the kitchen's far wall. The last time the Morrows had exchanged words, Misty got it bad. She always got it bad, whether she had anything to do with it or not. Momma directed all her rage at her daughter and hardly ever at her sons.

"You really are stupid, Ray," Wade said. "One day you're gonna cost us big . . . riskin' all of us gettin' caught so you can drink your troubles away."

"*You're* my trouble," Rebel bit back. "You ever think about that, old man?"

"Don't be so hard on him, Wade," Momma chimed in. "It's just a rough patch. It'll pass."

But Rebel had been going through that rough patch for as long as Michael could remember. It had been easier to steal booze as kids. Nobody expected a ten-year-old to smuggle hard liquor out the door of their shop. Now the calls were getting closer, the cashiers bolder. Michael knew better than anyone that it was only a matter of time before he wouldn't make it out of one of those stores, and Reb knew it just as well. It wasn't a rough patch; Reb was just a rough kind of guy.

"You wanna protect him? Wait 'til the police show up because of stolen booze," Wade said. "Wait 'til they start pokin' around, and then you can protect him some more. Tell 'em he's goin' through a phase."

Michael blanched at the idea. The meat was gone, but the bones were all still there, buried close to the shed.

"I don't want any more of these field trips, you hear?" Wade said.

"It's not your call." Rebel sneered.

"Wade, you leave him alone," Momma demanded. "Nothin' happened. Nobody's gone and followed them home."

"If he gets caught, he gets caught," Reb told his father, nodding at Michael. "I'll just take off. They'll have their man."

Michael didn't put his brother's statement together until a second later: the *he* in this equation was *Michael*. He blinked, opened his mouth to protest.

I thought we were friends, he wanted to say. *I thought we were in this together.*

Misty Dawn stiffened in her seat. "You're gonna leave Michael behind? Don't you dare—"

Momma cut Misty off with another rough yank of her hair, this one so vicious that it pulled the girl right out of her seat. Her macramé spilled onto the floor as she stumbled backward. All the while, Momma shoved her toward the back porch.

"What the hell did I say?!" Momma screamed.

Rebel shot a glance after his mother and sister, then grabbed the near-empty bottle and stomped out of the room like a petulant child.

Wade exhaled a defeated sigh and sank back into his seat. He plucked up the knife he had been sharpening minutes before and got back to work.

There was a crack of leather against flesh.

Misty cried out from somewhere on the porch.

Michael's mouth filled with the acrid taste of blood. He wanted to run up the stairs and shut himself in his room, but he didn't dare move from where he stood against the wall. He waited for Wade to notice him instead.

When Wade finally looked up, Michael whispered, "May I be excused?"

Wade nodded solemnly, and Michael took the risers two by two.

3

LAURALYNN MORROW LOOKED just like her mother, right down to her gilded strawberry waves. Her hair was the color of wheat during a summer sunset, blazing with hues of honey and gold. She was ten when she told Ray her secret in the quiet of the backyard.

"I don't wanna live here forever, Raybee," she said. Her nickname for him always made Ray laugh, made him think of rabid dogs foaming at the mouth. Ray cupped one of Lauralynn's baby rabbits against his chest, rubbing the fur between its ears. "I wanna be a teacher," she said.

"How you gonna be teacher, LL?" Ray asked. "You can't be no teacher unless you go to school. *Real* school, not just readin' story-books at the kitchen table the ways we do." Lauralynn had read *Where the Sidewalk Ends* to Ray and the others more than a half-dozen times. She wasn't great at reading—none of them were—but she'd practically memorized the poems. They came out smooth and lyrical whenever she'd recite them, turning each page with her pinkie finger raised aloft.

Lauralynn's gaze wavered. Her mouth turned downward at the corners, as if genuinely considering her eight-year-old brother's logic. "I guess you're right," she murmured after a moment, gingerly taking the rabbit from Ray's hands. "But don't you think it would be great, readin' books to a whole group of kids instead of it just bein' us?"

Ray liked it being just them. He'd like it even better if their six-year-old sibling Misty Dawn wasn't involved. Misty was always butting in with her dumb questions while Lauralynn read *Peter Rabbit* and *Winnie the Pooh*. The idea of there being even more kids and more stupid questions turned his stomach. Too many kids, and Lauralynn's attention would be so diluted that she'd look right through Ray as though he wasn't there at all.

"I thought you wanted to be one of them animal doctors," he reminded her.

"I do," she said. "But you gotta go to school for that too; and if I'm gonna go to school, I may as well be two things instead of one."

Had anyone else made that declaration, he would have rolled his eyes. But Lauralynn was the smartest person he had ever met. She could do anything, and for the first time, the idea put fear in his heart. He swallowed hard as Lauralynn kissed the top of the bunny's head and then released it back into its elevated cage.

"Do *you* think I can be a teacher?" she asked, giving her brother a questioning glance. But before Ray had a chance to answer, to tell her that maybe it wasn't the best idea, because it meant she'd have to leave him behind, Momma stepped onto the back porch and yelled.

"Girl!" Her voice carried across the expanse of the yard, and the light immediately left Lauralynn's eyes. "You do the dishes like I told ya, or are my eyes playin' tricks on me?!"

Lauralynn shot Ray a wide-eyed look, which Ray returned in kind. Ray had been the one who had wanted to play outside despite Lauralynn's chores. He was the one who had talked her into feeding the bunnies, just for a few minutes, before she cleared the breakfast dishes out of the sink. But Lauralynn was quick to replace her frightened expression with a brave smile. She ruffled Ray's hair and rose from the ground, dusting off the front of her dress.

"I'm comin', Momma," she called out.

Ray's mouth went dry as he watched her go, his fingers curling around the leg of the rabbit cage. Lauralynn climbed the back porch steps. She paused to listen to something Momma said, then disappeared inside. Ray tore at the wild grass that grew in tufts around the legs of the cage and fed it to Lauralynn's rabbits through the chicken-wire fence. Once, when he had asked Lauralynn why she thought Momma got so mad, Lauralynn shrugged her shoulders and said that she didn't know for sure but thought that Momma was sad. The answer hadn't made sense to him then, and as he waited for the inevitable crack of Momma's belt, it didn't make sense now. Sadness, as he understood it, brought tears; but rather than tears, Momma dealt blows.

The arc of a thick leather strap was silhouetted in the kitchen window.

He shut his eyes tight and covered his ears, but he could still hear it snap against skin. Lauralynn was silent. Tears would roll down her face, but not a sound would ever escape her throat.

Ray worried. Sometimes he imagined waking up to find Lauralynn gone. Her clothes would be cleared out of her dresser. The small suitcase she kept beneath her bed would be missing. He imagined her leaving to go to school to be a teacher or an animal doctor and whatever else she may have wanted to be.

It was then, watching Momma's belt slash through the air, that Ray decided he needed to do something to keep Lauralynn from running away. If Lauralynn wanted to be a teacher, Ray would find her a student.

●   ●   ●

That night, Ray snuck out of the house after the family had gone to bed. He pulled the door of Wade's shed open just enough to creep inside. With his fingers wrapped around the handle of an old ball-peen hammer, he moved across the yard to the dog pen out back. Rowlf was an old Russian wolfhound. He and Wade had found him along the side of the road years before, soaked to the bone and skinny as a rail. His white coat had been so dirty it was black in places. That giant dog had struck Ray as pathetic. After a few minutes of Ray pleading, Wade pulled a U-turn and they piled Rowlf into the back of the truck.

Ray's fascination with Rowlf was short lived. After a few days, Rowlf proved to be more trouble than he was worth. He barked all night, snacked on rabbit poop, and filled Ray's room full of noxious dog farts whenever the boy was nice enough to let him sleep inside. Rowlf was a real pain in the ass, and he was eventually exiled to an out-door pen, where no one paid any attention to him. But now, with that hammer resting heavy in Ray's palm, he was glad they had kept Rowlf around.

If the Morrows suspected foul play when he tearfully told them Rowlf had disappeared, they didn't show it. They had no reason to think that, rather than the old dog running away, Ray and Rowlf had gone for a long walk with Wade's old hammer jutting out of the kid's back pocket. Two quick swings and it was over.

"We gotta get a replacement," Ray sobbed. "We just gotta."

Wade had been reluctant—nobody had paid a bit of attention to that damn dog until he was gone. Momma was the one to succumb to his pleading.

"You go out with your daddy and get another after chores tomorrow," she said. "Ain't nothing could be bigger than that dumb dog anyhow. Stupid animal was starting to eat us out of house and home."

.   .   .

Ray spotted him from the truck after it took a sharp curve along a tree-lined road; a kid, maybe four or five years old. He was rolling a big rock up a slight embankment to the soft shoulder, where he'd set out a line of stones, arranged from largest to smallest. He had propped up a little cardboard sign that read ROX 4 SALE against the largest of the bunch.

Ray twisted around the bench seat as the pickup took the corner. And then he settled back, shot his father a look, and spoke.

"You gotta turn around," he said. "I just saw what I want."

4

M ICHAEL SAT ON the floor of his room, his back to the wall and his ear next to the crack of the bedroom door, listening for Misty Dawn's footsteps on the stairs. When he heard the light padding of her bare feet, he nudged the door open another inch and whispered her name into the hall.

"*Miss.*"

Misty stopped to look his way, her face swollen with tears. Her hair hung stringy across her cheeks, as if she'd just come from the shower, but the moisture wasn't water. It was sweat and saline—a ruinous mixture of self-pity and resentment. Michael's heart twisted at the sight of her. She looked defeated, frail. Submissiveness was a trait they both shared. It afforded them a kinship that someone like Rebel could never understand.

"You okay?" he asked, afraid to speak any louder.

Misty gave him a weak nod and shuffled past his door. There was a familiar wobble to her gait as she ducked into her room. Her unbalanced stagger guaranteed fresh wounds on top of crosshatched scars. Michael peeked into the hall, shot a glance in each direction, and scrambled to his feet. He closed the door behind him as quietly as he could before tiptoeing into his sister's room.

Although she looked up at him from her perch on the bed, Misty Dawn didn't say anything for a long while. She just stared at him, roughly wiping at her flushed cheeks with the palms of her hands. Michael pressed his back to the wall and slid down its length to the floor. When it came to Rebel, Misty had a knack for speaking out of turn; but when it was time to speak to Michael, she considered her words carefully. It was as though she had a limited supply, but Michael didn't mind. He liked to think that her hesitation was proof that she cared. The things Misty said to Reb were mostly barbs, while everything she directed toward Michael was laced with emotion. It was meaningful.

"Wade's gettin' tired," she said after a drawn-out silence. "I don't know how much more of Ray he's gonna take. Ray's pushin' on purpose." She didn't call Rebel by his chosen nickname as an act of defiance, a small protest against her big brother's cruelty. But no matter how paltry the uprising, Misty was more of a renegade than Michael would ever be.

Michael wasn't sure how to reply. It seemed to him that Rebel had been pushing Wade for as long as Michael had known him. There was an unspoken resentment between Reb and Wade, as though Wade had done something black and unforgivable. Michael had made the mistake of asking why Reb hated his father only once, questioning why he called Wade by his first name rather than "Dad." His inquiry was answered with a black eye and a kick to the ribs. Michael hadn't taken the attack personally. Some hurts were just too painful to talk about.

Misty coiled her arms around her knees, hugging them to her chest. "Why do you do it?" she asked. He looked up at her, shook his head to say he didn't understand the question. "Ray," she said. "Why do you do what he says?"

Michael frowned. It was something he didn't like to talk about out loud. It made him anxious. Afraid.

"Reb's smart," he murmured after a beat. "Smarter than Wade thinks, at least. He knows you can't hit up a place twice unless you're wearin' a mask, and he knows how fast to drive if the cops are on your tail. Reb knows a lot." He lifted his shoulders as if to tell her it was the best response he could offer.

"Except his name ain't Reb," Misty reminded him. "And he ain't as smart as he thinks. What're you gonna do if, tomorrow, Wade tells you to do one thing and Ray tells you to do somethin' else? Who you gonna listen to?"

Michael was compelled to listen to Rebel. He was like one of those dogs trained to drool at the sound of a bell. But he also knew that Wade was what the TV called "the man of the house"; he was supposed to be in charge. The TV didn't much talk about "the woman of the house," which Michael thought was kind of funny. If anyone had power at the Morrows' place, it wasn't Reb or Wade—it was Momma.

"I don't know," Michael finally said. "I guess Reb?"

Misty was shaking her head, and he tensed at her response.

"Wade?" he asked, backpedaling. "Hell, I don't know, Miss.

I just do what I'm told, you know? I do whatever I think will protect you more."

Misty smiled softly at that. "My knight in shinin' armor," she said. "All you need is a fast white horse."

"And some armor," Michael quipped.

"If you had a horse, would you ride away?" she asked. "Away from all this?"

He looked down at his hands and gave her a faint shrug. He thought a lot about the places on his postcards—Honolulu and New York City and San Diego. He wanted to see them in person, stare up at the lights of Times Square and feel the sand between his toes. But the idea of leaving Misty Dawn behind tied his stomach in knots.

"I don't know how to ride horses, Miss," he said, rising to his feet. "I just wanted to make sure you were okay."

"I'm okay," she told him. "Always am."

Michael turned to slip out the door, but Misty stopped him short.

"I don't think you should be so scared of Ray," she said. "Even if he did try to leave you somewhere, I don't think Wade would let him."

Michael tried to smile through a sudden pang of anxiety, his heart tripping over itself.

"I'll see you later, Miss," he murmured beneath his breath.

"See you," she echoed back.

But when Michael ducked into the hallway, he froze in mid-step.

Rebel was leaning against the wall at the far end of the hall, staring at him.

· · ·

Michael was surprised at how quickly he and Reb reached their destination. Typically, their marks were a good twenty to thirty miles from home, but this one seemed half that distance. Before Michael knew it, his brother was pulling the Delta onto the side of the road. It was a lonely stretch, twisting and flanked by trees. Rebel grabbed a pair of binoculars out of the glove box. Leaving the car behind, they climbed a hill that seemed to lead them deep into nowhere. Michael nearly asked if Reb was sure they were heading in the right direction, but Reb looked like he knew where he was going. Michael kept silent and stayed close to his brother.

When they reached the crest of the hill, Rebel motioned for Michael to get down. They sank to the ground like a pair of soldiers, slinking across the dirt and leaves until they could see over the top of the hill. A house came into view. It was simple, one story, what folks called a "charmer," not at all like the Morrows' ancient farmhouse. Theirs had faded clapboards and dirty windows that stared sorrowfully into the trees. This house was tidy, set back a good distance from the road. Its green shutters winked happily in the sunshine. A round bistro table and matching metal chair sat in the shade of a giant pine.

Rebel put the binoculars up to his eyes and fiddled with the focus wheel while Michael rested his chin atop his hands.

It was a nice change of pace, lying there with the sun dappling through the canopy of trees. There was something serene about this little house. It was secluded out there, with no neighbors to be seen, but it still looked joyful. The chirping of birds and the glint of sunshine made him feel dreamy as he studied it. Bushes flanked the walkway up to the front door. Tiny hot-pink flowers dotted waxy green leaves. Someone had left an axe embedded into a tree stump near the driveway, its handle jutting upward at an easy angle. A small birdhouse swayed from the branch of a tree just beyond the front door. There was even a ceramic garden gnome perched on the front doorstep.

That house filled his chest with secret optimism. Clumsy thoughts of his own future home and the leisure that would come with it filled his head. One day he'd spend lazy afternoons painting his own shutters that same perfect hue of green, then watch the birds while sipping a cold glass of lemonade. The future would be filled with birdsong and the whisper of an easy breeze. There would be no more screaming. No hard whack of a leather strap.

Reb was so quiet beside him that Michael allowed his eyes to drift shut. The sun was warm on his back. The twitter of birds made him feel safe. When Reb nudged him awake, the look on his brother's face suggested that Michael had been out for quite some time. He could fantasize all he wanted, but Rebel was still at his elbow and Momma was still waiting back at the house.

A woman emerged from the cottage. Michael reached for the binoculars and peered through them at her. She was pretty, but definitely not Momma's type. Momma liked her girls young. The woman who was crossing the front yard to the bistro table appeared to be in her early fifties. If she was any younger, time hadn't treated her well. She had tied her hair back in a tight ponytail, but the color looked fake—a reddish-gold straight out of the box. Her faded green T-shirt had a picture of a cartoon owl in the center, the slogan GIVE A HOOT, DON'T POLLUTE stamped in soft white letters. It looked strange on her, too junior, possibly stolen out of a daughter's closet. Her shorts were dumpy and unflattering, as though she had lost weight but hadn't bought any new clothes to celebrate. Her feet were shoved into a pair of brown leather sandals. Her knees drooped like frowning twins.

Michael shook his head, then gave Rebel a sidelong glance. "She's old."

"She ain't *that* old."

"Too old for Momma," Michael assured him, squinting at the woman. She had a tattered paperback novel in one hand and a can of TaB in the other. Taking a seat at the table beneath the pine tree, she took a sip, then flipped to where a bookmark jutted out from between the pages of what he assumed was some girlie romance. Misty Dawn was crazy for that stuff. She had a whole collection of Harlequin books with racy covers—women with giant breasts clinging to half-naked men. Michael had seen girls with big breasts before, but they hadn't ever struck him as all that attractive. Fear did strange things to a person's face.

Rebel snatched the binoculars from Michael's hands.

"Like *you're* the expert." He scoffed. "What do you know about what Claudine wants, anyway?"

Michael didn't know much about anything, but he knew the type of girls they'd hauled back to the house over the years fit a certain profile. None of them had been as old as the lady they were looking at now.

"You sure this is the right house?" The question tumbled from Michael's lips before he could cut himself off.

Reb lowered the binoculars and slowly turned his head. Their eyes met momentarily before Michael looked away.

"You got any more stupid questions," Reb asked, "or you wanna shut up?"

"Sorry," Michael muttered, ducking his head into his shoulders.

Reb continued to watch the woman for a while, as if admiring her just as much as Michael had the house. Eventually, his brother said, "She's perfect," beneath his breath, and the longing in his voice gave Michael the creeps.

"Perfect for what?" Michael asked, staring down at the dead leaves beneath him. He half-expected Rebel to smack him upside the head for talking out of turn. But rather than hitting him, Reb slid back from the crest of the hill, sat up, and dusted himself off. He gave Michael a weird sort of smile and shrugged.

5

___

THE FIRST DAY they had him, all Michael did was cry.

They didn't even know his name until Lauralynn took him outside to look at the rabbits and somehow got him to talk.

"His name is Merrell," she said. "But Raybee . . . he says he's only four."

"What difference does that make?" Ray asked, his arms crossed defensively over his chest. He had expected Lauralynn to be over the moon when he presented her with his gift, but all she had done was gape like an openmouthed catfish.

"He's scared," she continued. "We gotta take him back."

"Take him back?" Momma had stepped onto the back porch mid-conversation. She eyed her two eldest children while Misty Dawn tended to Merrell in the yard. "There ain't no takin' him back," she announced. "This ain't a dog." Her hard gaze stopped on Ray's eight-year-old face. "You stole 'im—now you got 'im for the rest of your life."

Ray and Lauralynn went silent as Momma whipped a rug against the banister of the back porch. Merrell started crying again, and Misty tried to calm him down. When Momma went back inside, Lauralynn turned to her brother and hissed out a whisper. "We gotta take him back, Ray, no matter what she says."

Ray narrowed his eyes. He had gone to the trouble of getting Laura-lynn what she wanted, and now she was throwing it back in his face?

"You heard what Momma said. We can't," Ray told her. "If you don't want 'im, I'll keep 'im for myself."

"Keep him for *what*? He's already got a family."

"That's right. He's got *us*." He turned away from Lauralynn, marched across the yard, snatched the kid up by the arm, and turned his new little brother toward the house. "Your name ain't Merrell anymore," he told the kid. "Your name is Michael. We're your family now, so quit your bawlin'."

. . .

The newly christened Michael kept right on crying, kept asking for his mom and dad, kept begging Ray to take him home.

He went on for so long and so hard that Ray felt as though his ears were about ready to bleed. No matter how much Ray tried to engage him, Michael turned away, faced the wall, and wept. Finally having had enough, he grabbed Michael by the arms and shoved him across the room.

"Don't you get it?!" he said. "Your family don't want you anymore! Why do you think they left you out in the front yard to get picked up the way you did? Now I know why they did it. You don't *shut up*!"

Michael's eyes went wide, Ray's monologue distracting him just long enough to stifle his tears.

"You're lucky, you know," Ray said. "Some kids don't get a second family. Some kids get taken to the woods and left for the wolves and the bears. You rather that happen to you? You want me to take you into them trees?"

Michael shook his head hard, his breath coming in post-sob hitches.

"Well, I *will* if you don't listen to what I say. Nobody wants you here but me. *I* decided to save you, you got it? That makes me your boss. You know what a boss is?"

Michael nodded reluctantly and wiped his snotty nose on his arm. At least the kid stopped blubbering.

The next day was better. Michael was still weepy, but Ray could tell his little speech had brought the kid around. And now that he wasn't screaming his head off, Lauralynn started to warm up to him too. She knew they couldn't take him back, just like Momma had said. She was smart enough to know that the police were already looking for Michael, or Merrell, or whatever his name was. The second they tried to take the kid home, the cops would be on them like flies on dog shit. And since Momma wanted nothing to do with Ray's new pet, Lauralynn had no choice but to play house. Ray watched Michael and Lauralynn from his bedroom window as they chased one of the bunnies around the yard. When Lauralynn pointed Ray out to Michael in the upstairs window, they both waved at their brother from below. Ray held up a hand and managed a smile. He did it not because Lauralynn was happy, but because now she had someone directly dependent on her.

There was no way she could leave. Not with a clear conscience. Not anymore.

6

A FTER ABANDONING THEIR perch on the hill, Rebel seemed in a particularly good mood. Rather than heading straight home, he guided the Delta into the town of Dahlia proper and eased it into a parking lot. There, in front of them, was a tie-dyed building with THE DERVISH written across the front in psychedelic bubble lettering.

"What're we doing?" Michael asked, marveling at the bright colors in front of him. The building looked like an ice cream sundae—orange, raspberry, lemon, and lime.

"I want to pick up some music," Reb said.

Michael furrowed his eyebrows. The Dervish didn't look like the type of place to stock a lot of KISS or Styx. It seemed more Misty Dawn's speed. The kind of store that was crammed with dusty vinyl from the sixties, blasted Bob Marley—who Rebel hated—and sold weird Vietnam-era curios.

"Here?" Michael asked.

"What's with you questioning every goddamn thing today?" Reb snapped. "Something crawl up your ass while you were napping on that hill?"

Michael slouched while Reb hauled himself up and out of

his seat. It was hot, and Michael didn't much feel like sitting in the car, but that was part of the deal. Michael didn't accompany his brother around Dahlia unless he was invited to do so.

Reb turned off the car. Michael hung out the open window, grimacing as a warm breeze blew across his face. The heat was stifling today.

Reb gave Michael a look—*What are you, stupid?*—"You comin' in or what?"

"I didn't know that you wanted me to." Michael blinked, surprised at the invitation.

"Don't look so shocked," Reb told him. "It makes you look dumber than you actually are. Roll the window up if you're comin' in. We ain't in the sticks no more."

Michael watched Reb turn and disappear inside the brightly colored building, then rolled up the window and slid out of the car. He let his gaze drift across the parking lot to the buildings beyond the road, his stomach growling at the sight of a pair of golden arches. The McDonald's "two all-beef patties" jingle immediately singsonged inside his head—that tune had been all over the place a few years back. The TV. The radio. Its catchiness had bored right into his skull. If he carried money, he'd have run across the street and bought himself a Big Mac. He'd had one only once in his life, during a particularly long stakeout, and only because Reb had sworn he was dying of starvation. It had been the best thing Michael had ever tasted—nothing like Momma's meat-and-potato meals. Maybe if he stopped asking so many stupid questions, Reb would let them grab a bite there before they headed home. Not like Momma had to know.

Michael followed Rebel inside. The interior of the record store smelled funny—like sweet smoke and faraway places. If the walls inside the shop were as colorful as those outside, he couldn't tell. There were too many posters tacked up, creating an intricate patchwork of smiling musicians and Day-Glo flowers. The Beatles greeted him in fluorescent suits of yellow, pink, and blue. The quartet stood in front of a huge crowd of people, flowers spelling out the name of the band at their feet. It was the *Sgt. Pepper's Lonely Hearts Club Band* album. Misty Dawn owned it. Michael's favorite track was "When I'm Sixty-Four." As expected, Bob Marley—another face he recognized from Misty's collection—grinned at him from various corners of the shop. Bob's head was thrown back in ecstatic joy, dreadlocks slithering across his shoulders like snakes. Janis Joplin gave a wicked smile courtesy of an old concert poster advertising a show at a place called the Alexandria Arena. Michael liked Bob and Janis all right, but not as much as he liked the Beatles. And while Misty Dawn would have preferred more pop than rock in her record collection, she didn't ever complain. Beggars couldn't be choosers, and Misty was certainly the former. All those albums had been stolen. When Michael had managed to stick ABBA under his arm, she'd screamed with delight. She'd played that album on a loop for what felt like a solid month. It seemed like the stylus should have cut that vinyl record right in half.

What looked like a black-and-white mug shot of Jimi Hendrix stared at Michael from the back wall. The poster was so massive that he couldn't help but imagine Misty going gaga over it. It wasn't Swedish pop, but Misty had eclectic tastes. Some of the stuff she listened to, even Wade liked. Sometimes Wade would go up to her room and listen to bluesy rock on her record player. Creedence Clearwater Revival would twang through the wall that separated Michael's and Misty's rooms. Michael would close his eyes and try to imagine himself in the stories Wade loved to tell. The jungle. Crawling through swamps. A rifle in one hand and a Lucky Strike tucked between his lips. Charlie just around the corner. Death only a few steps behind. And then there was Misty's other stuff—the Bee Gees and Peaches & Herb, Bonnie Tyler, and Rod Stewart. That was the stuff Rebel would yell for her to turn off because it was giving him a headache. That was the music Wade muttered about being "behind all the trouble with those fags in DC."

Michael looked across the expanse of wooden crates on top of what looked like homemade tables. The crates were packed full of record sleeves. Handwritten signs separated the tables into decades. Decades were portioned out by letters of the alphabet, and the most popular artists got their own tabs. Rebel stood close to the front window on the left side of the store, the sun shining on his back. He was leaning against the front counter, grinning at a strawberry blonde who was laughing too freely for the two of them to have only just met. Then again, Reb had a way with girls.

Rebel turned his head and regarded Michael with a nod. He was smiling, but as soon as their eyes met, his expression went hard. *Don't screw this up*, it said, and for a moment Michael didn't get what that could have meant. But then he saw the way Reb was looking at the girl. She was twisting a lock of hair around one of her fingers, snapping her gum between giggles. He supposed not screwing up meant not robbing the place. He was tempted to steal a whole armload of records and make Misty Dawn's day, but that wouldn't go over too well with the employees.

Michael looked away and stepped up to the nearest crate, flipping through record sleeves while the girl chuckled at something Reb had said. He kept his head down and his eyes diverted as he slowly moved from the front of the store toward the back. He was trying to place the song that buzzed through a speaker mounted in the top corner of the room, thinking about how Misty would have known it after the first few bars. It seemed like she knew every song on the radio—lyrics, title, artist, everything. Every time they caught *Name That Tune* on TV, she'd have a higher score than any of the contestants.

The song playing overhead was loud and rollicking with a fast beat and horn accompaniment. It was bouncy and buoyant despite its rough edge, as exotic as the smoke that curled up his nostrils and filled his lungs. Michael cast a glance at the speaker, waiting for it to reveal its secret as he listened, only to hear the slap of record sleeves against linoleum a few feet behind him. Sure that he'd nudged something in passing, he twisted around to see what damage he had done. But instead of finding an overturned crate at his heels—*Thank God, because Reb would have been pissed*—a girl was crouching there, collecting a few spilled records into her arms.

She looked up at him, her cropped black hair making her skin shine like freshly poured milk. Their eyes met, and Michael's heart tripped over its own beat. She looked like Snow White from Lauralynn's old book of fairy tales, except a hundred times more beautiful and wearing all black, looking about as modern as the music sounded. A smile crossed her lips, and she looked down at the floor, sweeping up the last record before rising.

"Sorry," she said. "You need help finding anything?"

Michael watched her lips move, mesmerized by the way she formed her words. He smelled spearmint. She turned to file a couple of records into the crate at his elbow. Her profile was astounding. The length of her neck. The way her earlobes seemed to flow into the angle of her jawline. She shot him another glance, raising an eyebrow at his lack of response. When he looked away a little too quickly, she chuckled to herself and lifted her shoulders into a shrug.

"Okay then," she said just beyond his shoulder. "If you change your mind, I'm easy to find. It's rockabilly, by the way. Brand new." She pointed to the speaker. "Stray Cats." Stepping around him, she left a waft of mint in her wake.

Leaning forward more than necessary, Michael allowed his hair to form a curtain around his face. There was something about her that twisted his stomach into knots—nervous excitement. A scary, forbidden longing. He had felt that dangerous hunger a few times before. Once, Reb had bent a girl over the hood of the Delta and pushed her underwear around her ankles. Her eyes had fixed on Michael through the windshield as she moaned. There had been a couple of times in the basement, as Michael stripped Momma's girls of their clothes. Each time had felt wrong, as though his body was responding to something prohibited, something poisonous.

He edged back to the front door, hoping Rebel would take notice and decide it was time to go. It didn't feel safe here. He felt vulnerable, as though at any minute he could fall into something he'd never be able to pull himself out of. Despite the horrors back home, at least there he had routine. Lingering beside the exit, Michael leaned against the shop window next to the door. He waited for the strawberry blonde behind the counter to stop her chatter so Reb could take notice.

As if on cue, Rebel looked back, rolled his eyes, and shoved away from the register with an easy shrug of the shoulders. "See you later," he told the girl, then pivoted on the soles of his boots and made for the door. Pulling it open, he grabbed Michael by the shoulder and shoved him outside.

Michael waited for Rebel to unlock the Delta's door, then slid back into the car and hunched his shoulders as he stared at his knees. Reb was clearly pissed, buzzing like an electric wire. He didn't say anything while pulling out of the parking lot, but he didn't have to. Michael knew he was spitting sparks, ready to ignite just as soon as they were on the road.

"What's wrong with you?!" he demanded once they put the Dervish and, to Michael's disappointment, McDonald's in the rearview mirror. "That girl was tryin' to talk to you, and you acted like a retard sprung fresh from Weston State."

"She just asked if I needed help," Michael murmured. "I didn't."

Reb laughed—a cold one, the kind Michael hated. "Yeah right," he said, "*you* don't need help. Man, you need more help than anyone I've ever met. I wonder about you, Mike."

"Wonder about what?"

"Whether you're human or not," he said. "Didn't you like that girl? She was hot. Even better than that chick at the counter. Probably freaky too. You see the way she was dressed?"

Michael didn't respond.

Reb sighed in frustration. "You like going into town, don't you? Wanna pick up some records for Misty every now and again?"

"Yeah."

"Great. So I'll take you into town with me more often, but you can't go actin' like a freak, alright?"

Michael nodded slowly, still unsure of Reb's intention.

"It's about time we start actin' more like brothers, huh?" Rebel said. "Stand united and all that crap. Like them protestors Wade loves so much."

"What about Momma?"

"Oh, fuck her." Reb just about spit the words. "She don't need to know what we do when we ain't workin'. Besides, *I'm* in charge, remember? If I say we're gonna have a good time, then we're gonna have a good time."

Michael looked out the window. It seemed to him that

Rebel always had a good time. He wasn't sure why he suddenly had to be involved.

. . .

Michael stared at the thick slab of meat on his plate, his Big Mac craving stronger than ever. There were no potatoes today, no vegetables, not even a slice of bread. Just a rare steak that oozed red against a chipped white plate.

The dining room was silent, save for the scraping of knives and Wade's chewing. It didn't matter what Momma put on Wade's plate—he always seemed to be working his teeth around a mouthful of rocks. The man could crunch tapioca pudding, his teeth gnashing against each other behind his lips. He stared across the table at Michael and Rebel as he ate, a look of suspicion pulled tight across his face.

"You boys were gone an awful long time today," he said. "Mind tellin' me where you two were at?"

Reb shifted in his seat. He looked uncomfortable but held his tongue, as if waiting for Wade's question to pass without requiring a reply.

Wade forced a tight-lipped smile at his adopted son. "Michael," he said, "everything okay?"

Michael swallowed the wad of sinewy meat he'd been gnawing and gave his father a slow nod.

"It don't look it," Wade said. "So . . . where you been?"

"We were scopin' out the new mark," Reb told the table. "Michael fell asleep on the goddamn hill, birds chirpin' around his head. Like Sleepin' Beauty."

Something about the statement made Misty Dawn smile. She gave Michael an almost dreamy look, like she'd fantasized about dozing atop a hill of her own.

"Sounds peaceful," she mused.

"Yeah, it was warm," Michael said, his voice below a murmur. "The birds were nice."

Wade gave Michael a dubious glance, as though he'd said something wrong.

"Don't be a fag," Rebel said, giving Michael a hard glance before continuing. "The place is out in the middle of nowhere. I mean *real* isolated."

"And you were able to find it?" Misty asked, something dangerous sparking behind the green of her eyes.

"Why the hell wouldn't I be able to find it?"

"I don't know." She raised her shoulders in an idle shrug. "Lots of things can happen between here and there, especially when you're good and drunk."

Michael winced at her boldness. Before he could give his sister a look that pleaded for her to shut up and not make trouble, Momma reached out and gave Misty's hair a vicious yank. Misty yelped.

"Hey, fuck you, Misty," Reb shot back.

"Enough from the both of you," Momma hissed.

"You best watch yourself, Misty Dawn," Wade said, his tone strangely solemn.

"Yeah," Rebel said. "You push hard enough and you'll end up at the grandparents' house with Lauralynn."

Both Wade and Momma tensed.

Michael could feel Reb itching to jump out of his seat, to launch himself onto the table and start kicking glasses into the walls, but he didn't understand why.

Momma stared at Reb like he'd just told the family he had called the police and turned them all in, having tired of his part in everything. The little color that had been in her thin, sallow face had faded. She stared at her son with wide, disbelieving eyes, the gold and brown tones in her floral-print dress making her skin look sickly and yellow.

They all sat in uncomfortable silence for a long while. Michael listened to the cacophony of everyone's breathing while Momma and Reb stared across the table at each other like a pair of vicious dogs. The quiet was finally broken when Momma shoved her chair away from the table. The legs screamed against the hardwood floor. She slammed her hands onto the tabletop. Everyone's utensils jumped and clanged against their plates. Her nostrils flared and the sinew in her neck stuck out like ropes. Michael had to look away when her lips turned up in a snarl.

"I don't never want to hear that name said in this house again," she growled, her eyes fixed on her oldest boy. "You understand me?" When Rebel didn't reply, her tone pitched toward a scream. "*You understand?!*"

Her arms jerked to the side in a mechanical sweep, sending her plate off the table and onto the floor. It shattered as soon as it hit the hardwood, bits of steak plopping onto the planks, red juice spraying the baseboard. She stepped behind Misty, who was now cowering in her seat, and grabbed her by the ears. "I'll deal with *you* later," she spoke into Misty's hair, then shot a final piercing glare at Reb before stomping out of the room.

Michael caught the startled shine in Misty's eyes, but she said nothing, and she didn't allow herself to cry. After a tense moment, Misty gathered herself up and began clearing the table as though nothing of consequence had occurred.

Wade left his seat without another word, and Michael half-expected Rebel to follow suit. But Reb sat wooden in his chair, like he'd been electrocuted. He gripped the seat on both sides, his head bowed, a man desperately trying not to lose control.

"Reb?" Michael chewed his bottom lip. His brother's posture was scaring him more than Momma's outburst had. Those same ropes that Momma had now stuck out against Reb's neck. Michael imagined him grinding his teeth down to powder inside his mouth. He dared to reach out—something he wouldn't have usually done, but Rebel's words from earlier were still fresh in his mind: brothers were supposed to stand united. It was time they started acting like a family, sticking together no matter what. But as soon as Michael grazed Reb's elbow, Reb windmilled both arms outward in a burst of energy. His chair went skittering backward as he stood.

"*Don't touch me!*" he yelled.

Michael's eyes went wide. He sat stock-still, afraid that moving would push Rebel over whatever edge he was toeing.

Misty slunk around the table to gather Wade's plate, her gaze flitting from Reb to Michael and back again.

"I shoulda gotten rid of you like she said," Rebel growled, the words so quiet he probably didn't mean for anyone to hear them. "Shoulda taken you out into the trees and did to you what I did to that stupid fuckin' dog."

Michael's stomach twisted around his dinner as Reb marched out of the room, leaving Michael and Misty to stare at one another.

"What's wrong with him?" he whispered, wondering if his sister had an explanation for Reb's weird behavior. When she didn't answer, he stitched his eyebrows together and frowned. "You shouldn't of said that," he told her, keeping his voice down. "The thing about him drinkin'."

"Well, it's *true*," she retorted. "And besides, he ain't got no right calling you names like that. Makes me mad."

"Except now you're in trouble," Michael reminded her.

Misty scowled at the plates in her hands and dropped a handful of silverware on top of the stack. Michael shook his head and slid out of his seat. Crouching next to Momma's broken plate, he began plucking ceramic shards off the ground, carefully piling them in the palm of his left hand.

"What would be so bad about goin' to the grandparents' place anyway?" Misty asked. "What would be so bad about that, huh?"

"I don't know, Miss," he said, murmuring toward the floor. "But we ain't never seen Lauralynn again after she went off there. You wanna go there forever?"

Misty looked like she was holding her breath in response to his question. Michael looked down to the bits of plate scattered around his feet, his chest suddenly tight. He knew Misty's answer without her having to say a word. Because anywhere was better than here. He only hoped that in the end he wouldn't be left on his own.

7

RAY COULDN'T REMEMBER being more excited. Wade and Momma rode inside the cab of Wade's pickup. Ray, Lauralynn, Misty Dawn, and Michael sat in the bed of the truck, chattering like a bunch of chickens, excited to arrive at the Cabell County Fair. Michael had been with them for nearly two years; he'd become part of the family and hardly ever asked about his other parents anymore. To Ray's chagrin, Momma had stuck him in Ray's room, and for the most part Michael drove Ray crazy with his endless questions and babyish ways. But today was going to be a good day. Today, Ray was going to spend his savings on corn dogs and cotton candy, and then he was going to make himself sick on the Ferris wheel. He was going to ride that thing until he puked.

The Fair was a big deal, and Lauralynn and Misty Dawn were wearing matching dresses for the occasion—a set they had outgrown but that Momma still squeezed them into because there was no money for fancy things like Sunday best. Momma's own mother, Grandma Jean, had given the girls their dresses during a rare visit a few years back. Grandma Jean was meaner than sin, and even Momma looked uncomfortable when Grandma Jean and Grandpa Eugene spent a week at the Morrow farmhouse. Ray had laughed when Misty and Lauralynn had come downstairs in their matching getups. They had pulled their hair up in pigtails and stood at the foot of the stairs, Lauralynn stoic as ever, Misty clawing like a helpless chimp at the fabric that bit into her armpits.

"You all look like you got tangled in them window curtains," Ray had cackled, pointing to the ugly drapes that flanked the window of the front room. When Grandma Jean whacked him in the mouth with an open palm, he'd stared at her in a wide-eyed daze. Later that afternoon, Ray had spotted Lauralynn sitting on Grandpa Eugene's lap on the back porch. The skirt of her new dress was piled up on top of her thighs. Grandpa Eugene's left arm circled her shoulders to keep her close, his right hand lost somewhere in the ugly fabric of her skirt.

As Wade's truck bounced along, Ray tongued his chipped front tooth, remembering the way Grandma Jean's wedding ring had smacked against the enamel. Lauralynn smoothed the skirt of her too-small dress over the tops of her legs. Her hair shone in the sunlight like a pink-and-gold sunrise. She looked prettier than Ray had ever seen her.

"Now, you know there's gonna be lots of people," Lauralynn told them as the truck turned down a rural road. "Lots of chances to get lost. Ray, since you're the second oldest, you're takin' care of Misty."

"Aw, man!" Ray cried, but Lauralynn ignored him.

"Michael, you're still just a baby, so you stay with me."

"I ain't no baby!" Michael protested, but again, Lauralynn wasn't swayed.

"You all can keep complainin' and stay in the truck, or you can keep quiet and have a good time at the fair," she told them. "So which is it gonna be?"

Ray and Misty met eyes. She pulled a face at him as he scowled. He supposed it could have been worse—LL could have paired him up with Michael. If that had happened, the entire day would have been ruined for sure.

"We should just leave 'em with Momma and Wade," Ray murmured.

"That way we can go on the big rides instead of gettin' stuck on them stupid baby ones."

"I don't want to stay with Momma and Wade!" Misty shrieked. "That ain't fair!"

The sound of Misty's complaining made Ray's skin crawl. He wondered how sad Momma and Wade would really be if she just up and disappeared.

"You're not stayin' with Momma and Wade," Lauralynn told her, fixing one of Misty's curls. "You're stayin' with Ray, and we're *all* gonna stick together. But in case we get separated, you gotta hold on to Ray, okay?"

Misty nodded in approval and stuck her tongue out at her big brother in triumph, then smoothed out her skirt, mimicking Lauralynn. Momma had cut along the side-seams of Misty's dress and filled it in with different material so she could still squeeze into it. But the skirt rode up so high that, if she bent over, the entire fair would see her underpants. Ray supposed the only reason Momma didn't care about Misty flashing her undies was because she was only eight years old. If it had been Lauralynn, Momma would have had a conniption fit.

The Morrow kids waited patiently as Wade paid their admission. Wade had been worried about taking Michael to the fair, but Momma waved his trepidation away. The fair was a good distance from Dahlia, and besides, Michael had grown quick. He didn't look at all like he had when Ray and Wade had snatched him from his front yard two years earlier.

As soon as their tickets were torn, the Morrow kids ran through the gates like a pack of wild horses busting out of a corral. Ray grabbed Lauralynn by one hand and Misty by the other while they dragged little Michael behind them like the tail of a kite. The chain of them ran for a row of food vendors. They bought candy apples and buttered popcorn with the pennies they'd saved all year. They washed the salty sweetness down with orange sodas and shaved ice flavored like cherries and watermelon.

After a round of bumper cars, a queasy spin on the Roll-O-Plane, and a couple of go-rounds on the Paratrooper ride, the quartet went back for greasy corn dogs and soft pretzels dotted with big cubes of salt. Ray gave himself a personal challenge and stuck his grubby hand into a barrel while the vendor wasn't looking. He stole a giant dill pickle before bolting into the crowd, laughing madly as the vendor screamed for him to stop. Some fairgoers looked on in amusement. Others shot disapproving glances at the culprit. But none were motivated enough to stop the pickle thief.

They rode the Sky Whirl and the Octopus and sang along to "California Dreamin'" while on the Ferris wheel, kicking their feet high up in the air as they swayed side to side like four best friends. Ray spotted the massive clown's face at the back of the fair from the crest of the wheel, pointing it out to his siblings. Its mouth was a giant gaping hollow. Its eyes looked crazed rather than inviting. It dared only the bravest of children to enter its lair.

"That's next," Ray announced. "I bet it's got a mirror maze and everything."

"That looks scary." Misty Dawn seemed unsure.

"It's only scary if you're a dumb chicken," Ray told her. "You can stay outside."

Ray crossed his fingers that both Misty and Michael would be too scared to tag along and would, instead, wait for him and Lauralynn next to the ring toss and the water-gun game. Once they got closer to the giant clown head, Misty decided that staying behind was a good idea, as long as someone gave her enough money for a funnel cake. But Michael clung to Lauralynn's hand and gave her and Ray a brave five-year-old's smile.

"I ain't scared of no clown," Michael declared. "It's a *fun* house, so it's gonna be fun."

Ray nearly protested, but he smiled to himself and patted Michael on top of his dumb head instead. This was going to be fun indeed. Ray would make sure of it.

Michael lost it in the hall of mirrors. With seemingly no escape from the darkened room, their reflections warped and leered at them like demons trapped just beyond the glass. Terrified, Michael threw his head back and screamed.

Ray thought it was funny at first. He took the opportunity to terrorize his little brother by circling Michael and Lauralynn, bounding from foot to foot like a crazy jester. But that was fun for all of thirty seconds; after that, all he wanted was for Michael to shut up again. The way he was screaming was just like how he had gone off in Wade's truck the day Ray had swept him up off the side of the road. There was a level of terror in Michael's wail that gave Ray a secret pang of joy, but it was also the kind that made other people nervous. Nervous enough to remember them.

"Hey, shut up, stupid!" Ray yelled as a pair of teenagers gave the trio a curious look. They were deciding whether they should get an adult to help or forget about the screaming kid and be on their way. "Shut up," Ray repeated, more for the teens than for Michael's sake. "It's just mirrors, see?" He danced in front of one of them, putting on a decent show of trying to calm his kid brother down. The older kids shrugged and left them behind.

Lauralynn crouched in front of the screaming six-year-old. She wrapped her arms around him and cooed into his ear as she rocked him back and forth.

"It's okay," she whispered. "There, there, Mikey. I'm here with you. It's all right."

Ray stood by and watched the exchange while something ugly twisted into his guts like a rusty old screw. When he couldn't look at them anymore, he peered at the endless walls of mirrors instead. That's when he lost his breath. The way the mirrors were angled, the three of them only cast a reflection of two. There was only Lauralynn and Michael, the two of them clinging to each other like castaways with no hope of rescue.

Ray twisted where he stood, startled as he took in each reflection, which seemed to trail off into infinity. Somehow, by some weird trick of angles and light, the fun house had erased him. His big sister held his replacement tightly in her arms.

Ray turned and stumbled out of the fun house, pale as a sheet. Misty Dawn was leaning against some metal railing near the exit. Her mouth was smeared with powdered sugar, and her eyes glinted with mischief.

"I thought it was only scary if you were a dumb chicken." A smile of wicked satisfaction pulled at the corner of her mouth. "Guess you're a dumb chicken, huh?" She giggled, then folded a wad of funnel cake into her cheek. A moment later, she nearly choked on the pastry. Ray socked her in the arm as hard as he could before stomping away.

During the ride home, Ray sat on the opposite side of the truck bed from everyone else. He tried not to look at his siblings. But anytime he caught a glimpse of them, he could only note a single detail: Lauralynn was still holding Michael's hand.

8

REBEL WAS IN a foul mood. He had hardly said a word as he lumbered around the house, waiting for Michael to get his boots on. Once the boys were in the Olds, he cranked the Rolling Stones so loud that it made Michael's head hurt. They drove for a while. Eventually, Reb parked the car along the side of the road and slid out of the driver's seat. Michael's ears rang in the silence. He could hardly hear the crunch of old leaves beneath his feet as he followed Reb up the hill.

They crawled across the crest the same way they had before. Michael folded his arms and rested his chin on top of his hands while Reb studied the green-shuttered house through his binoculars. Michael didn't like this part of the job. Scoping out marks involved a lot of waiting, sometimes in the blazing heat of the car—but he did like it here. Maybe it was the songbirds. There were tons of them in West Virginia, but it seemed that there was a greater concentration in this particular corner of the mountains. He closed his eyes and considered the possibility. Maybe there was magic in this spot. The thing that drew the birds to this location was probably what made him feel so at ease as well.

But just as he began to drift, Reb's impatience jolted him awake.

"Let's go." His words were gruff, testy.

Michael blinked his eyes open. He shot his brother a questioning glance, then turned his attention back to the little house below them with a curious look. He expected to see the woman sliding out the front door with her romance novel and a cold can of soda, but the yard was empty. The house looked abandoned, and with the garage closed, there was no telling whether she was home or someplace else.

"You saw her?" Michael asked.

That was the number one rule when hunting sedentary marks: Reb and Michael had to get a visual, establish the routine. It was their job to know when the mark came and went. How long they stayed out. How long they slept. Who they knew, and who would care if that person suddenly vanished off the face of the earth. Drifters were easier. That's why their prime targets were wayward girls hitching rides along empty highways. They didn't have to establish a damn thing when it came to transients. Even if those girls did have family, it didn't matter. Hitchhiking came with risks, and someone shoving them into the trunk of a car was one of them.

"I don't see her," Michael murmured, reaching for the binoculars. "Where is she?"

"I don't care," Reb said. "I'm tired of waitin'. We're leavin'."

"We're givin' her up?" Michael's fingers slid along the strap of the binoculars, tugging it lightly so that Rebel would let him see, but Reb wasn't in the mood. He jerked the binoculars away from Michael's hand and sat up in plain view, throwing caution to the wind.

"Did I say we're givin' her up? No, I didn't."

"But we're leavin'?"

It didn't make sense. Michael knew Reb was still sore about the whole thing with Momma from the night before. But abandoning their post would put them behind schedule, and being behind schedule put Misty Dawn at risk.

Rebel stood, dusted off the seat of his jeans, and began to stalk down the hill toward the car. Michael stared at him from where he lay on his belly, somehow convinced that Reb wasn't serious even though he was walking away. A mild form of panic set in when his brother put twenty paces between them. Michael skittered down the slope so he was out of view of the house, sat up, and stopped him with an almost pleading remark.

"But we *can't*."

Reb twisted to look over his shoulder. "Stay out here, then," he said. "I'll come back for you in a couple of days."

The suggestion was enough to make Michael scramble to his feet, his pulse banging against the interior of his skull. "We've gotta clear this," he said. "Either that or find someone else."

Rebel didn't look back this time. He raised his voice while tromping away. "Don't you worry. It's clear."

Michael rushed after him, sure that Reb really would leave him out there if he didn't follow. It scared him that what they were about to do would put them both in a bad situation.

"How can it be clear?" he asked, catching up. "We've only

been out here one time before this, Reb. We don't know nothin' about her."

Rebel narrowed his eyes. He bowed his head, kicking last winter's leaves with the tips of his scuffed-up boots. His sharp, angular features looked harsher than usual.

"*You've* only been out here once," Reb said, then cut himself off with a snort. "Don't be such a pussy."

"But we're gonna get in trouble."

Rebel came to a stop.

"How're we gonna get in trouble?" he asked. "You gonna tell?" He gave Michael a stern shove. Michael stumbled backward, nearly toppling over when a pine branch rolled beneath his foot. "You rat me out, you rat us both out. Claudine will beat the livin' crap out of you first, and then I'll take my turn, because nobody likes a snitch."

"I'm not gonna tell," Michael insisted. "I just don't wanna—"

"Don't wanna what? Do what I tell ya?"

Rebel grabbed Michael by the arm, suddenly twisting it behind his back. A flash of pain bit into Michael's shoulder.

"Reb, don't!" he pleaded, but Rebel refused to let go.

"You've been a real pain in my ass these past few days, you know that?" He pushed Michael forward, forcing him to march like a prisoner of war. "*But Re-eb,*" he mock-whined. "*We're gonna get in trouble. When are we gonna get me some more maxipads?* How about we make a new rule for the retard? How about we say the retard ain't allowed to ask any more stupid questions? How's that grab you?"

"Please, Reb." Michael stumbled forward. "You're gonna break my arm."

Rebel gave him another shove, letting him go. "Brothers united . . . remember?"

Michael rubbed at his shoulder, frowning as the Olds came into view through the trees. "I remember," Michael murmured. He was worrying for nothing. Rebel had the brains. Hell, Rebel was smart enough to clear the mark on two visits and Michael didn't have the slightest idea how he did it. That's how smart his brother was.

Sliding into the passenger seat, Michael pulled his seat belt into place and kept his eyes down. Reb sat motionless on the driver's side, the plastic eight ball that was attached to his keys hanging down from his hand. He mumbled something beneath his breath, too quiet for Michael to catch, and then shoved the keys into the ignition and left the hill behind.

.   .   .

Seeing the Dervish blaze bright and colorful in the summer sun made Michael sick. He felt like he'd swallowed a family of squirming eels, all of them collectively trying to gnaw their way out of his belly with tiny needle teeth. Those sweet, sherbet colors sent a quiver of nausea up his throat. Rebel was defying Wade's set rules—rules that had been made to keep the Morrows safe. They were supposed to clear their marks. They weren't supposed to visit the same place twice in a short amount of time. And they certainly weren't supposed to be getting friendly with the locals, whether those persons of interest had strawberry-blond hair or not. The Morrow boys were to be ghosts, leaving behind nothing of themselves or those they took from the world.

Michael opened his mouth to protest, but he couldn't find the words. Every argument that tumbled through his head made him feel guilty, because he and Rebel were supposed to stand united. Brothers in arms. But despite all logic, despite every reason as to why going back to the Dervish was the worst idea in the history of bad ideas, Michael managed to convince himself that Rebel would never put the Morrows in danger. Reb knew what he was doing because Reb was the smart one. If Michael didn't trust in his brother and best friend, it would serve him well to pray for a little more faith.

He hoped that Rebel wouldn't read into his silence. But when he finally looked over to his brother, Reb's expression was severe. His mouth was pulled into a tight line and his eyebrows had stitched together. The ridge of his brow threw his weird gray-green eyes into shadow. It was the look of a killer—the kind of expression murderers wore just before wrapping their hands around a victim's throat. And yet, as soon as their eyes met, Rebel's face changed from harsh to oddly amicable. For half a second, Michael was caught off guard by that strange expression. It was almost plastic, as though his brother had pulled a mask over his face, hiding his true feelings behind a distant grin.

Rebel leaned back in the driver's seat and casually turned so that he was fully facing Michael rather than looking out the windshield. He stretched a hand toward the stereo and turned the music down. Cleared his throat. Gave Michael what looked to be an embarrassed smile.

"So, that girl in there," he said, nodding toward the Dervish. "Her name is Lucy. And I know what you're gonna say before you even say it. You're gonna tell me how we ain't supposed to be doing this kind of thing because it's dangerous. Because Wade put all them stories about bein' followed and found out and whatever else inside your head."

Michael shifted in his seat, caught the inside of his cheek between his molars, and frowned as his brother spoke.

"But I'm tellin' you that Wade is full of shit about that stuff. It ain't half as dangerous out here as he makes it out to be. The old man thinks every fuckin' place is 'Nam. He just wants to keep us under his thumb, you get me?"

"Why?" Michael asked.

Reb scoffed. "*Why?* Hell, maybe because he don't got no one else to control but us, huh? Maybe because he's married to an old battle-axe that tells him when to eat, shit, and sleep. No army man can really be comfortable with that, you know?"

Michael slouched in his seat, lifted his hand to his mouth, and chewed on a nail.

"You get what I'm tryin' to say? The old man is using fear to keep us in check. It's what them fancy folk call *manipulatin'*, except that I'm tired of it, Mikey. I'm tired of someone else tellin' me how to live my life. I don't care how many people he killed out there in the swamps. That don't mean he's better than me. I'm twenty-three years old. I'm ready for a steady girl. But

I can't have one if I follow Wade's rules, can I? Naw. And you can't have one neither. Not now or never."

Michael nodded and looked down to his hands. He understood where his brother was going with this, although he was really trying to sell it hard.

"It's fine," Michael finally said. "I ain't gonna tell."

Rebel's face lit up, and suddenly his sharp, birdlike features melted into something good-looking. He looked like the handsome guys in the magazines or the ones that did cigarette commercials on TV. It was strange how fast Reb moved through emotions. Not more than a half an hour ago, he had been pissed off and brooding; now he was wearing the biggest smile Michael had seen in all his life.

"All right," Reb said, looking satisfied. "That's great. You ain't gonna regret it, Mikey. You'll see." He pushed open his door and began climbing out of the Olds when he stopped short, noting Michael's lack of response. "What's with you? Ain't you comin'?"

Michael shrugged. "You go on ahead," he said. "I think I'll just stay in the car."

If Reb wanted to pick up chicks, that was okay; Michael knew how to keep a secret. But he sure didn't know how to keep up when it came to playing the game. The idea of standing in that record store made him queasy. Snow White was in there, and with Rebel preoccupied with Lucy, she'd have nothing better to do than strike up a conversation. Michael didn't know how to talk to girls. That weird, uncomfortable yearning would come back. It would swallow him, and she'd see it in his face; she'd see what Michael really was.

"What do you mean, you'll stay in the car? That's crazy," Reb was shooting for lighthearted, but Michael could hear the aggravation leeching into his tone.

"I don't feel so good," Michael explained.

"Then you're *really* not stayin'," Reb assured him. "What are you, afraid of girls?"

The more Michael thought about it, the less it made sense. Even if Rebel and Lucy hit it off, what did he expect would happen? He couldn't take her back to the farmhouse, couldn't ever tell her what he did or who he was.

"I just don't feel like it," Michael insisted, waiting for Reb to reprimand him for being a loser. When his brother didn't fire back an insult, Michael dared to look up from his hands. Reb's expression had changed. But rather than glaring at Michael with a look that could kill, he was now watching him the way someone would look at a wounded animal along the side of the road. *How sad*, it read. *How totally pathetic.*

"Fine, suit yourself." Reb finally relented. "But I'm gonna be a while, so if you cook in here . . ." He shrugged, sliding out of the car. "Just think about what I said about Wade, huh? We work hard, Mike. We work hard for him and Claudine and we don't never get nothin' in the way of thanks. Don't we deserve a good time?" Then he slammed the door and trudged across the parking lot. Michael watched him disappear into the store.

. . .

Michael stepped inside the Dervish a few minutes later, but not because he wanted to. It was because he knew his brother well, and one girl may not have been enough. The idea of Rebel bending Snow White over the hood of the Delta compounded the nausea he already felt. If he didn't show an interest, Reb would take that to mean Snow White was fair game. Michael didn't know the first thing about what he was doing, but something about the idea of his older brother having Lucy *and* Snow was too much to bear.

The little bell jingled when he pushed open the door, that exotic scent hitting him square in the chest. He took a deep breath and stepped inside. Reb was standing at the front counter, leaning against it with one hip cocked. He shot a look over his shoulder at Michael, and when their eyes met, Michael could read Reb's expression with ease. *Don't waste this opportunity*, it said. *Don't let Wade boss you around no more.* Rebel grinned at Lucy. Her hair cascaded down her back in soft, easy waves. She tucked her ear against a raised shoulder and gave Reb a bashful smile as he reached out to draw his fingers down the delicate line of her jaw. Lucy's gaze darted from Michael to the back of the store, then returned to Reb again. She caught him by the hand and stepped out from behind the register, pulling him along. Michael followed them with his eyes—a pretty girl leading a grinning jackal to what Michael guessed was a storage room. They slid beyond the door and shut it behind them with a quiet click.

Michael blinked at the seemingly abandoned store. He

twisted around to look at the posters on the walls, the ones closest to the front windows discolored by the sun. He recognized the music coming through the speakers as Van Halen; Reb played them in the Delta every now and again. David Lee Roth *ooh baby baby*'d his way into the open room, accompanied by the constant groan of an air conditioner battling the West Virginia heat.

He nearly jumped at the sound of the tiny bell above the door and glanced back at the Dervish's new patron. A woman wearing a floor-length skirt in loud oranges and greens stepped inside. Her stick-straight hair was so long it hid her entire back. Henna tattoos spiraled down her bare arms and decorated her hands in intricate paisley patterns. She gave Michael a lazy smile and murmured "Hey, man" while drifting down an aisle of crates.

Pulling records from the stacks with little to no thought, she created a pile of vinyl that would make Misty Dawn quiver with jealousy. Michael watched her from behind his hair for a while. His eyes occasionally darted to the storage room door, and he wondered if Lucy was going to come back out in time to ring the woman up. With an armload of records, the long-haired lady gave Michael a questioning look. She then moved across the store and dropped the stack onto the checkout counter.

"Is nobody working this place today or what?" she asked. "Where's Lucy?"

Michael opened his mouth, not sure how to reply. Explaining that Lucy was in the back room doing God only knew what with Rebel didn't seem right. Michael didn't want to get her in trouble, but before he could stumble through an awkward sentence and explain that someone *was* there, that they were just . . . *busy* . . . a sweet voice saved him the embarrassment.

"Lucy's at lunch."

Snow White appeared seemingly out of nowhere. Michael imagined her hiding behind a stack of crates, appearing in a puff of glittery smoke like Glinda the Good Witch.

"Hi, Barb," Snow White said, giving the woman a wide smile.

"Seems a bit early for lunch," Barb said, glancing over her shoulder at Michael. Snow White began to sort through the records on the counter. "Maybe you should hire Robert Plant to help you run the place." Barb hooked a thumb over her shoulder.

"Yeah, maybe I should," Snow said with a half-smile. She cast a glance in Michael's direction before punching a series of buttons on the register.

The attention made him feel self-conscious. He stepped away from the bank of windows and moved down one of the aisles, his back to the girls. Wade had taught him to avoid conversation. People were unpredictable. They asked a lot of questions, and sometimes finding appropriate answers was hard. Reb had agreed on that point up until now, and that left Michael in a vulnerable position. He could talk to Snow White and risk her asking about things he couldn't talk about, or he could ignore her completely and have his brother engage her instead.

"Or maybe Lucy ran off because you're playing *this* stuff,"

Barb said, pointing to one of the speakers. "A store full of music and you pick this?"

"We try not to discriminate." He couldn't see her, but Michael could hear the amusement in Snow's voice.

"Yeah, well, maybe it would suit you to be a bit more choosy. Discrimination is one thing, but free love isn't unconditional, man."

Snow chuckled. "Is that new ink?" she asked.

"Yeah. Got it done when I drove up to Charleston. Picked up some new sound equipment for the station. Though I gotta say, we're probably switching to cassettes soon."

"Aw, what? Tapes?"

"Hey, they're starting to sound better these days. Get your boss to stock 'em, huh? Anyway, say hi to Lucy for me when she gets back," Barb said. Michael listened to the crinkle of a paper bag. "And put on another record for me. Please."

"Will do," Snow singsonged. "See you later, Barb."

"Back in a few weeks. Later days, babe."

Michael chewed his bottom lip as Barb walked his way. She slowed her steps, as if to get a better look at him, then shot a glance over her shoulder, flashing a grin back at Snow.

"He's decent," she announced. "A possible fox." The chime of the bell marked her exit.

Michael looked down to the records in front of him. One of the tabs was marked FLEETWOOD. Misty Dawn loved that Stevie Nicks chick.

"That's Barb Callahan."

Goose bumps.

Snow White had, for a second time, pulled a magic trick. Instead of being behind the register, she was now at Michael's right elbow.

"You know," she said, responding to Michael's silence, "Barb Callahan from J104?"

Michael shook his head. His heart thudded so hard it felt as though it was ready to punch its way straight out of his chest.

"Don't you listen to the radio?" She gave him a smile.

"Not really." That was a lie. The name Barb Callahan sounded familiar. So did the station's call sign. More than likely, it was one of Misty Dawn's regular spots on the dial, but Michael was way too nervous to say any of that. His throat felt dry. His words sounded gravelly. He could smell that spearmint scent coming off Snow White in waves. She canted her head to the side, her cropped black hair exposing a long slope of neck. Grinning toward a crate of records, she filed one away into its rightful spot and shrugged.

"Yeah, me neither," she said, her words colored with easy amusement. "But I tell Barb I do. Too much hippie-dippy crap for my taste. I'm pretty sure she still plays Simon and Garfunkel, which is just . . ." She pulled a face, like she'd tasted something bad. "But if I told Barb that, I'd never get her to leave."

Michael was afraid to look at her, partly because if he did, he'd be committing himself to the conversation. But he was also terrified that she'd look into his eyes and see him for what he really was. But he couldn't *not* look at her. She was less than two feet away, so close that he wanted to reach out and touch her, if only to feel the warmth of her skin. He watched her from his peripheral vision. Her fingers walked along the spines of record sleeves. The way she rolled her neck, trying to loosen a sleep-strained muscle—it was tempting. Sexy.

"You, on the other hand." She filed another record, then turned to face him fully. "You sure know how to make a girl feel interesting with all that talking you do."

Michael forced an unsure smile and pushed himself to meet her head-on. When he finally managed it, he truly saw her for the first time, and what he saw made his heart ache. She wasn't pretty like Lucy. Lucy was more of a generic, everyday pretty rather than genuinely beautiful. Michael had seen that kind of pretty more times than he could count. Snow White was ethereal, as though she'd been plucked from the pages of a storybook. She was all eyes, and despite her black attire, he imagined her living in a tiny cottage tucked into the hills where she'd feed fawns and bluebirds by hand. Her face was framed by her short hair, the fringe of her wispy bangs cutting across a pale forehead. She shifted her weight from foot to foot, the heavy combat boots on her feet looking too heavy for her petite frame.

"See?" she asked. "I look a little freaky, but I'm not that bad. Probably why your Romeo of a brother likes Lucy a lot more than me." She cast a glance at the storage room door with a smirk. "Isn't that weird?" She looked back at Michael, eyebrows raised. Michael mimicked her, arching his own eyebrows in a questioning glance.

"Weird?"

"That they'd just go back there like that," she clarified. "I mean, would *you* do that?"

Yes, he'd do that. If Snow White caught him by the hand and led him to that back room the way Lucy had led Rebel, he'd do it because he wouldn't know how to say no. He'd do it because when he looked into her eyes, he saw magic. Maybe facing his fear and allowing their limbs to tangle together would cause some of that magic to rub off on him. Maybe drawing his hands across her bare skin would make him a better person. Perhaps it would erase all his wrongs, would let him start over, be someone new.

"No," he said softly, looking away from her. "I wouldn't do that."

"Okay," she said, shaking her head, this time with a bit of a laugh. "Just making sure it, like, doesn't run in the family or something. Because that would be, I don't know . . ."

"Weird," he finished for her.

"Exactly. *Really* weird. Almost creepy."

Michael thought *creepy* was a good word for it, but it wasn't quite right.

"I'm Alice."

She offered him her hand.

Another beat of hesitation.

If he took it, would she suddenly pull back? Would she be able to sense the blood that had washed over his fingers for so many years; would she hear the screams he'd never done a thing about?

He cautiously took her hand in his and gave it a delicate squeeze, not sure how long he was supposed to hold it. He only let go when she gave the floor an antsy smile and slowly pulled away from his touch.

"This is the part where you're supposed to introduce yourself," she said, looking almost embarrassed. "Unless you don't want to, I guess."

Memories of Rebel giving girls false names came flooding back. One time he was Ted. Another time he introduced himself as John Wayne. When the girl had laughed and asked *"Like the cowboy?"* he had said, *"No, like the killer,"* and hit her in the temple with a tire iron before she could run.

"I'm Michael," he told her. "Michael Morrow." An electric thrill shot up his spine. Revealing his first name was a no-no, but revealing both his first and last names was a cardinal sin. He'd never told anyone his full name before, had never revealed his identity, because that was one of the rules you simply didn't break. But Rebel said today they were breaking rules.

"That sounds like a name you'd see in lights," she mused. "Michael Morrow." Alice smiled again, but this one was more thoughtful. Her gaze drifted across his face, paused on his mouth for a beat before she turned away with a blush. Michael wanted to tell her that *her* name sounded like one you'd read in a fairy tale—Alice was one of the most famous princesses of all. Lauralynn never did own the Alice book, but she'd told them the story as best she could. And from her telling, Michael knew that Alice wasn't the kind of princess to sit around waiting for Prince Charming. She was a girl of action, one that fought a monster that Lauralynn had called the Jibberjabber—a giant beast that she somehow defeated because she was pure of heart.

"Are you in a band or something?" Alice asked.

"Me?" He shook his head, caught off guard, as though the mere idea of it was impossible.

"You never know," she said. "Lots of famous musicians come from the sticks. Dahlia, West Virginia, could be next."

He wasn't sure what to say to that, only that there was no chance of him being the next big thing. If Michael's name ever appeared in lights, it would be alongside Rebel's on the nightly news.

"I haven't seen you around before." She grabbed the small stack of unfiled records off of one of the crates and moved to his opposite side. The sweet scent of spearmint surrounded her like an aura. "Other than seeing you yesterday, I mean. You *are* from Dahlia, aren't you?"

"The outskirts," he told her.

"So, the boonies of the boonies." Alice chuckled. "Sounds fun. Kind of like *Deliverance*."

Michael didn't know what *Deliverance* was—he guessed some kind of a movie—but he didn't ask. He didn't want to sound as stupid as he felt, so he tucked his chin against his chest and acted interested in the artwork on a Foreigner record sleeve. Michael watched the muscles of Alice's forearms flex as her fingers worked the records into place. Two small numbers were tattooed on the inside of her left biceps: 10:15. She caught him looking and glanced down at it as if having forgotten it was there.

"It's a song," she said. "You like the Cure?"

"I don't know." The memory of the 10/6 printed on the Mad Hatter's giant green top hat was distracting. He'd seen it in one of Lauralynn's picture books. Alice. The Hatter. It was enough to convince him that she really was from Wonderland.

"You don't know, as in you have no opinion, or you don't know because you haven't heard them?"

"I haven't heard 'em."

Another round of silence.

Another exchange of awkward smiles.

"Well, what *do* you like?"

"Whatever my sister has," he said, not stopping to think about how strange that must have sounded.

Alice raised an eyebrow at his response. "And what does your sister listen to?"

"Just old stuff. She actually likes Simon and Garfunkel," he said. "And the Beach Boys."

Alice stared at him as though he'd just told her his deepest, darkest secret. She wrinkled her nose in disbelief. "I was right, weird *does* run in your family. Romeo is promiscuous and you . . ." She narrowed her eyes and pursed her mouth, trying to find the right words. "Freaky deaky."

Well, at least it wasn't hippie-dippy.

She pivoted on the soles of her combat boots and turned toward the front of the store, motioning for Michael to come along. Stopping in front of a bank of crates, she plucked a record from the center of the bunch and held it out for Michael to see. The cover was a reverse black-and-white exposure of leafless trees. The sky was pitch-black above trunks colored neon-white. THE CURE, A FOREST was printed across the middle.

"The Beach Boys are for shark bait," she told him. "This is super rare. It'll change your life."

"I ain't got no money," he said, afraid to reach for it without any cash in his pocket. But rather than rolling her eyes at him, which he fully expected her to do, she exhaled a quiet laugh instead.

"I'm not surprised, spaceman," she teased. "Just take it. Consider it a loan. We'll dig you out of that nineteen-sixties grave yet."

Michael looked down at the record, his fingers drifting across its glossy surface. "Do *you* like this?" he asked.

"No," she said, sliding a finger across her tattoo. Michael gave her a curious look, and when she chuckled beneath her breath, he laughed too.

"Wow," she said. "Finally a genuine smile."

He diverted his gaze once more, looked down at the album cover in his hands. She made him feel awkward, vulnerable, scrambling his thoughts with the curve of her lips. His heart palpitated with the way she shifted her weight from one foot to the other, as though dancing to a beat only she could hear.

"If you don't like it, just bring it back," she said. "We've got a store full of records at our disposal."

Michael took a breath, on the verge of asking why she was being so nice. What made him so special for her to treat him so well? But before he could figure out how to string together the words, the click of a lock disrupted their silence. Both he and Alice shot looks toward the back of the store. The storage door swung open. Rebel stepped out first, followed by Lucy, who looked a bit more disheveled than she had when they had first disappeared inside.

Alice and Michael exchanged a look—one that made him want to laugh in spite of himself. Alice mouthed a silent *Oookay* before turning away from him completely, focusing her attention on her friend.

"Barb stopped by," she announced. "She asked for you, so I told her you were doing it in the back room with some dude."

Lucy gave her friend a bug-eyed stare, as if refusing to believe what had just come out of Alice's mouth.

"What?" Alice asked, flashing Lucy an innocent look. "That's what you two were doing, right? Or are Michael and I mistaken?"

Rebel walked across the store and met Michael next to a crate marked IMPORTS. Glancing down at the record in Michael's hands, he was like a parent eyeing a kid who had already spent his weekly allowance. "You gonna gyp that or what?"

"I'm borrowin' it," Michael said, avoiding eye contact by staring at the cover. That dark forest reminded him of the woods behind the farmhouse.

"Borrowin' it," Reb echoed. When Michael finally looked up, Rebel was wearing a strange sort of smile—one that didn't quite reach his eyes. "Guess that means we're comin' back later, don't it?"

When Michael failed to reply, Reb swept a pair of fingers up and away from his forehead in a casual salute, giving the girls a wink. "Catch ya on the flip side," he told them, then pulled open the door and stepped out of the store.

Michael glanced across the shop to the register. Lucy was watching him with a vague sense of curiosity. Alice stood beside her, a ghost of a smile touching her lips. He raised a hand in a silent good-bye. Alice mimicked his action. She mouthed *See you*, looking even more beautiful than she had during their few minutes alone. Even more stunning than she had the first time he had laid eyes on her. His heart twisted up on itself, and suddenly the last thing he wanted to do was leave. He didn't want to go back home, didn't want to go back to his old life, didn't want to see Momma or Wade or even Misty Dawn ever again. He wanted to start over, forget who he was and become the person he knew Alice could make him. He wanted to stay in that very spot, right where he stood, for the rest of his life.

But instead, the sound of the Oldsmobile's engine drew his attention away from the girls. He slowly turned away and stepped out into the summer heat.

9

MICHAEL RUSHED OUT of the Olds, hopped up the back porch stairs, and stepped into a kitchen heady with the scent of garlic and onions. Momma was standing over a pot at the stove, stirring something with a long aluminum camping spoon. She glanced over to Michael, but didn't speak until Rebel followed him inside. "Dinner's at six," she told them, then turned back to her cooking. Michael darted out of the room and all but leapt up the stairs to get to Misty Dawn's room, with Alice's record beneath his arm.

He stopped short, just inside Misty's door. She was sitting on her bed, a fresh bruise swelling up her cheek. Her eyes were red-rimmed and raw, and when she tried to smile at him, it only made her look worse.

"What happened?" Michael asked, eventually finding his voice again.

She shrugged her shoulders as if to say she didn't want to talk about it, but explained it with a single word.

"Momma."

"What'd you do?"

"Nothing." She looked almost offended by the question.

"When do I gotta do anythin' to get her mad? She's been in a mood, gettin' impatient again."

"But we just had a girl," Michael said.

"And then Ray went and said somethin' about Lauralynn. You know how she gets."

It must have been about fifteen years earlier that Momma had shipped Lauralynn off to Grandma and Grandpa Westfall's place out in North Carolina. One day Lauralynn was around, and the next day she was gone—poof, like magic, a disappearing act that only went one way. The grandparents had always scared him. Grandma Jean had the face of an old witch—the kind that lives in gingerbread houses and cooks children for supper. Grandpa Eugene carried a cane and whipped it across the small of people's backs when they were too slow to get out of his way. Michael suspected that Momma had learned how to be cruel from her own parents. Maybe their meanness had been so severe that it had rubbed off on Claudine like a contagious disease.

"What's this?" Misty Dawn leaned forward and snatched the record from beneath Michael's arm. She peered at the cover, then gave her brother a curious glance. "Where'd you get it?"

"In town."

"You had money?"

"I'm just borrowin' it," Michael said. "The girl that works at the store said it's a loan."

Misty's expression flickered from inquisitive to suspicious. "A girl?" Her mouth quirked down at the corners. "What *kind* of girl?"

"Just a girl who works there." He tried to sound indifferent, as though Alice couldn't have caught his interest if she had pulled her shirt over her head and shimmied back and forth. Except if she had really done that, Michael would have dropped dead of a heart attack. If Alice had leaned in a little closer than she had while standing above those crates, he would have vomited his nerves all over the Dervish's inventory.

"What kind of a girl lets you borrow a record for free?" She narrowed her eyes at him. "What did you do—give her somethin' in exchange?"

"No." Michael forced a breathy, incredulous laugh from his throat, but it only made him sound guilty. "I didn't even want it," he told her, "but she said to take it anyway. It's supposed to be rare or somethin'."

He took a seat on the edge of Misty's bed, but she popped off it as soon as he sank into the mattress, as if not wanting to be close to him just then. She approached the old RCA portable record player sitting on top of her dresser instead, then carefully removed the vinyl that had been left there. Sliding the new record that Michael had brought out of its sleeve, she dropped it onto the turntable, hit a button to start it spinning, and lowered the needle into place.

They listened to the track in silence, Misty standing motionless in the center of her room as if mesmerized by the spinning disc. Michael was fascinated by the weird, almost watery-sounding guitar and the strange, brooding vocals. The lyrics struck him as both haunting and alluring, as though the singer wasn't only singing *to* him, but *about* him. By the time the song was over, Michael was in love.

Before he could ask Misty to replay it, she lifted the needle from the record and placed it back at the outer edge. Michael closed his eyes, allowing the moodiness of the music to sweep him away. By the time the second verse hit, Misty had her arms over her head, her hips swaying to the dark, sexy rhythm. She turned to him as she danced, giving him a look he had seen before, a look that always managed to set his teeth on edge. But Michael was too engrossed in the song himself. With his head lolling back and forth, his thoughts were ten miles away. He was back inside that brightly colored store, pretending Misty was Alice dancing to this very song. It was an image that shifted his storybook perception of her to something far more human. Sitting there with his head bobbing to the beat, he longed to inhale spearmint. He wanted to smell sweet, exotic smoke.

What he got was the stale scent of cigarettes instead.

Misty had danced her way across the room to stand in front of her brother, swaying her hips as she ran her hands along the length of her sides. She placed a hand on his chest and strad-dled his legs, then lowered herself onto his lap as he swallowed his nerves.

"Misty," he croaked, desperate to get away without pushing her aside. He didn't want to hurt her feelings; she didn't need another wound to nurse.

"Come on," Misty whispered. Leaning in just enough, she let her lips drag across his temple. "How do you expect to handle the record-store girl if you've never been with a girl before?"

Michael squirmed. He dug his fingers into the blanket

beneath him and clenched his teeth, wanting nothing more than to bolt upright and run out the door. When her lips grazed the lobe of his ear, he squeezed his eyes shut as tight as he could. He willed himself to imagine Alice in her place, but the scent of nicotine kept him from disconnecting. Had Misty been chewing spearmint gum, Michael would have lost himself completely. A kiss from a girl like that—he could only imagine it. And what he *did* imagine lingered on the fringes of heaven.

Misty's hands slithered across his torso. She gyrated on top of him, her mouth trailing away from his ear, beginning a slow descent toward his mouth.

Michael's pulse drowned out the music. He felt queasy, skittish, afraid to open his eyes, knowing that as soon as he saw Misty's face so close to his, he'd twist away from her and plead for her to stop.

But they snapped open anyway, responding to three harsh words.

"What the *fuck*?"

Before Michael knew what was happening, Rebel was jerking Misty off him and shoving her across the room. Michael opened his mouth to speak—to explain that it wasn't Misty's fault—but Reb's fist crashed against his teeth. A bloom of hot pain mingled with a sudden metallic taste. Reb pulled back and nailed him again, splitting Michael's lip.

Blood filled Michael's mouth. He ducked into a protective position, shielding his head from his brother's blows.

Rebel didn't hold back. He pounded his fists against

Michael's shoulders. His arms. His back. He aimed for Michael's kidneys before stumbling backward, haggard with rage.

Michael peeked out from behind his hair in time to catch Reb veering around. He grabbed Misty by the front of her fringed shirt and slammed her hard into the wall. The needle on the record zippered across the black plastic grooves.

"You filthy fuckin' whore," he hissed into her face. "You're disgusting." He gave her a parting shove and stomped out of the room.

Michael watched Misty straighten her halter and pull back her shoulders in a prideful sort of way. He admired her for being able to shake it off, but he wasn't as composed. Gathering himself up off of Misty's bed, he kept his head down as he slumped to the door. He couldn't look at her, couldn't even bring himself to apologize for the trouble he'd gotten her into. He simply slipped out of her room and back into his. He curled up on his bed, his head still encased in his arms, the sorrowful lyrics of that song spiraling through his brain.

．　．　．

Michael joined the Morrows at the dinner table for their usual six p.m. ritual. He slid into his seat and bowed his head as if in silent prayer. Wade's eyes jumped from Michael's split lip to Misty Dawn's bruised face. With a furrowing of eyebrows, he finally spoke. "I miss somethin'?"

Momma shifted in her chair and dropped a fresh-baked roll onto her plate, then offered the table an indifferent shrug.

Every now and again, Michael pictured her the way she must have been as a girl—distant, distracted, stuck inside her own head.

"The girl needed to be shown her place," she said, serving herself a heaping spoonful of mashed potatoes.

"And Michael?" Wade's attention shifted to the youngest member of their brood.

Michael kept his head down as he pulled at the strings of his frayed jeans. Rebel cleared his throat and leaned back in his chair.

"These two like pretendin' they're best friends," Reb explained. "I figured they'd want to match."

Michael looked up and caught Rebel grinning. Momma was too. Neither one was looking at the other, but both of them were leering like a pair of electric eels.

10

RAY HAD LEARNED how to steal from his mother. Momma never took Lauralynn or Misty Dawn anywhere, but Ray, being the only boy, was occasionally spoiled with a trip into town. These sojourns were little more than a visit to the local grocery store to pick up milk and eggs and, if Ray was lucky, a box of Hamburger Helper or some Sloppy Joe sauce and buns. But grocery stores had lots to steal, and he livened up these mundane journeys with his own brand of fun.

From as early as he could remember, he watched Momma pull things off of shelves, consume them, and stash the empty containers in other aisles. She did this with Cokes and Popsicles and bakery items. During one trip, she let Ray eat an entire box of cookies, then casually left the empty packaging in the bread aisle.

Ray was only caught once. A store manager grabbed him by the ear and searched him for the roll of Lifesavers he'd shoved into his pocket only seconds before. Momma materialized behind them with her hard stare and her line-tight lips. The manager demanded an apology, but when Momma laughed in his face, both she and Ray were booted from the store.

But the first *real* thing that Ray stole hadn't come from a grocery store, but a fireworks tent along the side of the highway.

He was eleven and the Morrows were on their way back from their yearly visit to the county fair. Ray had spotted the tent on the way over, and he banged the back window of the truck to get his father's attention. Wade raised a hand as if to tell the boy to hold his horses. The vehicle rambled onto the dirt shoulder and Momma and Wade slid out of the cab while the Morrow kids bounded out of the truck bed. Ray was the first to step under the tent's scalloped vinyl canopy, those red-and-white stripes making him think of candy canes and circus clowns. The setting sun gave the glossy shrink-wrapped packages of bottle rockets and aerial repeaters a mystical glow.

Ray didn't know he was going to steal anything until he saw the box of bright-red balls marked CHINA CHERRIES. Had they been black and five times larger, they'd have been straight out of a cartoon. Ray shot a look over his shoulder. His siblings had gathered around a table display featuring enormous variety packs. It was the wimpy stuff that the fireworks manufacturers tried to pawn off as "fun for the whole family," but all you ended up with was a bunch of duds and a headache from all the smoke. Two men worked the tent, both of them distracted. One was packing things up at the far end of the pavilion. The other was chatting up Momma and Wade, probably crossing his fingers for one final sale. Ray looked back at the box of cherry bombs, grabbed one in each hand, and shoved them into his pockets.

Wade ended up splurging on a pack of sparklers for Michael and the girls, which Ray had zero interest in. Wade deemed everything else as too expensive. "It's like settin' good money on fire," he had complained. "We may as well sit on the back porch and light dollar bills." Ray normally would have whined, but he kept quiet and tried not to draw attention to himself while the cherry bombs sat lumpy in his pockets. He kept his hands perfectly positioned against his legs and idly wandered back to the truck. If he had tried to be any more casual, he would have been kicking at the dirt and whistling the jingle from the *Andy Griffith Show*.

He did his damnedest to be patient, but patience didn't come easy to ten-year-old boys. He managed to hold out for two whole days before stepping into the backyard, nervous but casual. Lauralynn was fussing over her rabbits. Misty Dawn was sitting in the sunshine on a ratty old blanket. She was brushing the hair of a naked baby doll with a missing arm—the kind that opened and closed its eyes depending on how you held it. Michael was skirting the trees, hunting for beetles or worms or bird feathers. Ray squared his shoulders and crossed the yard to meet his brother along the edge of the woods.

"Hey, Mikey," he said. "Got somethin' for ya." Ray ducked behind Wade's tool shed, motioning for Michael to follow.

Michael dropped what he was doing and ran after his big brother, a wide smile spread across his six-year-old face. "Whaddya got?" he asked, excited to see what Ray would produce out of the depths of his front pocket. Ray pulled out one of the bombs, holding it for Michael to see.

"Candy?" Michael asked, wide-eyed.

"No, dummy, it's a firework. Got it for your birthday."

"Really?" Michael's face lit up with excitement. The Morrows didn't know when Michael's birthday really was, so they had switched it to the anniversary of his arrival instead. It was coming up on three years since Ray had brought home the wailing, blubbering kid who had told them he was four.

"Hold out your hand," Ray instructed. Michael did as he was told, and Ray placed the bright-red sphere in his brother's small palm. "This is a special firework," he explained. "I'm gonna light the fuse, and when I do you gotta cup it like this." Ray put his hands together as if holding a bird. Michael mimicked him. "And when it goes off, you're gonna get a real big surprise, see? But you gotta hold on to it, otherwise it ain't gonna work."

"Is it gonna be cool?" Michael asked.

Ray fished a lighter he'd stolen from the kitchen out of his back pocket.

"Oh yeah," he said with a grin. "It's gonna be *great*. You'll never forget it." Kind of like how he'd never really forgotten Lauralynn holding Michael in that fun house, how Ray had vanished, so easily replaced.

He sparked a flame at the top of the old BIC lighter and leaned in, lighting the cherry bomb's one-inch fuse. It caught and began to smoke as Michael stood there with a smile, cupping the explosive just as Ray had told him to.

"Now don't move," Ray told him as he backed away, light-headed with the sudden rush of adrenaline. This was it—it was really going to happen. That cherry bomb was going to go off, and it was going to blow that stupid kid's hands clean off. Hell, maybe it would tear his arms off entirely. Maybe the blast would be so strong that it would obliterate half his face and blind him in the process. Ray grinned to himself, knowing that Michael wouldn't be seeing the inside of a hospital no matter how bad it was. Momma and Wade didn't believe in doctors. They said hospitals asked too many questions and doctors stole people's money. When Ray had fallen out of a tree and broken his arm at Michael's age, Wade had slapped a couple of scraps of wood together and made a hillbilly splint. Breaking his arm had hurt, but it hadn't been all bad. The pain had won Ray his first taste of whiskey. For the two months he wore that wooden arm around, he could take swigs of booze anytime he wanted, no questions asked.

But Michael would need more than liquor for this. He'd need a miracle, and even that wasn't guaranteed to save his life. He'd bleed out quick. He might even be dead before Wade and Momma figured out where the bang had come from.

Ray narrowed his eyes as the fuse burned down toward Michael's hands. Lauralynn would be upset—it was the only thought that nearly convinced him that this plan was a bad one. But Lauralynn would get over it. She was strong. Ray would get her another kid if she wanted—a girl this time . . . someone who wouldn't step on his toes.

Ray turned his head away from Michael for a moment to look back at Lauralynn and her rabbit cage. But rather than seeing his sister and her bunnies, he saw Wade coming up fast. In his anticipation, he hadn't bothered to check where Wade and Momma were, and Wade had been not more than ten feet away, inside the shed.

Wade shoved Ray to the side so hard that the boy went skidding onto his ass. He watched his father grab Michael's hands, pluck the bomb out of his palms, and chuck the firework into the trees. The thing exploded with a massive *BOOM!* before it ever hit the ground, sending a few branches of a dead pine flying to the forest floor. Michael jumped at the noise. He stared into the woods with wide, startled eyes, then looked to Wade with confusion.

"But I was supposed to hold on to it," he said. "That was mine!"

Ray winced and began to scramble to his feet to avoid whatever was coming to him, but he wasn't quick enough. Wade came up behind him, grabbed him by the back of the neck, and shoved him inside the tool shed. That's where he proceeded to beat the hell out of him with the buckle-end of his belt. He beat him so badly that by the end of it, Ray couldn't tell if it hurt anymore. He left that shed with the back of his shirt bloodied and the seat of his jeans so numb he could hardly walk straight. When he hobbled past Momma on the back porch, she didn't say a word. She didn't even bother looking up from the string beans she was working on, snapping the ends off with the flick of a wrist, much like the way Ray wanted to snap Michael's scrawny neck.

Ray had to crawl up the stairs to get to his room, and when he finally reached the top, his lips pulled back in a sneer. He resented the fact that his bedroom had been split in two, one side for him, the other for the kid he'd nearly wiped off the face of the earth. Pulling himself into the room, he looked out the window, rage boiling the blood in his veins. One story below, Michael was surrounded by his siblings and father. Lauralynn had wrapped her arms around him in her usual protective embrace. Even Wade was squatting in empathy, bringing himself down to Michael's line of sight. Ray never got that kind of attention. When he broke his arm, Wade told him to suck it up and Lauralynn's doting tapered off after a few days.

Later that day, Wade raided Ray's side of the room and came up with the second stolen bomb. When he found it, he raised his arm over his head, ready to lay into his firstborn again. But he had shown mercy when he saw the blood on the back of Ray's shirt. Had it been Momma, compassion wouldn't have entered the equation.

The next morning, Ray gritted his teeth as he watched Wade and Michael stick that cherry bomb into the hollow of a pine and blow it sky high. *His* dad. *His* bomb. His stupid little brother clapping his hands like a gleeful idiot while Ray sat upstairs, locked in his room. Forgotten.

11

THE BEDROOM DOOR swung open so fast it hit the back wall with a loud crack. Michael jerked awake. His gaze fell onto Rebel's silhouette. His brother appeared to be fully dressed despite it still being dark outside. "Get up," he said, and he didn't sound amused.

"What time is it?" Michael murmured, his throat still too dry with sleep to project much more than a croaky whisper.

"You think it matters?" Reb stepped inside the room and jerked Michael's blanket off of his legs. "I said *get up*."

Michael sat up and shoved wild, slept-in strands of hair behind his ears. He imagined himself to look like a seventies rock-band reject, groggy and disheveled, nothing but hair and a sloppy, beat-up face.

"Get dressed," Ray told him. "We're takin' a little trip."

Michael got to his feet, but he had to catch himself on the wall the moment he left his mattress. His head spun, still not quite recovered from the blows Reb had dealt him hours before. The ache in his jaw had metastasized into a killer headache, one that throbbed white-hot with every whoosh of his pulse. But there was no time to consider the gnawing ache that continued to squirm behind his eyes. Rebel was in a mood, and when Reb was moody, Michael did whatever the hell he was told.

He grabbed his discarded jeans off the floor and pulled them on as his brother loomed over the simple pine desk beside Michael's window. It was old and had been in that room for as long as Michael could remember, having belonged to Lauralynn before Momma sent her off to North Carolina. If Reb had awoken anyone else, they weren't making themselves known. The house remained silent.

Michael shoved his bare feet into his boots and pulled his unruly hair back with the rubber band from around his wrist. He looked up just in time to catch Reb pushing his hands into the pockets of his denim jacket.

"I'm ready," Michael said. It had taken him all of sixty seconds to pull himself out of bed and prepare for whatever it was Rebel had planned. But despite Michael's haste, Reb still grabbed him by the shoulder and shoved him out of the room like a disobedient child. Michael was surprised Reb didn't throw him down the stairs as they descended to the first floor. Reb had pushed him down that staircase a few times in the past. Once, after Reb had a barn burner of a fight with Wade, he had launched Michael off the top riser, and Michael went tumbling down the stairs like a sack of meat. It was a wonder he hadn't broken his neck—no doubt Rebel's intent. Momma had rushed to see what all the ruckus was about, only to scold her eldest son from the bottom of the staircase. *You break this house and I'll make you rebuild it with your two bare hands, Ray!* And then she had shot Michael a look and told him to *Get up off of that floor* before returning to her TV show.

Still groggy with sleep, Michael nearly lost his footing on the back porch steps. The deep blue of the sky suggested it was three, maybe four in the morning. Despite the heat of those blazing summer days, it still felt crisp at that hour. The air was always better when the world was sleeping. It made it easier to breathe.

Rebel pushed Michael toward the Delta and peeled away from the dozing farmhouse in a blast of loose gravel and dirt. Michael stared at the house in the side view mirror as the Oldsmobile bounced down the rutted dirt road two miles shy of the highway. The house looked haunted in the darkness, pale moonlight reflecting off its front windows. The cold white glint of light gave the weatherworn clapboards an almost iridescent silver sheen. The farmhouse had belonged to Wade's mom and dad once, grandparents Michael had never met because they were long dead by the time he came around. Sometimes it made him wonder about his adoptive father and how it had been for Wade as a boy. He wondered what room Wade had and whether he had been happy or sad. But Michael never had the nerve to ask and always settled on sadness. He couldn't imagine anyone being happy in that house. Anytime he heard laughter inside, it seemed as though the rooms sucked up the sound and squelched it beneath a veil of discolored wallpaper. If that house were alive, it would feed on happiness and breathe out nothing but screaming and hate.

Just before the house disappeared from view, Misty Dawn's

light clicked on. If she'd gotten up to check what was going on, she was too late, which was for the best.

They drove for nearly an hour before Rebel turned onto another road and followed the winding path deep into Appalachia. The endless twists and turns and the thick darkness that lay heavy over the landscape was disorienting. It made Michael sick with nerves. When Reb finally pulled over and told Michael to get out, his anxiety rose to a panicky, fevered pitch, but he climbed out anyway.

Something about this entire scenario felt so wrong, yet so familiar. When he spotted Reb pulling an old shovel out of the Delta's trunk, Michael was overwhelmed by a sickening sense of déjà vu. He'd been here before, wherever *here* was. He'd seen that look in Reb's eyes in his nightmares—a single recurring dream he'd been having for the past fifteen years. Michael opened his mouth to speak, but no sound came. He usually loved the forest, but now the smell of pine and sap made his skin prickle with nauseous apprehension. He would have traded anything to be back in his bed, the fresh scent of nature replaced by stale sheets and dusty floors.

Rebel threw the shovel at Michael without warning. Michael caught it reflexively, the spade's cracked and splintered handle biting into the palm of his hand. "Let's go." Reb motioned to the moonlit trees, to the nowhere that Michael knew existed within those branches. He had been afraid of this moment for as long as he knew, and now it was happening. There was no one around to save him. Like Momma's girls, so far away from civilization that gagging them seemed pointless, Michael could scream all he wanted; nobody would hear him. At least not anyone who could help.

He stumbled into the trees, his boots flopping around his ankles. They felt too big without socks on, his feet swimming in shoes that were otherwise a perfect fit. He held tight to the shovel, his fingers squeezing the dry, weatherworn handle hard enough to make his palm ache. A voice inside his head screamed for him to spin around, to drop to his knees and beg his older brother for mercy. *Please,* he'd say, *please don't do this. I'll do anything.* But he continued walking, knowing that begging would only make it worse.

They walked for a good fifteen minutes before Reb muttered "Here's good," and pointed to the ground at Michael's feet. "Start diggin'."

Michael's bottom lip began to quiver.

Rebel was serious. He was going to go through with it.

"Start diggin' what?" Michael whispered, unable to help himself. But he was already digging despite the question that slipped past his lips.

"Whaddaya think?"

Michael didn't want to think, didn't want to know. This was just like in his dreams, where he always ended up dead. He sank the spade into the soft earth and choked back a sob. Reb could have at least let him say good-bye to Misty. He might have allowed Michael that small indulgence.

He dug while Reb watched from a few yards away. His brother had taken a seat on a large fallen branch and was holding his chin in one hand, as if considering his next move.

Again, Michael was seized by an urge to plead, because if Reb killed him, Misty Dawn would be alone. If Reb got drunk and Momma got tired of waiting, Misty would be in her cross-hairs. Wade would be the only one left to protect her, and Michael wasn't so sure that Wade cared enough to make the effort.

"That's good enough," Reb said, as if speaking up to cut off Michael's train of thought.

Michael looked down at the hole at his feet. It was easier to see now. The sun was starting to come up. The sky was a sickly sort of purple, like a blood blister just starting to heal. The hole wasn't big enough for Michael's body, not nearly deep enough to bury the dead. Rebel rose from where he sat and closed the distance between them, grabbed the shovel from Michael's grasp and glared. "On your knees."

Michael's heart sped up, thudding so fast and so hard that when he sank to the ground, he had to lean forward and press his palms to the earth to keep himself from passing out. He shut his eyes, waiting for the world to stop spinning. When he opened them, he stared at a few of his most prized possessions, dropped into the hole he'd just dug.

A small plastic toy stared up at him from its grave. It was a tiny pink pig Misty had won out of a coin-operated machine when they were kids, the kind of cheap stuff that came in clear plastic eggs. He stared at the picture postcard of Times Square printed on beat-up cardstock. Someone had made the back out to a guy named Travis. WISH YOU WERE HERE! LOVE, BRENDA. Honolulu was there too, the back of it blank, its corners soft and worn from being thumbed for some many years. A *Garfield* comic Michael had cut out of a newspaper obstructed Hawaii's beachside view. They were all things he had squirreled away, the things that made him feel a little more human. But among them was one item that didn't belong, something he was sure Reb had tossed into the mix on purpose. It was a business card from the Dervish, the store's name scripted in colorful, bubbly, Woodstock lettering. Michael's mouth went dry at the sight of it. Reb had included it for no reason other than to remind Michael of Alice, the girl he'd never get to know because he was about to be dead.

Rebel crouched in front of the hole, reached across it, and caught Michael by his chin. He squeezed hard. Michael's freshly split lip cracked with a sizzle of pain and began to bleed again. "Does Misty turn you on?" he asked, his words spoken through clamped teeth. "You wanna sleep with your sister?" Michael winced as the sting of his swollen lip blossomed, the pain leaching into his gums and teeth. "You see this stuff?" Reb released him and scooped up the items he'd tossed into the excavation in the ground. "Who does it belong to?" Michael was afraid to answer, but Reb insisted, shoving the memorabilia into his face. "Who does this shit belong to, Michael?!" His voice rose an octave. His patience was dwindling.

"Me," Michael croaked.

"That's right," Rebel said, crumpling Times Square in his fist. "And how does *this* feel?" he asked, shredding the comic into pieces and letting the fragments drift to the ground like big flakes of snow.

"Bad," Michael whispered, staring down at his destroyed possessions.

"It feels bad for someone to mess with your shit, huh? It feels bad for them to do what they want with it like it belongs to *them* instead of *you*, don't it?"

"Yeah." The word was nearly inaudible.

"*Don't* it?!" Ray yelled.

"What do you want?!" Michael yelled back, the world going wavy behind a veil of tears.

Reb rose to his feet as Michael swept up a few pieces of the comic, wondering if he could tape it back together—he probably could, if he found all the bits.

"Bury it," Reb said flatly.

Michael looked up, his breath hitching in his throat.

"You heard me. Bury that shit—see how it *really* feels to lose somethin' you care about."

Michael swallowed. He crawled a short distance to the small mound of dirt and pressed his palms against it. He hesitated, not wanting to do it, afraid that burying his things would make him different. That it would disconnect him from his secret hopes and dreams, leaving nothing but this life. The farmhouse. The Oldsmobile. The screaming girls.

"But Reb," he whispered, ready to beg, not caring if it made his brother angry or not.

Rebel didn't give him the chance to plead. He shoved his knee between Michael's shoulder blades and grabbed him by the hair. He craned Michael's neck back so he was staring up at the wisteria-colored sky, up into Reb's snarling face.

"Misty Dawn is *my* sister," he hissed. "You don't touch her unless I say you can touch her. You don't even *look* at her unless I say you can."

"I'm sorry," Michael said. "It wasn't what—"

"Shut up," Reb snapped. "I don't want to hear no stupid excuses. I saw it with my own two eyes. You wanna call me a liar?"

Michael shook his head, still held captive in Rebel's grasp.

"If Wade tells you to do somethin', you ignore it. If Momma tells you to do somethin', you don't do a fuckin' thing until you come to me and clear it. And if Misty Dawn tells you to do somethin', you tell her to get bent. You've gone and forgot rule number one. . . ."

"I haven't."

"Then what is it?"

"You're the boss."

"And you don't goddamn question me."

"I don't question you," Michael quietly repeated.

"And if you do, what happens?"

"We go into the woods," Michael whispered.

"And do *what*?" Reb yanked on Michael's hair, craning his neck back at a painful angle.

"Leave me there."

"Leave you there for what, asshole?"

"To die." Michael squeezed his eyes shut against the words, only to fall forward when Reb shoved him, releasing his hair.

"I'm sick and tired of your shit, Michael. This is your last chance. Next time you piss me off, we're takin' this same drive, takin' this same walk, but instead of diggin' a tiny hole, you're gonna dig your own grave, and then I'll kill you. Shit, I might kill you on your own fuckin' birthday. How great would *that* be? Live fast and die young."

Michael slowly looked up at him. He didn't doubt Rebel would follow through on his threat, but he couldn't help wondering how his brother would get his booze without getting caught. How would he snatch girls off the side of the road without them escaping? How would he deal with Momma and her insatiable urges while juggling alcoholism and Wade's disapproval? Rebel acted like he was in charge, like he had it all figured out, but he never once stopped to consider that anytime there was a job to do, anytime they needed *results*, Michael was there to help . . . was there to do most, if not all, of the work. A spark of bitterness ignited in the pit of his stomach. *Brothers in arms, my ass,* he thought. Rebel didn't see Michael as a brother; hell, sometimes it seemed as though Reb didn't see him as a human at all. Michael was a means to an end. A tool. That was it.

Anger bubbled up his windpipe like bile, but he said nothing, digging his fingers into the dirt instead.

Rebel let his head flop back on his neck as he stared up at the sky. He released a frustrated sigh, then shot Michael an annoyed glare. "All right, get up. Just remember, if you ain't my friend, you ain't friends with no one."

"I thought I *was* your friend," Michael muttered toward his hands. "Besides, ain't being family better than that?"

Reb paused, as if considering something, but he shook his head, dismissing the thought. "Grab that shovel," he finally said. Then he began his trek back through the trees.

. . .

On the way home, Rebel stopped at a gas station along the side of the road. The place was closed, and Michael considered protesting, but he decided to take his fury out on the gas station's front window instead. Locating a brick next to the door—one the owner probably used as a makeshift doorstop—he smashed the glass. He risked going in twice despite the wail of the alarm, dumping armloads of bottles into the Delta's trunk. It was their most successful haul yet, one that would keep Rebel off Michael's back for weeks. But Reb didn't look the least bit satisfied. He simply took silent swigs of cheap bourbon as he drove, not once looking in Michael's direction. The lack of interaction solidified Rebel's threat inside of Michael's head. No matter how angry Michael was with his brother for making him feel worthless, Rebel would make good on his warning. He'd take him out into the woods, slash his throat, and leave him for dead.

But just as he was ready to accept the fact that Rebel didn't care about him, that the whole brothers-in-arms thing was a lie, Reb sighed and cast a sideways look his way.

"You're a good brother, you know," Reb said. "I'm sorry."

It was the first time Rebel had apologized for anything. Ever.

And suddenly, all Michael wanted to do was cry.

12

I T FELT THAT the more Michael became a Morrow, the less part of the family Ray was. It was as though there was only room enough for one boy, and when Ray had dragged Michael into the mix, he'd diluted his own importance within the group. And now, after the cherry-bomb incident, Ray felt on the verge of exile.

For Michael's seventh birthday, Michael was assigned a job that solidified his place in the Morrow household. Wade gave him a kid's rifle—one of Ray's old Christmas presents—and gave Michael the task of going into the woods and foraging for food. Ray had never actually used that gun—he was too impatient for hunting—but it still stung. It was *his* gun, one of the best gifts he'd ever gotten from his pop, and Wade hadn't even asked if Ray minded whether Michael used it or not. *Use it or lose it,* Wade liked to say. Punishment for the cherry-bomb affair, no doubt. Ray had never liked his dad much, but now he was really starting to hate him.

After Wade issued Michael Ray's old rifle, Michael would get up early every morning while Ray rolled around in a tangle of sheets. Mid-morning, he'd bring back chipmunks and squirrels, foxes and raccoons. Momma had nearly laughed herself into a fit the day he brought back a skunk. Rather than eating the stinky animal, Wade taught the boy how to skin it and make a hat out of the hide. Michael ran around wearing that stupid thing all winter long, a skunk tail dangling down the back of his neck. He'd shampooed it a half dozen times, but it still smelled like shit.

As far as Michael's new hunting job was concerned, Ray held out for as long as he could, but eventually his curiosity took hold. He wanted to see his little brother in action, hardly able to believe a seven-year-old could bag so many forest animals on his own. He followed Michael into the woods, the rifle slapping the back of Michael's legs as it bobbed behind him on a strap. Ray kept his distance as he watched the kid stalk through the trees, searching for something to kill. Nearly a mile from home, Michael fired off a shot at a family of gobbling turkeys and Ray couldn't help but be struck by the fact that *this* was the boy Wade had wanted. Ray had never fit the profile of a good son, and now that Wade had Michael, Ray had been reduced to a shadow of what could have been but never was.

Michael missed the turkey. As the flock squawked and dispersed, Michael screwed his nose up in disappointment and sulked. That was the start of his dry spell. It was as though Ray's presence had cursed the young hunter to return home empty-handed day after day, resulting in Michael going to bed earlier so he could get up sooner. By the fifth unsuccessful day, Michael turned in before the sun set, pulling his blanket over his head to block out the light. It amused Ray how affected Michael was by failure. He found solace in the idea that, despite being in Wade's favor, Michael may have been a disappointment after all.

On the sixth morning of Michael's dry spell, Ray woke to the sound of his adopted brother stumbling around, getting dressed in the dark. Ray rubbed his eyes and waited for them to adjust, but Michael didn't notice that he was awake. He simply pulled on his pants, stuffed his feet into a pair of pip-squeak-size shoes, pulled a tattered Salvation Army sweater over his head, grabbed his gun, and slid out the door as silently as he could.

Ray sat up in bed and yawned. It couldn't have been later than four in the morning. If Michael thought he had a better chance of shooting something because of the hour, he hadn't considered that he wouldn't be able to see a damn thing as soon as he stepped into the cedars and elms. But Ray was intrigued. He rolled out of bed, sidled up to the window, pushed the curtain aside, and watched from above. The back porch light eventually clicked on, illuminating a good part of the yard with a dull yellow glow. Michael wandered across the property, his steps a bit wobbly, still groggy with sleep. He took one step into the forest just beyond the yard and stopped, seemingly struck by something he hadn't considered. Ray's blank face shifted into a mean-spirited grin when his little brother veered away from the dark and scary woods.

Stupid kid, Ray thought. *Idiot forgot he's afraid of the dark.*

Michael vacillated along the border of trees. He marched up and down their perimeter, waiting for the darkness to lighten with the onset of morning. Or maybe he was trying to make some momentous decision with his mushy six-year-old brain. Ray was about to collapse back onto his bed when Michael started to make his way back toward the house. Something about the way he was walking made Ray hold his post in front of the window for a beat longer. The way Michael had angled his chin down against his chest sent weird, long shadows across his face. Despite his age, he looked crazed, like something out of a movie. Like those freaky glowing-eyed kids from *Village of the Damned*.

Michael was making a beeline for Lauralynn's rabbit cage. When Ray realized what was happening, he shook his head in the dark.

He don't have the guts, he thought. *He wouldn't. She'll know.*

But Michael was really going to do it. He unlatched the door of the cage, reached in, and drew out a white rabbit that Lauralynn had named Snowball. Ray's pulse quickened. He pressed himself against the glass as he watched with wide, disbelieving eyes. Michael latched the door, then thought better of it and left it wide open before turning his back to the house. With Snowball tucked against his chest, he walked back to the trees.

Once he got to the forest's perimeter, he crouched down, placed Snowball on the ground, and swung his rifle from his back to his front. Snowball just sat there. He looked like a tuft of lint on an otherwise pristine swath of black silk. Michael watched the animal through the scope of his gun, standing not more than six feet away. Eventually, Snowball hopped a few steps deeper into the woods. Michael stepped in behind the rabbit, and though his figure faded into the shadows, Ray never completely lost sight of his brother.

A muffled pop rang through the early morning silence; not loud, but enough of a report for Ray to know Michael had gone through with the deed. He expected to be outraged, pissed enough to march downstairs and beat the living hell out of the kid for doing something so heinous, especially when it came to Lauralynn. She'd be devastated as soon as she realized one of her babies was missing. She'd cry and cry, and Ray's heart would twist at the sound of her sobs. And he'd be partly responsible for her pain, because he had seen the whole thing. Instead of opening the window and yelling that Michael better not even think about it, Ray had simply watched. He had let it happen.

But rather than rage, Ray pressed himself against the cool window and smiled. The feeling of vindication was something new, something that made him feel so alive it was almost electric. Because Lauralynn *deserved* it. She had abandoned Ray. She had replaced him with that stupid kid. And now she was going to get what was coming to her.

Michael eventually surfaced from the shadows of the forest carrying an animal that was no longer fluffy and white. His rifle was slung across his back again, and a skinned rabbit hung from his small right hand by its long, powerful back legs. He was bringing it home for dinner.

And Lauralynn would eat her precious pet as punishment for what she'd done.

Ray stepped away from the window and paused at the sight of his own reflection. He was no longer grinning—he was *leering* at the idea.

It was perfect, so damn perfect it was almost poetic, and he had that stupid little shit Michael to thank.

13

REBEL SLID OUT of the Oldsmobile, slammed the door, and marched up the embankment that would take him to the hill that overlooked the little green-shuttered house. Michael rolled the window down, allowing the sound of songbirds inside the car. He leaned out the window and inspected his busted lip in the side view mirror. It had healed enough over the last few days that the swelling and the purple color were nearly gone, but the cut was still visible—a deep burgundy line that ran from the bottom of his lip to inside his mouth. It was scabbed over, glued shut on the outside, but it still stung where it rubbed against his teeth, and it tasted like blood when he tongued the laceration. He frowned at his reflection and tried to think up a convincing story to tell Alice when she asked about it. Falling down the stairs seemed too obvious, not to mention too embarrassing. He could say the rifle kicked back while he was hunting and he took it in the mouth like some amateur marksman. *No,* he decided. *Don't bring up hunting.* Killing was the last thing he wanted to discuss.

Rebel hopped back into the Delta a few minutes later. Gray clouds were rolling in, thundering overhead, threatening to tear open and pour. Despite being winded by his quick trek, Reb was in a relatively good mood. Michael hadn't seen much of him in the last seventy-two hours. As expected, he had locked himself away in his room and busied himself with his freshly pilfered booze. He was going through the bottles, Michael assumed, the way a fat man went through hot dogs at an eating contest—one by one, with hardly a break in between.

Michael rolled up the window and patted his lip with a fingertip. "What do I say if she asks about this?"

Reb gave Michael a look as he guided the Oldsmobile down the winding road toward Dahlia, then stared out the windshield in silence as he mulled it over. "Tell her you fell down the stairs."

"But that sounds fake, don't it?"

"Tell her you got into a fight with your boyfriend." Reb cracked a grin at his own joke. "Shit, I don't know—just tell her I popped you in the mouth for being smart. You think she's gonna care?"

Michael hoped she would, but he didn't say as much.

"You ain't gonna be weird again, are you?" Reb gave Michael a once-over. "You'll freak her out if you're weird, you know. Freak a girl out good enough and she might never wanna see you again."

The idea of their outing being a date sent an electric thrill through Michael's limbs. But it also turned his stomach inside out.

"It's gonna ruin the whole point," Reb continued. "I don't even wanna see this flick, but chicks dig these kinds of movies. They like bein' scared. It gets 'em excited, and excited is good."

"I'm not gonna be weird," Michael said, but he sounded less than convincing. He'd never been to an actual movie theater before, and he was genuinely excited to see a new release. But the idea of doing it all with Alice at his elbow turned him into a nervous wreck. What if he said something wrong? What if she asked too many questions that he couldn't answer . . . *wouldn't* answer? She'd get suspicious. She'd know something was off.

Reb parked the Delta in what had become their standard spot in front of the Dervish, and Michael stared ahead at the record store a few yards away. Its melted-ice-cream paint scheme made his heart thump a little faster. It looked oddly bright in the setting sun, but those joyful sugary colors now only made his stomach churn.

When Michael and Rebel stepped inside, Alice was at the register closing out the day. Lucy was nowhere in sight. Alice smiled at them from behind the counter, motioning to the hallway when Reb gave her a questioning glance. "She's in the back," Alice said. "Getting ready."

Reb breezed past the counter and stalked down the hall, leaving Alice and Michael alone at the front of the store.

"Hi," she said, giving Michael a meek sort of smile.

"Hi," Michael echoed, his guts seizing up with sudden realization. "Shit." He had meant to whisper it, but the curse came out louder than he had intended.

"What?" She angled her head toward one of her shoulders.

"I forgot the record." It was still in Misty's room. After what had happened between him and Misty and Ray, he was afraid to go and retrieve it. And since he had no way of listening to it without Misty's record player, there hadn't been much point.

Alice dismissed his worry with a wave of her hand. "Forget it," she said. "Unless you didn't like it."

"No, I loved it," he told her, his response a little too quick.

Alice gave him a look, her mouth turned up at the corners. "So you've got some taste after all," she said with a wink. "Good to know. Though I already suspected that." Her gaze drifted to the storeroom door, and she gave a quiet laugh. Michael didn't get the joke, but he liked the sound she made—airy, light, carefree, like a perfect summer evening. "What happened to your lip?"

"Um . . ." He touched the cut, looked down to his feet then up again. "Me and Reb got into it a few days back."

"Reb?"

"Ray," Michael corrected himself.

"What's Reb stand for?"

He cleared his throat quietly, then muttered "Rebel" beneath his breath.

Alice cracked a wide smile, as if attempting to hold back a laugh. She shifted her weight, her forearms sliding across the countertop. "Come over here," she said, nodding for him to get away from the front door and close the distance between them. He hesitated but did as she requested. "Got into it about what?" she asked. The bridge of her nose wrinkled in what he assumed was innocent curiosity—just something to talk about, that's all. She wasn't trying to corner him; just keeping the conversation afloat.

"Just stuff."

"Stuff." She didn't look satisfied with the answer.

"Family stuff." He lifted his shoulders up as if to say it really wasn't that big a deal.

Alice pinched her eyebrows together as she sorted through receipts, her smile fading while she jotted down numbers in a green-sheeted ledger.

"Does that happen often?" She tipped her chin down in a way that brought her to eye level with his still swollen lip. "Does he have a temper or something? Should I be worried about Lucy hanging out with him the way she does?"

You should be more than worried, Michael thought. *You should never want to see either one of us again.*

"No," he told her. "He's okay."

"So you're saying you provoked him?" Before Michael could answer her, she cut him off. "You don't seem like the type."

Michael's gaze drifted across the counter. He was suddenly uncomfortable with the conversation. He was eager to find something else to talk about, wondering what was taking Rebel so long. His eyes stopped on a spiral-bound notebook, but the pages were blank rather than ruled. Three equally sized squares were drawn lengthwise across the page. The beginnings of a sketch decorated the inside of the first, so faint it was nothing but a ghostly trace of graphite.

"What's that?" he asked, forcing himself out of his shell enough to steer the discussion in a safer direction. Alice pulled the notebook toward the center of the counter and flipped the page, the previous sheet of paper decorated with a carefully drawn comic, like the *Garfield* one Reb had ripped up and made him bury. The panels were pictures of a girl who looked just like Alice—short hair, almond-shaped eyes, dark clothes.

"It's my life," she said after a beat, as though stopping to consider whether putting it so plainly made her seem lame. "Or at least I hope it will be."

In the panels, the girl was sitting at a counter that looked just like the one Michael was standing at now. The girl slouched behind it, her chin in her hand, a look of bored desperation across her face. The panels were identical to one another save for a single detail. The second square had a thought bubble filled with nothing but three dots in a row. The third had the same thought bubble, but words replaced the dots: I SHOULD REALLY QUIT MY JOB.

Michael looked up from the drawing to Alice, then back to the animated girl on the page.

"You don't like it here?"

"Would *you* like it here?" she asked, a moody scoff crossing her lips.

The truth of it was, Michael would love working at the Dervish. It was new and exciting and mysterious, and there were thousands of album covers to admire and just as many records to play. It smelled like a distant land, like Caterpillar pipe smoke must have smelled, as Lauralynn had described. Those stories—told from memory—enchanted all of them back then, even Reb. And the glossy patchwork of posters that covered every inch of the shop walls made Michael feel like he was in some magical den, a place like Wonderland, where everyone was happy and nobody got hurt.

"It don't seem so bad," he confessed.

"I guess it isn't *that* awful." Alice seemed to be trying to convince herself. "I just . . ." She paused, shook her head, looked up at him, searching for answers. "I need to get the hell out of West Virginia." She broke eye contact, looked down to her hands. "I just feel like I'm suffocating. Don't you ever feel like you don't belong somewhere, like you're out of place?"

Her question left him breathless. It was as though she had reached inside his head and pulled out his thoughts. As though they had appeared in a thought bubble like the one in her comic, and she had plucked them out of the air and stuck them in her mouth, talking them back to him as her own ideas.

"But don't you got family?" he asked. The question was automatic, the importance of family beaten into his DNA.

"I've got my mom, but we aren't close. She's always had this . . . *thing*. Depression, you know? I can't really remember a time when she was actually happy."

"Not even on holidays?"

"Especially not on those, and especially not after my dad died. She likes to wallow in it, I guess. You know what they say—some people get addicted to feeling bad because whenever they feel good they feel guilty. I'm pretty sure that's her deal."

"What happened to your dad?"

"He was a miner, died about five years back, in the Scotia Mine disaster out in Kentucky. There was an explosion—over twenty men died, and he was one of them. After a while, my mom just got hard to look at, so I moved in with Lucy." Alice nodded down the hall, Lucy's and Reb's voices were muffled in the distance. "I felt bad about it for a while, visited three times a week to make up for it, but it didn't really seem like she cared. We'd just sit around the living room and watch TV without saying anything, so I stopped visiting. We live less than ten miles apart and we talk maybe once or twice a month. Last time I was at the house was on Christmas . . . and I know she's trying. I mean, I can tell something's different, you know? This past year it seems like she's really tried to fix herself up, but I don't know." She shrugged, laughed a little, shook her head, and slid a pair of fingers across her mouth, as if surprised by how much she had just revealed.

Michael liked hearing her talk. It was nice to know that despite the storybook picture inside his head, Alice didn't dance with the bluebirds after all. It was comforting to know that she was a real person, that she had her own problems, that maybe she had her own secrets. Not on the level of Michael's, but secrets nevertheless.

"What about you?" Alice asked. "If you got into it with Ray . . . or *Rebel*, or whatever, does that mean you two live together?"

Michael gave her a faint nod. "With Momma and Wade and Misty Dawn."

"Is Misty Dawn your sister?"

Another nod.

"And Wade?"

"That's my dad."

"Then why do you call him Wade instead of Dad?" she asked, and honestly, Michael didn't know. Reb had never called Wade by anything but his first name. He wasn't sure he had ever heard Ray or Misty call Wade *Dad* at all. But he imagined that if he ever tried to call Wade *Dad* or *Father* or even *Pop*, Reb would just about kill him for it. *Wade* was safe. *Dad* was too possessive, too close.

"Where will you go?" Michael asked, changing the subject for a second time.

"Hmm?"

"You said you don't wanna live here . . . so where are you gonna go?"

"Oh." She snorted. "You mean where *won't* I go. God, anywhere. . . . I'd say New York City, but that sounds so, I don't know, like . . ." She lifted a hand, looping it in the air. "Everyone says New York City, you know? It's a fantasy. New York is so cramped with dreamers, it's a wonder they aren't crawling out of the sewers like rats."

"I had a postcard from there."

"Yeah?"

"From Times Square. But I lost it."

"Who sent it to you?"

"I found it in a parking lot," he confessed, then looked away when she gave him a funny look. A momentary silence passed between them, one that didn't feel as uncomfortable as the last. Michael let his shoulders slump as he gave her an unsure sort of smile. "Maybe I'll go there one day. Probably not to live, though; I don't think I could."

"Millions of people do it, so why couldn't you?"

"I dunno." He rubbed at the back of his neck. "I guess maybe I'd miss this place."

Alice scoffed. "You're kidding, right? No way. Even Pittsburgh or Columbus, Ohio, would be better than Daliah. At least there I'd have a chance with this." She tapped the sketchbook with a finger. "Here? Forget it."

"What do you mean 'a chance'?"

"A chance to make this my career." She flipped through a few of the pages, each one bearing a carefully inked strip. "You know, like get into the newspaper, drawing dailies or something?" She fell silent, flipped the sketchbook closed, looked up at him. "I'm talking too much. You know all this stuff about me, but I don't know a thing about you. What do *you* do?"

"What do you mean?"

"Like, for work."

"Oh." He pursed his lips, winced when his bottom lip shot a jolt of pain into his gums. "I catch things." He immediately regretted saying it. It sounded bad. *Wrong.*

"*Catch* things? You mean like hunting?"

Yeah, you could say that.

"Yes." Michael's nerves buzzed again. "For my family."

There was no thrill in that confession, no jolt of excitement like he'd felt when he revealed his full name. It hit too close to home, as though at any second she'd come to realize exactly what he meant. Her eyes would grow impossibly wide. She'd open her mouth to scream. She'd gasp for air, and he'd have to lunge over the counter and grab her by the throat before she made a sound. Because if she yelled, Rebel would realize she knew the truth, and that would be the end of Michael and Alice both.

"You mean to eat, right?" Alice looked unsure. "You don't just hunt for fun."

His eyes darted to the hall.

How long are they going to be down there?

It seemed like an eternity since he'd last seen Reb. What if Lucy had said something that had made him mad? What if he had decided that going to the movies was a bad idea and snapped her neck instead, pulled out his switchblade and stabbed her in the stomach a hundred times?

Michael couldn't get a decent breath in. He imagined himself turning blue right before Alice's eyes, choking on nothing but his own viselike anxiety. And then he remembered what Wade had said while teaching him how to hunt as a kid, and he spit the statement out as his own.

"We don't have hardly anything," he recited mechanically. "We gotta make do with what the land gives us."

Alice didn't respond.

Michael swallowed against the beat of tension.

He watched Alice put away her receipts and her ledger, Reb's insistence that he not be weird echoing inside his head. He had said something wrong—he could see it in her face.

He nearly breathed an audible sigh of relief at the sound of Rebel and Lucy coming down the hall, and for a moment Michael was sure Alice looked relieved too. Maybe she *had* seen something in his face—a momentary flicker of hesitation, a brief pause that told the whole story. He swallowed against the tightness of his throat and turned to face Reb. An unlit Lucky Strike dangled from his brother's bottom lip.

"You all ready to rock 'n' roll?" Reb asked.

"Yeah," Michael said, inching away from the counter and toward the front door.

"Sure," Alice said, giving the three of them a smile that was a few watts shy of her standard grin.

Michael waited for the group to start moving toward the door, but Reb waved him out. "Be out in a minute," he said. "Wait by the car."

Michael's gaze flitted back to Alice, but she failed to return the look.

He suddenly felt panicky, as though it was the last time he'd ever see her. Something about the way Rebel was leaning against that counter, cocky and as smooth as the Marlboro Man, made him want to scream. It was one of Reb's personalities—a mask he put on for the hunt. He'd become the suave and seductive Raymond "Rebel" Morrow with the killer smile and the bedroom eyes, the gentle touch and the long eyelashes girls went nuts over. Reb had once told Michael that if he wasn't so awkward, Michael could have been even better at it than Reb was.

Faggy or not, he had said, *chicks dig that long hair.*

For a moment, Michael froze with his hand on the doorknob. He was unsure whether to comply with Rebel's request or refuse to leave the girls alone with him while they locked up the store. Reb noticed his hesitation and chuckled.

"Come on, man," he said, a little plea in his tone. "I just need a minute. We'll be right behind you."

Michael only realized he was scowling after he turned away from the group, the muscles in his face momentarily relaxing as he stepped out of the store and into the early evening heat.

14

THE DAHLIA CINEPLEX had three screens. *The Empire Strikes Back* was playing on one. *Urban Cowboy* was on another. And Rebel's movie of choice—*The Shining*—played on the third. Michael inhaled the lobby air, which smelled so heavily of buttered popcorn it made his mouth water as much as passing a McDonald's did. Reb bought four tickets at the window outside, and they entered the lobby. Fascinated, Michael watched a couple of teens fill drink cups from a soda fountain and scoop popcorn into paper sleeves while his brother stood in line for concessions. Michael wasn't sure where Reb had gotten the cash, and he certainly wasn't about to ask.

Lucy giggled beneath her breath and Michael turned her way.

"What?" he asked.

"Nothing," she said. "Just that you're looking around the place like you haven't ever seen the inside of a theater before."

Michael pushed his hair behind his ears and shook his head. "I haven't."

Lucy furrowed her brow, trying to figure out whether he was making a joke. "You're serious?" She looked over her shoulder just in time to catch Alice stepping out of the ladies room. "Hey Allie, did you know that Michael hasn't ever been to the movies before? Isn't that bananas?"

Alice joined them in the middle of the lobby. Her expression matched Lucy's—intrigued, curious, mystified. "Really?"

Michael raised his hands as if to show them he wasn't playing tricks.

"Man." Lucy shot Alice a look. "That means he hasn't seen *Amityville* or *Alien* or anything."

Reb sidled up to the group, handing out tickets.

"What about you, Ray?" Lucy asked. "This isn't *your* first time at the movies, right?"

Rebel gave Lucy a look like she'd lost her mind, and Michael glanced away from his brother to the paper ticket in his hand.

"I love the chick that played the space woman in *Alien*. I forget her name. CiCi or something?" Lucy shrugged, then looped her arm through Reb's as they turned toward a door marked SCREEN 3. He squeezed the ticket in the palm of his hand, imagining Reb coming to this very movie theater while Michael was upstairs, or wandering through the woods, or down in the basement, working his knife between the vertebrae of a fresh kill. *Brothers united,* Michael thought, and something twisted inside his chest.

"Hey." Michael nearly jumped when Alice's fingers brushed across his arm. She pulled her hand back as soon as he moved, but rather than appearing afraid, she looked concerned. "You okay?" she asked. Her soft tone was comforting. It pulled him inside an invisible box that only the two of them occupied.

When Michael didn't respond, she offered him a faint smile. "Let's get some snacks," she suggested. "I'll buy." And then she grabbed him by the hand and pulled him to the concession stand.

By the time Alice and Michael stepped inside the theater, it was 75 percent full. They searched for Rebel and Lucy for a minute or two, Alice holding a paper sleeve of popcorn and a box of Junior Mints while Michael palmed two cups of TaB. But after a while Alice motioned to the two empty seats closest to them with a shrug. "Let's just sit here," she said and slid into place. "They probably want to be alone anyway. Unless you *want* to sit next to them." She looked skeptical, and Michael shook his head to say that the two seats Alice had chosen were just fine.

As they settled into their seats, Alice took a sip of soda and tore open her box of Junior Mints. "You have seen movies, though, right? You guys have a TV at least?"

"Yeah, we got one," Michael said.

"Then what's your favorite movie that you've seen?" she asked.

He looked down at his soda and pursed his lips, not sure whether he should be honest or make something up that sounded at least a little cooler than the truth. She smirked, noticing his hesitation.

"Come on," she said. "Out with it."

Michael squirmed and took a breath. "I like *The Wizard of Oz* pretty well."

She gave him a look—another one that assured him he was too weird to live. "What do you like about it?"

"I dunno. I guess I like that Dorothy gets to escape to a place where it's colorful and magical instead of livin' in Kansas all her life." He paused, then added, "Those flyin' monkeys were pretty good too."

Alice looked thoughtful, as though considering just how good the monkeys had been. She met his gaze a moment later. "But you realize that isn't what the movie is about, right?"

"What do you mean?"

"Dorothy thinks Oz is amazing until she realizes it's full of danger and sadness and evil. In the end, she's happy to go back to her old life on the farm."

He couldn't help from frowning at that. Whenever Michael would watch that movie with Misty, they'd turn off the TV before Dorothy went back to Kansas. For them, the mantra of there being no place like home meant something entirely different.

"Oh no. I didn't ruin it for you, did I?" Alice matched his frown with her own. "I mean, it's just my interpretation. It doesn't mean you have to watch it like that. It could mean whatever you want it to, I guess."

Michael wondered if there was some truth to Oz. Perhaps longing for his own escape seemed full of wonder because it was nothing more than a pipe dream. Maybe if he ended up going out in the world, all he'd want to do was crawl back to Momma and Wade.

Alice opened her mouth to say something else as Michael held fast to his silence, but the lowering house lights cut her off.

He sat through the majority of *The Shining* with his eyes

wide and his mouth slightly open. The movie itself paired with the scope of that massive screen transported him to the Overlook Hotel. For nearly an hour he sat motionless, having forgotten all about his TaB and the beautiful girl on his right. She nudged him, holding out a half-empty sleeve of popcorn, her own gaze fixed forward. When he turned to look at her, the way the lights danced off her face, the way he could see the movie reflected in her eyes, overwhelmed him with the sudden urge to kiss her. His heartbeat drifted down his chest and settled low in his stomach, throbbing like an electric pulse. His face flushed at the memory of one particular girl—not nearly as pretty as Alice, but the prettiest one he had seen up until then. She had smelled of oranges and pine and had given fourteen-year-old Michael an ache at the very base of his guts. It had been an urge that he soothed by standing in the farthest, darkest corner of the basement, snuffing it out with anxious abandon, his eyes fixed on her dead and naked frame.

Alice noticed him staring. She pulled her attention away from a wild-eyed Jack Nicholson, and gave Michael a faint smile. Leaning in, she whispered into his ear. "Are you having a good time?" Michael nodded, and her smile brightened a notch. "Me too," she murmured, catching her bottom lip in her teeth. And then she slid her hand into his.

• • •

The credits rolled and people began to shuffle out of the theater. Some were grinning and chatting. Others looked dazed, like they'd just sat through a three-hour lobotomy that would leave them forever changed. Michael couldn't believe it was over, which was part of the reason he hesitated getting out of his seat. He wanted the projectionist to play the movie again so he could figure out exactly what he had watched. Part of him loved the fact that Wendy and Danny had escaped Jack's wrath. But the other half of him—the darker half—couldn't help but think their escape was nothing but wishful thinking.

"Bullshit, right?" Rebel asked with a laugh, suddenly standing next to Michael and Alice's seats with Lucy hanging off his arm. "There ain't no way those two would get out of there alive. No way. That Wendy was too stupid."

Michael looked over to Alice. She shrugged, but she was grinning. He grabbed his nearly empty cup of soda and took a watered-down swig.

"So, what did you think?" Lucy asked, her gaze fixed on Michael. "First time at the movies. . . ."

"I wanna see it again," he said. Lucy and Reb laughed at his response and exited with the rest of the crowd, leaving Michael and Alice alone again. When Michael glanced over to her, Alice nodded at him.

"I know what you mean," she said. "I want to see it again too."

. . .

Lucy and Reb debated about it the entire way back to the Dervish. Was Jack Torrance insane, or were the things he had seen real? Was it all in his head, or was the Overlook actually haunted? Michael and Alice sat quietly in the backseat, listening to them banter back and forth. Two blocks from the record store, Alice scooted more toward the middle of the seat, letting her thigh press against Michael's leg.

. . .

Rebel flipped down the driver's seat and left the door open for Michael and Alice to crawl out, then followed Lucy across the parking lot to her car. When Michael made a move to step out of the Delta, Alice gently caught him by the wrist to stop him. Her eyes lingered on Reb and Lucy in the distance before they focused on the boy beside her. Michael's pulse whooshed against his ears, her touch electrifying him, making every hair on his body stand on end.

"I had fun," she said softly.

He looked down at the seat, his hair curtaining the sides of his face. She leaned in, her hands rising to pull his hair back, her fingertips sweeping across each cheek with a butterfly's touch.

"I like that you're shy. It makes you special." Her lips grazed the corner of his mouth, her warm spearmint scent drifting across his skin. His fingers curled against the upholstery of the backseat before daring to graze a denim-covered knee. And for a flash of a moment, he pictured her dead on the basement floor, stripped and cold-skinned, her eyes wide open, her lips a grayish-blue. He pulled back, simultaneously revolted and undeniably turned on. He yearned to touch her, but the idea of doing it while she was breathing scared him. It was different when there was potential for humiliation, rejection, disgust.

Alice nodded faintly when he pulled away, as if to say she understood. "See you soon, I hope?"

"Yeah."

She hesitated, as if contemplating something, then slipped out of the Oldsmobile without another word.

.   .   .

When Rebel finally slid into his seat, he smelled like Lucy's perfume. Michael had switched back to the passenger side. He had watched his brother kissing and groping through the windshield while Alice waited in Lucy's Honda hatchback. He couldn't shake the fact that he had pictured Alice dead—a murder victim laid out on the basement floor.

"What's wrong?" Reb asked. "You say something stupid?"

"I don't think so," Michael murmured.

"Then what?"

Michael shook his head, not daring to explain.

Reb rolled his eyes and slid the key into the ignition. "Yeah, bet you said something dumb, but whatever—she likes you."

Something fluttered inside Michael's chest—hope, elation, an eagerness to come back and see her again, even though they had yet to leave the parking lot.

Reb gave Michael a skeptical glance. "You like her?"

"Yes." The word was almost breathless.

Reb pulled the Delta onto the road, smiling to himself. "Good," he said beneath his breath. "Glad to hear it, brother. Glad indeed."

15

MICHAEL SPENT NEARLY all of the following day sitting at his desk, scribbling pictures into the margins of old newspapers. He used whatever blank space he could find to draw panels like the ones he had seen in Alice's sketchbook while music cut through the silence of the upstairs rooms. Neil Diamond's "Cherry, Cherry" filtered through the wall on what seemed like endless repeat. His sketches weren't much more than crude line drawings, like primitive art scratched onto a cave wall. Because Alice had drawn her own life at the Dervish, Michael decided to follow her lead and draw things about himself as well. They were things he'd never be able to show her, but putting them on paper made him feel closer to her. He sketched himself sitting in the Delta with Rebel behind the wheel. He drew them both lying on their stomachs on top of a hill, spying on the next mark. There was the farmhouse and Misty Dawn dancing in the backyard, Momma with an angry face, looming in the background, watching her from the shadows.

By the time he had switched from sketching the subtle horrors of his own life to the tall buildings of New York City, Reb barged into his room. The smells of that evening's dinner drifted in behind him. Michael jerked his head up from its unnaturally bowed position and winced at a sudden bite of pain. He'd been huddled like that for so long his poor posture had given birth to a wicked crick in his neck.

"What've you been doin' in here?" Reb asked, stepping behind Michael and snatching the sheet of newspaper off his desk. "Haven't seen you all day." Michael made a swipe for the paper, but Reb twisted away, peering at the doodles in the margins. He gave Michael a weird smile. "Don't Alice draw stuff like this? You fallin' madly in love, little brother?"

Michael didn't respond. He simply extended an arm for Reb to return what was his.

"Must be nice knowin' someone's taken an interest in you, huh? Must feel good to get some attention instead of bein' ignored all the time."

Rebel's tone was strained, and Michael could smell the alcohol wafting off of him—a sharp, fermented stench. Reb acted strange when he'd been drinking, seesawing between self-pity and aggression. Sometimes he'd ramble on about how nobody appreciated him. Once, during a particularly rough night, Reb stood on top of his chair in the middle of dinner and announced that he was nothing but a slave. Used and abused. Never paid. Undervalued. Wade had laughed. Misty had rolled her eyes. Momma had told him to get his dirty goddamn boots off her chair, as though she hadn't heard a word he'd said. But Michael had felt bad for him. Even if the declaration held no merit, the fact that Reb had said it meant he felt it. Michael didn't know much, but he knew feeling that way couldn't have been good.

"You're drunk," Michael murmured, catching the paper by its corner, but Reb yanked it away again.

"You don't think you've got a real shot with her, do you?" He tossed the newspaper at Michael's outstretched arm.

"Why not?" Michael turned his back on his brother, smoothing the wrinkles out of where he had crumpled the page in his hand. "If you can get with Lucy, why can't I get with Alice?"

"Because you ain't *me*, you stupid shit." Reb smacked the back of Michael's head with an open palm. "We ain't even related by blood. Think about it." He gave his own forehead a few rough taps. "Can you think about it, Mikey? You able to process that little nugget of hard fuckin' truth?"

"What do you want?" There was only one reason Rebel came into Michael's room, and that was to tell him to get ready to hit the road. Sometimes their trips would be quick. They'd get lucky and find a girl wandering the side of the highway, hitching in the dark, a thumb pointing upward whenever a pair of headlights shined along the horizon. On those nights, they were back home before the sun came up, but hitchhikers weren't that easy to find. Reb said they were like winning cash at a card table—if you knew what you were doing, you could usually get lucky. But even lucky players came up empty now and again.

"First, I want Miss to stop playin' that goddamn song. How many times has it been now?" He scowled at the wall that separated Michael's room from his sister's. "Then I want you to stop askin' stupid questions. But since *that* ain't happenin', I want you to get your shit and meet me downstairs." He turned to go, then paused in the open bedroom door. "We're out of tape. Grab a fresh roll."

Michael frowned at his poor attempt at artwork while Rebel's boots banged down the stairs. When he had drawn himself and Reb in the Delta, he had imagined them driving to the Dervish to see the girls. But the more he looked at it, the more he understood that wasn't what was happening in the picture at all. Ray looked too serious, his expression both determined and hungry. Michael appeared too defeated to be excited by the prospect of seeing Alice again, his gaze turned out the window. Those two crudely rendered people weren't headed toward social interaction. They were speeding down a darkened highway toward screams garbled by fear and desperation.

Michael had drawn them on the way to work.

I should really quit my job.

Rebel called up from the first floor. "You comin' or what? Jesus Christ, Misty! Turn that shit off!"

Michael gritted his teeth. He jerked his desk drawer open to clear its top. He grabbed a broken red crayon from the corner of the drawer and scribbled red wax over Reb's face, pressing down as hard as he could. The red blotch spread involuntarily, spilling onto Michael's drawn face. Onto Misty Dawn dancing in the yard. Across the entire sheet of newspaper. He pushed into the desk until his hand ached, the crayon wearing down to a nub within seconds. The newspaper was suddenly in his hands. Crumpled. Torn. Strips of black and white and red flying through the air, Neil singing *She's got the way to move me* over and over and over again. Breathing hard, he shoved himself away from the desk, his pulse blinding him with its bass-like thump. His fingernails bit into the flesh of his palms. And then, just as quickly as the rage had consumed him, it was gone. Michael turned away from the mess strewn across the floor and left the room.

He grabbed a roll of duct tape from the hall closet and stepped into the night.

. . .

The little house with the green shutters looked different in the dark. Michael couldn't decide whether it was because he hadn't seen it at night or because of the angle. He'd only ever peered at it from the hill that was now behind him, not from the crushed gravel of the driveway that rolled out toward the garage. A few lights shone through curtained windows, and the flicker of a TV screen flashed against the interior walls in shades of blue. He'd wrapped girls up in tape dozens of times, but he'd never been brazen enough to pull someone out of their home. Something about abducting a woman out of her living room felt like far worse a crime than shoving a hitcher into the car trunk. Home was supposed to be safe. There was no place like it.

"I'm goin' in." Reb buttoned up his jean jacket as if doing so would somehow conceal his identity. "You watch the clock, give me ten minutes, then come in through the back."

"How do you know it's gonna be open?" Michael asked.

"Gotta hunch."

"But what if she ain't alone?" Michael's gaze flitted to the front window. This whole thing still felt premature. Sloppy. If

Rebel walked in and found the woman lounging on her couch with a man at her side, Reb would either end up seriously hurt or the man would end up dead. Michael assumed the former was more likely, though he'd never tell Reb that to his face. And if that woman *did* have a boyfriend or a husband, he was probably a logger or a miner, a tough West Virginian son of a bitch who'd swat Rebel across the room like a fly. His brother wouldn't stand a chance, and Michael wouldn't have enough time to get the hell out of there before Mr. Miner came running into the yard. Teeth bared. Big arms held over his head like a grizzly. Ready to crush the skull of whoever had thought they could screw with his woman.

"She's alone," Reb murmured beneath his breath. Despite the fact that Michael had only seen this house twice before tonight, Ray was somehow positive. The mark was clear. It was safe.

"You don't want me to just go in with you?" It seemed like a better option. They could tape her up in the living room. If it was just Reb, she'd go racing around all over the place. Sure, the house was in the middle of nowhere, but keeping her quiet was a good idea. You never knew when a car was going to pass by or when some night owl was going to take Fido out for an evening stroll.

Rebel narrowed his eyes and Michael shrank away from the glare. "I told you, ten minutes." He stepped out of the car, leaving the door wide open behind him. Michael fumbled with the dome light. He turned it off as Reb stalked along the wild grass and ducked around the side of the house, probably looking for open windows or an unlocked door.

There wasn't much to fear in places like this. That's why people moved out to the country. It seemed safe and peaceful and perfect until you caught a lunatic crawling through your bedroom window. Michael glanced at the analog clock recessed into the Delta's dash, its phosphorescent hands glowing weakly in the dark. Then he opened his door, looped his hand through the fresh roll of duct tape, and slid out of the car.

He crossed the front yard to the small bistro table beneath a tree and took a seat in its metal-backed chair, waiting for some sign of struggle—a scream or the breaking of glass. The inevitable noise of someone watching their life flash before their eyes. When it remained silent, Michael got up and walked the dozen yards it took to get to the darkened road. He knew he shouldn't have gone so far from the Delta—Reb had told him to be ready—but he had seven more minutes to wait.

Stepping onto a small boulder along the side of the road, he balanced there, wondering if Rebel was into old ladies. Maybe his brother was discovering his own tastes rather than letting Momma dictate them with her MO. Reb wanted to break the rules, and this one seemed as good as any to break.

There was a bang from inside the house. Michael turned to look at the cottage from the edge of the road. He hopped off the rock he was balancing on and hurried back to the Oldsmobile. There was no screaming—just the sound of things being thrown. He imagined Rebel dodging table lamps and crystal ashtrays, wondered what he'd do if the woman actually got the better of him and came bursting out the front door. What if Reb didn't come bolting from the house after her because he was unconscious on the living room floor? What if it was because she had stuck a kitchen knife through his neck? Would Michael let her get away? His pulse quickened at the possibility of the woman slashing Reb to ribbons, of his brother dying on a cheap Formica floor.

"I'll let you get away," he whispered. "Just kill him. That's all you gotta do."

He blinked at his own words. Did he really mean that? If Rebel really did die, what the hell would Michael do then? He'd drive the Olds back to the house, grab Misty, and leave Momma and Wade in dreamland. They'd drive into town and find Alice, and the three of them would take off to New York City.

Even Pittsburgh or Columbus, Ohio, would be better.

He chewed on his still-tender lip, wondering if any of that was possible. Would he be able to get out of Dahlia and start a new life if there was no one there to stop him?

At the eight-minute mark, Michael pushed away from the Delta and followed Reb's path around the side of the house. Reb had left the back sliding-glass door open a crack, and Michael quietly pushed it over before slipping inside. A strangled cry sounded from down the hall. Pivoting on the soles of his old boots, he trotted down a picture-lined hallway until he reached an open door.

Rebel held the sobbing woman down on the bed by her wrists, quiet pleas escaping her throat.

"Please, Michael, don't. . . ." she croaked.

Michael froze in the doorway, the world momentarily tilting on its axis when his name slipped past her lips. How did she know . . . ? Had Rebel told her that his brother, Michael, would be there any minute, ready to help?

He swallowed and stood idle at the threshold. Reb shot a look across the room, his jeans unzipped, his most private parts exposed. Michael looked away, squeezing his eyes shut as though he'd walked in on something he wasn't supposed to see.

"What the hell are you doin'?" Reb snapped. "Get *over here!*"

Michael forced his eyes open and shifted his weight to his toes. He moved fast, already peeling a strip of duct tape from the roll.

The woman was weeping. Her hair, which had been pulled into a ponytail, was now halfway down. The rubber band barely held back an unnatural reddish-blond. Rebel had bloodied her face, most likely with a swift whack to the nose. The blood dribbled across her mouth and chin, staining her powder-blue tank top. A golden *M* glinted from a chain tucked into the hollow of her throat.

"Grab her hands," Reb demanded. Michael took one of her arms and wrapped the duct tape thrice around a wrist. He yanked it toward her other hand, and then taped them together as quick as a rodeo star. Rebel let her go, then tucked himself back into his jeans while Michael taped the woman's mouth shut. "Take her to the car," he said, shoving his fingers through his hair. It was then that Michael realized the woman wasn't wearing any pants. A pair of plain white panties were skewed around her hips, half on, half off. Michael stared at the woman's hips, reluctant to push her out of the house without at least giving her something decent to wear.

"What's wrong with you?" Reb asked, shoving Michael out of the way when he hesitated to move. His brother grabbed the woman by the back of her neck and shoved her into the hallway.

Michael blinked and followed Rebel out the front door and to the car. The woman was now fighting like hell, thrashing and bucking in Reb's arms. Halfway across the yard, they stopped and Michael tied her legs together at the knees with a thick binding of tape. He then moved down to her calves, and finally her ankles, repeating the process. Rebel dragged her the rest of the way to the Oldsmobile. He popped the trunk and dumped her inside before marching around to the driver-side door with a dissatisfied grunt. Michael was left with the woman staring up at him, her eyes pleading, begging him to reconsider, beseeching him to be her savior. When she tried to scream around the tape stuck across her mouth, he slammed the trunk closed.

He expected Rebel to yell at him as soon as he fell back into his seat, but his brother said nothing. He simply threw the Delta into reverse, peeled out of the driveway, and fishtailed it onto the road.

But halfway home, Rebel broke his silence with a laugh. It was a severe, heartless titter that made Michael's skin crawl, a sound that he'd never heard escape Reb's throat before. Michael wrapped his arms around himself and stared out the window, watching the headlights slash across the trees. He wondered where Reb had gone, because Reb *was* gone. Not here. Lost somewhere along that winding rural West Virginia road.

When they finally turned onto the road that would take them back to the farmhouse, Michael dared whisper a question into the Oldsmobile's cab.

"How'd she know my name, Reb?"

Rebel didn't answer. He just laughed again.

16

THE MORNING RAY had watched Michael unlatch the rabbit cage and pull Snowball from behind the fencing, he lay in bed, waiting for Lauralynn's wail. She was usually the first of them up, but the fact that Ray was waiting with baited breath turned the minutes into hours. By the time Lauralynn screamed, Ray had actually started to drift back to sleep. As soon as he heard her, his eyes darted open. Michael, who had snuck back into bed after he'd done the deed, didn't move when their sister cried out. He was faking sleep so hard it seemed that he had paralyzed himself in the process.

Ray bounded out of bed and hopped over to the window, shoving the dingy curtains aside just in time to catch his older sibling kneeling in front of the rabbit cage. But to Ray's surprise, it wasn't just Snowball who was missing. The cage was completely empty. Michael's plan had worked like a charm. He nearly said something to his kid brother, thought about congratulating him on a job well done, but rushed downstairs in his pajamas instead.

Misty Dawn had her arm around her big sister's shoulders. Michael drifted onto the back porch a minute later, but he kept his distance. He sat on the bottom porch step with his hands covering his mouth. Ray was tempted to say something—*Don't look so guilty, you idiot.* Michael had done a bang-up job covering his tracks, and now he was going to give himself away with that pathetic look of shame plastered across his face.

"What happened?" Ray asked in his best *I'm-super-concerned* voice.

"My bunnies!" Lauralynn's words were nearly indecipherable around her sobs.

Ray widened his eyes in a dramatic sort of way as he stared at the empty cage. "Oh *no!*" He almost cracked a grin at how ridiculous he sounded. "They got away?"

Lauralynn didn't reply, because she couldn't speak. She was crying so hard now that she could hardly breathe. Misty Dawn rubbed her back and whispered, "There, there, we'll find 'em," like the dumb little girl she was.

Find 'em? Ray thought. *Sure, you'll find 'em—just wait 'til dinner.*

Ray turned to look at Michael, who was still petrified upon the steps. "What's wrong with *you*?" he asked, padding back up the porch steps. "It almost looks like *you* opened the cage."

Michael jerked his head up and stared at his brother with wide, glassy eyes, and then he burst into tears. But rather than dodging back into the house, he ran for the girls, threw his arms around them both, and wailed "I'm sorry, Lauralynn!"

Neither of the girls deciphered his apology. Michael had practically confessed to the crime, and they mistook his admission for mutual sadness.

The day dragged on, and Ray's siblings spent most of it among the trees just beyond the backyard. Even Michael was helping Lauralynn look for her fluffy babies, as though finding at least one of them would somehow redeem him from the evil he'd done. Ray hung around the back porch, listening to them calling out bunny names—*Snowball! Blackie! Mr. Buttons!*—as if the things had the capacity to respond like dogs.

"They're pretty stupid," Ray told Momma as he buzzed around the kitchen. "They think them rabbits are gonna come hoppin' back outta those trees because they heard their name or something? Bunch of idiots, if you ask me."

"I don't think nobody 'round here *did* ask you," Momma replied, not once turning to look at her boy.

When Momma finally called them to the table, Ray had to cover his mouth to keep from laughing. It was as if she'd done it on purpose, leaving the rabbit intact the way she did. She presented the roasted critter on a platter the way any other family would present a turkey on Thanksgiving. Snowball lay on a bed of leafy greens, surrounded by steamed carrots, like the punch line to a particularly gruesome joke. She hadn't even bothered to chop off the head. The ears had wilted in the heat, and the eyes were nothing more than black cigarette burns, but there was no mistaking it for what it was. Lauralynn screamed so hysterically when she saw it, Ray was sure she was within inches of a puking fit.

He expected her to turn tail and bolt up the stairs, slam her door and refuse to come out for a few days. But rather than escaping the dining room in a flurry of tears, she screamed at Momma instead. "You *did this!*" she wailed. "*YOU killed my bunnies, you bitch!*"

Ray's mouth fell open in shock.

Misty Dawn and Michael were also unable to hide their surprise.

Ray had never seen Lauralynn so angry, and he'd never *ever* heard anyone speak to Momma that way. He looked from Lauralynn to Misty Dawn and Michael, dumbstruck, the three of them sitting there like openmouthed trout. Wade covered his face with a hand, as if not wanting to see what was about to come next. When Ray laid eyes on Momma once more, his secret amusement was gone. Sure, Lauralynn deserved some of what was coming to her, but the satisfaction of a little poetic justice burned away at the sight of Momma's bubbling outrage.

Her gaunt face was as red as if she'd stuck her entire head into a boiling pot. Her mouth was pulled into a line so tight that her lips all but disappeared. But her eyes scared Ray the most. Just as he'd never heard

Lauralynn so angry, he'd never seen such hostility, such obvious loathing radiate from Momma's stare. For a second, Ray was sure Lauralynn had sealed their fates. Momma would murder them all, and then she'd boil their bones and go back to being Claudine Morrow—childless, happier.

Ray shot a look at his adopted brother. This was all *his* fault. Michael was the one who had turned Lauralynn against him. Michael was the one who had taken Snowball and skinned him under the cover of night. Ray considered outing him right then and there, telling the entire table that he'd caught Michael red-handed earlier that morning. But he was almost positive Michael would get a free pass. He was little, and he hadn't successfully brought in a kill for dinner in nearly a week. He had killed Snowball out of desperation, out of *loyalty*. And what was Ray doing? Betraying him by tattling. Ray bit his tongue against the temptation. No, if he kept it to himself, he'd have something to blackmail the little bastard with. If he kept it to himself, he could hold it over Michael's head for the rest of the kid's life.

All of this flashed through Ray's mind within the time it took Lauralynn to horrify the table with her outburst. And Momma reacted exactly as expected. She stood up, the legs of her chair screaming against the hardwood floor. Wade got up too, as if ready to stop the inevitable, but he kept silent. It was as if he'd risen from his chair to get a better view, his hands gripping the table in front of him. Lauralynn made like she was about to run, but Momma was faster than any of them gave her credit for. She grabbed Lauralynn by the hair and used her daughter's momentum to shove her into the wall. Except Momma missed the wall and pushed Lauralynn directly into the corner of an old armoire.

Lauralynn stumbled backward, choking out a winded breath before falling onto her rear. Her hands flew to her face like frantic birds and came back bloodied. Ray couldn't tell where it was all coming from, her nose or her mouth, but there was a lot of blood . . . so much that his fascination turned into panic. He jumped up from his seat, ready to run to his big sister's aid, but Momma gave him a look so threatening that he froze in his tracks. When his gaze darted back to Lauralynn, two teeth were swimming in a pool of crimson against the white of her palm.

"Okay, everybody upstairs," Wade said, rushing Misty and Michael out of the dining room. Ray hesitated, then shoved past Wade to help Lauralynn up. *Everybody* included LL, but Momma caught him by the shoulder and gave him a stern glance, assuring him that he was mistaken. Lauralynn wasn't going anywhere.

"Everybody but her," she said, that terrifying look twisting her face into someone Ray hardly recognized.

"Momma, please," he whispered, surprised by the warble of his own voice.

"Get outta my sight," she seethed through her teeth, sinking her fingers into the meat of his neck, and giving him a ruthless shove out of the room.

When Wade ushered Ray upstairs, Michael was sitting on his bed, looking as aghast as Ray felt. Ray didn't comfort his brother. When he heard Lauralynn shrieking downstairs, he slapped his hands over his ears and faced the wall.

.   .   .

Ray couldn't sleep. He kept replaying Lauralynn's fall in his head. Kept seeing the way her hands fluttered around her face like trapped moths. Remembered the small bits of pink-stained bone lying in her hand like rotten, oozing fruit.

And then there was Michael, his steady breathing slowly driving Ray insane. He was sleeping like nothing had happened, like he didn't have a care in the world, when this was all his fault. Ray imagined leaping across the room and pounding his fists against Michael's scrawny seven-year-old body until the cries and pleas for mercy faded into nothing. Ray wanted to beat him until he heard bones snap. Until blood soaked the bedsheets. Until he could no longer recognize the face he'd come to know over the past year—a face that he'd seen once on the news and on a missing-child poster at the grocery store but never again. When Ray had told Michael that his parents no longer wanted him, it had been an easy lie . . . but now he had to wonder if maybe he had been right. Michael was a blight on the Morrows, so it only made sense that the little shit had been a nuisance to his original family too.

Ray shoved his sheets aside and stepped up to the window. He stared down at the empty rabbit pen and wondered if it would stay that way or if Wade would feel sorry for Lauralynn and get her replacement bunnies despite Momma being against the whole thing.

He watched a long shadow shift across the yard. Someone was standing on the porch, the light to their back. When Wade finally came into view, he was carrying something in his arms. Lauralynn's bare feet bobbed up and down with each step, her skirt fluttering in the light night-time breeze. Her long hair hung down in easy waves, streaked with something that almost looked like oil in the gloom. Wade stopped in front of the rabbit cage for a moment, as if in consideration, and then stepped around it and moved toward the trees, the same way Michael had done just that morning.

Ray refused to understand what he was seeing. He couldn't process the possibility, the reasons for why Lauralynn had kept screaming for a good fifteen minutes when every other time Momma had attacked her she had remained silent. He didn't want to entertain the idea that maybe Momma . . .

. . . that she had . . .

. . . that . . .

His eyes went wide when he saw Wade come out of the trees empty-handed.

Ray leaned against the wall, his cheek pressed to the cool glass of the window, his knees threatening to buckle beneath him. Something inside him was tearing itself free and it hurt. His eyes began to water. His hands trembled. Something was inching its way up his esophagus— a sob that he was determined to swallow whole.

Wade's shadow trailed behind him across the yard as he walked back to the house. It reached for the oaks and maples, as if afraid to separate itself from the girl whom he had left in the dark. A second shadowy figure met Wade's, and Wade stopped to regard it at the foot of the porch steps. When he turned back to the trees, his hands were hidden inside a pair of old work gloves. The handle of an old shovel stood out in the weak yellow light. He was moving slowly, as if reluctant, but he never stopped, and he never looked back.

Ray pressed his palm to the window pane. He stared at his own reflection, just as he had before the sun came up. But his expression couldn't have been more different from what it had been that morning. What was once dark amusement was replaced by a set of wide saucer eyes, that sinister smile now an *O* of shock, a refusal to believe, a silent scream.

The Ray in the window looked monstrous with grief, and then he disappeared. Momma turned off the porch light and Ray vanished, swallowed by the darkness of the room.

● ● ●

The Morrows sat silently as they ate breakfast around the kitchen table. Ray's eyes were fixed on Lauralynn's empty chair, and the silence was enough to make him want to scream. He shot his mother a deadly serious look and split the quiet with a question he knew she wouldn't want to answer. "Where's Lauralynn?"

Momma and Wade exchanged glances, but neither one responded. Ray considered having his own outburst. He wondered what would happen if he stood up and flipped the table over, wondered what they'd do to him if he told them he had seen Wade carrying his sister into the woods.

But before he got up the nerve, Momma settled her gaze on him and answered.

"We sent her up to North Carolina. She'll be livin' with your grandparents from now on."

"North Carolina?" Ray asked, daring her to continue the lie. "In the middle of the night? Without takin' any clothes?"

"She already has clothes there." Momma's words were clipped. "And it ain't none of your business anyhow."

Ray fell silent, glowering at his plate of rubbery scrambled eggs.

"Momma?" Misty Dawn blinked up at her mother, her small face drawn in concern. "She was reading us *Winnie the Pooh*. When's she comin' back?"

"I said that ain't none of your business."

"She's our sister," Ray pushed.

"Will *you* read the rest to us?" Misty asked quietly. "Me and Michael wanna know what happens next."

"When's Lauralynn coming back?" Michael whispered toward Misty, looking confused. Misty shook her head to say that she didn't know. "Was she bad?"

Ray's attention snapped to his younger brother. His pulse whooshed in his ears. How dare he ask such a stupid question about an event that *he* had caused? Dropping his hands to his lap, his fingers gripped the edge of his chair, his teeth gritted behind a close-lipped sneer.

"Of course she was bad," Momma snapped. "Did you lose your eyes and ears last night? She was bad and now she's gone . . . and let that be a lesson to all of you, you understand? Any of you step outta line and it's off to the grandparents. You won't be settin' foot back in *my* house again."

Michael turned his sorrowful eyes toward Ray. "Like you said, Ray," he whispered. "Into the woods to get lost by yourself."

Every muscle in Ray's body tensed.

"Except she ain't in the woods," Misty murmured. "She's at

Grandma's." She wrinkled her nose at the idea, most likely imagining her older sister living out the rest of her life in window-curtain dresses.

"I hope she comes back soon," Michael mused. "We've gotta finish *Pooh*."

"Oh, you're both idiots," Ray spit at his siblings. "Don't you get it? She ain't coming back." Michael and Misty looked startled. Ray scowled, hating them for being so stupid, and then shot a look at Wade. "Really, North Carolina?" he asked, giving his father a chance to come clean. But Wade let the opportunity pass him by, holding on to his silence.

Ray's gaze then jumped to his mother. She now appeared to be assessing her eldest son, sizing him up, probably considering whether Ray was worth the trouble of keeping around. That calculating look both enraged and terrified him; there was no love in his mother's eyes, no compassion. He was sure it was the last thing Lauralynn saw before Momma had gone forward with whatever she had done—tightened her fingers around his big sister's neck, or maybe slashed her throat. It didn't matter how Momma had done it; it would never matter. But the fact that she had lied about everything, about where Lauralynn had gone—for that, he would never forgive her.

For that, he would never call her Momma again.

17

MICHAEL HELD THE pillow over his head and squeezed his eyes shut. He was trying to block out the wailing in the backyard with happier thoughts of his next visit to town. He wondered whether spending too much time with Alice, whether getting too close, would reveal the tired dismay in his eyes. Maybe someday, after he'd heard one cry too many, he'd open his mouth to speak, but rather than words, screams would pour out instead. And yet Michael could still talk, could still smile, could still enjoy himself at the movies and forget the horrors of his daily life. Somehow, despite his circumstances, he could still *feel* things. Like the flutter of excitement when he saw the Dervish come into view. Or what might resemble peace while he lay on a sun-dappled hill. It should have been a comforting thought—the fact that he'd somehow managed to remain human despite the things he had seen and done—but it wasn't. If Alice only knew, his ability to disconnect would make him look like that much more of a monster. Cold. Heartless. A demon personified.

Outside, the pitch of the woman's screaming changed. Michael could read those shrieks like a mother deciphering an infant's cry. The woman had started out desperate, but that had soon slipped into defeated terror. The cries that were coming now weren't as much for salvation as they were for death. She was getting tired, probably woozy from the blood loss.

The woman finally went quiet, and Michael pushed his pillow aside. He lay motionless on his mattress and listened to the silence hum in his ears as he waited for Momma to call his name. The crickets had chirped for a full minute before his curiosity got the best of him and he rose from his bed to glance out the window.

Outside, the woman's body wasn't more than a few steps from the back porch. Her face was turned skyward, her eyes wide open, as though she'd been waiting for Michael to appear. Her arms were outstretched on either side, and her legs were bent at the knees. She looked as though she was running away, even in death.

A shadow then drew long across the back lawn—Momma, he thought—but it was Rebel who moved down the back porch steps instead. He slowly circled the body. The woman's tank top was so saturated with blood that its pale-blue color had all but disappeared. The fluffy cartoon sheep in its center now looked like a slaughtered lamb. With his hands deep in the pockets of his jeans, Reb looked up as if trying to determine what was in the dead woman's line of sight, and caught Michael in the window.

Michael's stomach flipped. His skin prickled with nerves. He had seen dozens of dead bodies, had gazed down on more than a few in this very manner, waiting for Momma to call him.

But Rebel had never circled the fallen like a vulture, and he had certainly never looked up at Michael this way.

Reb pulled his right hand from his pocket and held it up in a silent wave, offering Michael a peculiar smile. It was the same young man who had driven them home a few hours before—Reb's body, Reb's face, but not his brother.

"Michael!" Momma called up from the base of the stairs.

Michael turned away from the window, Rebel's weird grin birthing goose bumps up and down his arms. When he stepped into the kitchen, Momma was washing a knife in the sink, its wooden handle water-worn and faded from decades of use. Reb stood on the back porch looking straight through the open door. He was still wearing that bizarre expression, as though his mind were a million miles away.

"Bring me a flank on your way up," Momma said. "Leave it in the icebox. I'll get it in the mornin'."

Michael was only halfway listening, unnerved by Reb's distant smile. Momma turned away from the sink with an impatient frown.

"You hear what I said?"

"Yeah, Momma, I heard." Michael turned away from his brother and stepped up to the sink next to his mother. Momma never did offer much comfort, but at that particular moment, Michael wanted to be near someone, *anyone*, and other than Rebel, she was the only one around. "What's Reb waitin' for?" he asked under his breath.

Momma lifted her chin and glanced out the kitchen window, as if noticing Reb for the first time. She shrugged, indifferent, and went back to washing the knife, scrubbing the blade with an old rag. "Ray's being Ray," she said. "Just ignore 'im and go about your business."

Michael stepped onto the back porch, avoiding eye contact with his brother.

"Have fun," Reb said as Michael passed.

He wasn't sure why, but those two small words sent a chill down his spine, worse than any dead body ever had.

• • •

Michael threw open the storm door that led to the cellar and began his descent down the wooden staircase. He carefully placed his feet on each step as he went, pulling the woman along behind him by her ankles. The staircase was old and rickety and narrow, and there wasn't a handrail. Her head thudded against each step as she slid into the bowels of the Morrow farmhouse. Michael only noticed her sliding to the outer edge of the staircase when her body was torn from his grasp. Inertia pulled her over the side of the steps and to the concrete floor ten feet below. She landed on her neck, a distinct *snap* cracking through the quiet. Michael winced and stalked down the rest of the way. It would have been a lot easier to shove bodies down into the basement like that, but he didn't like doing it. Something about the way they fell, their dead weight pulling them down like stones, their limbs spread out like life-size rag dolls; he hated seeing them that way. He was to blame for their final denigration—an act that he was required to perform. Any dignity he could offer them in the meantime, he did. It felt better to treat them well until there was none of them left.

He crouched beside the woman with a frown. "Sorry," he whispered, then straightened out her arms and legs and pulled her to the center of the room. A moment later, he climbed back up the steps to shut the both of them inside. Taking a seat on one of the middle risers, he stared down at Momma's—or did this one belong to Reb?—latest victim, the golden *M* around her neck glinting in the harsh fluorescent light. Nothing about her made sense, but Michael found some comfort in his own confusion. If he didn't understand it, it meant he was different, that he still had a chance.

His body went through the motions, but his mind remained separate, never really connecting the dots. Rebel had explained it to him once, when they had dragged the first girl home— something about Momma, about Grandpa Eugene doing bad things and Grandma Jean looking away. Somehow, Reb was able to justify his actions; Michael supposed that, to a point, he did as well. The Morrows had swept down from heaven like angels and plucked him out of harm's way, swaddled him and taken him into their home when nobody else had wanted him. In a world where he owed them everything, he often reminded himself that this—the basement, the bodies, the blood—was his bounden duty. He had been saved.

He stripped the body first, cutting away the blood-soaked tank top with a pair of kitchen shears. He counted eighteen stab wounds, most of them centered around the stomach, a few near the shoulders, one in the neck. Momma liked knives.

When she wasn't stabbing, she sliced jugulars instead. Once, she'd cut a girl's throat so deep that, when Michael dragged her down into the basement, her head had nearly come clean off as it bounced down the steps.

He cut away the woman's underwear and stared at the triangular patch of velvet between her legs. That's when he started to feel that familiar twist. It was a rolling ache at the base of his guts—the same feeling that had overwhelmed him when Reb had bent that nameless girl over the hood of his car. That arousal made him hate himself even more than he already did. Something Rebel had said echoed in his mind: *You're human, ain't ya?* It was wrong to feel it. He knew that. But he *was* human. Only a genuine monster would never feel anything at all.

Michael shot a look up to the storm door. He was alone, would be for hours. His hand trembled as he placed it on the woman's breast, gently kneading it with his fingers. He leaned over her body and let his eyes flutter shut, holding his breath as his lips brushed across hers. He tried to imagine Alice naked, alive but lying perfectly still, breathing in and out. But the memory of Reb's leering grin tainted the moment. This was the same woman who bucked and fought against his brother just beyond her front door. He pulled back, imagining Reb sneaking up on her, throwing her to the floor, forcing himself on her. Except that the woman's dead eyes and gray lips were replaced by Alice's face, her expression shifting from a smile to inexplicable horror, desperately trying to fight Rebel off, pressed into a mattress, her gaze turned toward an open door, Michael standing there, staring, a roll of duct tape circling his right wrist.

Please, Michael, don't. . . .

The ache between his legs was gone, replaced by a rush of queasiness that threatened to fold him in half.

He leaned back on his heels, furiously wiping his mouth on his forearm, the taste of the woman still lingering there. The wave of sickness took a moment to pass. When it did, his gaze settled on the gold necklace around her throat—M for Misty. Unclasping it, he slid it into his pocket, then tipped his chin skyward. A meat hook winked at him from overhead.

It wasn't much different from field dressing a deer. With the body hanging by bound ankles, he sliced open the neck and waited for the blood to slither down the drain. The rest he did on autopilot: Making an incision just below the breastbone and up to the pelvis. Spilling out the cooling guts and preserving the stuff Momma liked in half-gallon plastic bags and old containers she'd saved up. He cut along the Achilles heels and drew what looked like stocking seams along the back of the legs with the tip of his knife. The seams continued across the body, making the woman look more like a sewing project than a human being. Sliding his fingers beneath one of the seams, he loosened skin from muscle before giving it a firm downward tug.

Rebel had asked Michael to save a girl's skin only once. He had tried to fashion a leather jacket out of the hide but had failed miserably. So he made the remains into an ugly little leather doll he had given to Misty Dawn instead. When Misty discovered it was made out of a person, she shrieked and threw it out her bedroom window. For all anyone knew, it was still out there somewhere, rotting among the wild grass and weeds.

Dismembering the body was the final step. It used to take Michael a better part of six hours, but now he could do it in less than three. He knew exactly how to twist arms and turn legs to pop them out of their sockets. He knew just where to stick the knife blade to separate tendon from bone. It was quick, precise, clean. He wrapped each butchered body part in paper and stacked them in the standalone freezer that hummed in the corner of the basement. Michael saved a thick haunch of thigh for Momma, leaving it on top of the freezer as he hosed down the floor.

By the time he was done, there was hardly any sign that something so brutal had occurred there. It was just a basement, upgraded with a drain in the middle of the concrete floor, a hook in the ceiling for field dressing, and a freezer in the corner for preservation. Michael assessed his clean-up job, and when he was satisfied that everything was in order, he grabbed the fresh hunk of meat he'd wrapped from the top of the freezer and climbed the cellar steps. Upon entering the house, he tucked the brown package into the refrigerator, got a drink of water, and went to his room. There was no point in thinking about how Momma would use the meat, no use in mulling over what he'd find on his dinner plate. As Wade had put it, and as he was fond of reminding them anytime they needed a refresher, folks like the Morrows didn't have much. They got by living off the land or, as Momma had made it, off of whatever wayfarer they found along the road. Thinking about it only made a hard life that much more difficult. So Michael didn't think about it. Any more guilt and he'd buckle beneath its weight.

. . .

Kneeling in front of his bedroom window, Michael retrieved a rusty framing nail from his desk drawer and pushed the frayed curtain aside. His fingers drew across a series of notches beneath the sill, tucked away where no one would see them. Ducking down so he could see what he was doing, he added a fresh notch next to the others—almost thirty in all—and then he crawled into bed and closed his eyes.

He held the golden *M* in his closed fist as he drifted off to sleep, wishing it was an *A* instead.

. . .

Despite Michael's long night, when Rebel appeared at his door and announced they were driving in to Dahlia, Michael's exhaustion evaporated like rain on a hot summer day.

"Can you give me half an hour?" Michael asked, his fingers crossed that Reb was in a decent mood. He had never asked for extra time before. But rather than scoffing and telling him to get his ass downstairs in five minutes, Reb shrugged and muttered "Whatever," before stalking down the hall.

Michael showered, shaved, brushed his hair and left it loose, remembering the way Alice had looked at it the first time they had met.

Are you in a band?

He searched his closet for the cleanest pair of pants he had—not an easy feat, seeing as how his standard pair of jeans hadn't been washed in over six months. He pulled a T-shirt that he had picked up at the Salvation Army but hadn't worn in years over his head. It was a little small, but he liked the design. A man Michael didn't recognize appeared in black and white with an electric-blue and pink lightning bolt painted across his face. When he brought it home, Misty had told him it was the coolest shirt she'd ever seen. *She* had known who the guy on the shirt was, but Michael couldn't remember his name. And he wasn't about to ask her what it was now, sure she wouldn't take kindly to him dressing up for the record-store girl.

When he finally appeared downstairs and met Rebel on the back porch, Reb stared at him as though he'd never seen Michael before in his life. Wade looked up from his newspaper, and Momma glanced up from mending a sweater, noting Reb's surprise.

"Shit," Reb said, "I hardly recognized you."

Wade was more suspicious. "Where you two off to?"

"Town," Reb told him.

"What for?"

Reb exhaled an aggravated sigh and turned to fully face his father. "To see what the hell we're gonna do about Michael's birthday. Shit, seems like I'm the only one who even remembers."

Wade raised an eyebrow, then gave Michael a half-hearted smile. "I didn't forget," he said, but he wasn't altogether convincing.

"Yeah, okay." Reb rolled his eyes. "Either way, we're goin'."

"Dinner's at six," Momma said automatically—a statement

she hardly had to voice. Dinner was always at six. "Don't be late."

"Wouldn't miss it." Reb caught Michael by the elbow and dragged him down the steps.

Once they arrived at the Delta, Rebel paused before pulling open his door. "Jesus H," he said, "You got it *bad,* huh?"

"Got what bad?" Michael asked.

Reb shook his head and laughed. "Nothin'. Never mind. Get in."

. . .

But the closer they got to the Dervish, the more uncomfortable Michael felt. It was as though the woman from the night before was reaching out from beyond the grave. He imagined her nails scratched down his cheeks, leaving deep gashes across his face like trails in soft earth made by the dragging heels of the dead. *You've got blood under your nails.* Michael's eyes darted to his hands, but they were clean. *Except they'll never be clean. They'll NEVER be clean.* Michael twitched and grimaced, and Reb gave him a guarded glance.

"The fuck," he muttered. "You finally losin' your shit or what?"

Michael wrung his hands in his lap. What did he expect to happen? For he and Alice to live happily ever after? Pretend that he had never full-body tackled a girl as she ran along the soft shoulder of a highway? Forget that he knew exactly where to cut to make someone bleed out in less than sixty seconds? Pretend he never suspected what was on his plate?

It was like a bad joke: *Hey, have you heard this one before? Two serial killers walk into a record store . . .*

He and Rebel weren't even hiding. Hell, Reb drove a metallic-brown yacht and dressed like an Appalachian John Travolta and nobody batted an eye. It was a cosmic wisecrack, a dirty trick that was made that much more wicked because nobody knew it was being played.

I catch things.

She'd figure it out. She'd look across the record stacks and see the face of a killer. She'd smell it on his breath. Except that maybe they'd be married by then. Maybe they'd have two grown kids. Maybe she'd be into gardening and he'd make a living fixing cars or selling furniture—an honest living—when he wasn't visiting Momma and Wade out of the sense of guilt he felt for leaving them. When he wasn't climbing into Reb's Delta and going on joyrides that would end with a hitcher in the trunk and dismemberment in the basement.

Rebel had told him stories about women married to axe murderers before, completely oblivious that the monster was *in* the bed rather than under it. That's what had happened to that John Wayne Gacy guy, but Michael still wondered if something like that could be true.

When you got someone that close, Reb had said, *it's safer to have 'em in on the deal.*

In on the deal. As though killing people was as innocent as fishing or joining a bowling league.

"You ever think about quittin'?" Michael asked, slowly turning his head from the trees that zipped by his window to give his brother an indirect glance. He looked down to his hands before Rebel could catch his gaze.

"What?"

"All this," Michael said, motioning to the interior of the car, as if its steel dashboard and eight-track player would somehow clarify his question.

"What're you talkin' about?" Reb asked, but the tone of his voice suggested he knew exactly what Michael was saying. It nearly screamed *I knew this was coming!* Like a parent faced with delivering the sex talk. Reb was suddenly the brother who had to explain why being an accessory to murder was nothing to worry about. Just a fact of life. A growing pain.

When Rebel pulled the Oldsmobile onto the highway shoulder just outside of town, Michael swallowed against the wad of nerves that had clambered up his throat. Reb gave him a stern look. "You bein' serious?"

Michael pulled his shoulders to his ears, as if dismissing his own question. "I guess not." He peered at the frayed denim of his jeans. "I just wonder if maybe you ever thought about leavin' home."

"Why would you wonder about somethin' stupid like that?"

"Because Alice said she thinks about it. She said she wants to go to Pittsburgh or Columbus or someplace. Maybe even New York City."

Reb scoffed. "Yeah, New York my ass. You know how many losers dream about New York City?"

So many that the dreamers crawl out of the sewers.

"She ain't goin' nowhere, Mike." From the way Reb said it—

so matter-of-factly—Michael actually believed it. "People like us don't leave. We don't go nowhere. She's gonna die in this shithole just like you and me. And no, I *don't* think about leavin'. You wanna know why?"

Michael nodded faintly, but he was afraid of the reasons.

"Because blood is thicker than water, and maybe you're too dumb to get what that means, but—"

"I know what it means," Michael cut in. "It means family comes first."

Reb leaned back in his seat, looking impressed. "Huh. This comin' from a kid whose parents dumped him on the side of the road. That's pretty good."

There was a beat of silence.

Michael shifted his weight uncomfortably.

Rebel leaned against the steering wheel.

"Besides, ain't nobody keepin' you here, are they? I don't know about you, but I don't see any handcuffs around your wrists, no shackles around your feet. You wanna blow outta here, blow outta here. Ain't nobody gonna beg you not to go."

Michael looked up, trying to judge whether Reb was being earnest or not. Could it have possibly been that easy? Could he just stuff his knapsack full of clothes and leave the Morrows behind?

"Except maybe for Misty," Reb said, cutting into Michael's thoughts. "She'd probably care. If you bail, you'd be ditchin' me, and if you ditch me, Claudine ain't gonna be getting a steady stream of girls. So you know . . ." His words trailed off as Michael slouched in his seat. He didn't need to hear the rest. "Your mind's gettin' muddy. You ain't thinkin' straight. She's got you all screwed up. Good thing I've got a way to fix your problem, though."

"What do you mean?" Michael looked up, curious, and Reb smirked at his eagerness.

"You show her you mean business. Show her you ain't just some passin' John, right? Show her that she belongs to you and she ain't goin' nowhere unless you say so."

Michael frowned. That plan sounded complicated—besides, who was Michael to say Alice belonged to him? What if she didn't like him as much as he liked her? That made a difference, right? There wasn't some switch you could flip in someone's mind and make them your own.

Rebel reached out and patted Michael's knee in a chummy sort of way. "I just want my little brother to be happy," he said. "Believe me, Mikey, you follow my lead and you can have her forever."

18

I T WAS STRANGE how quickly Michael's feelings toward that tie-dyed record shop could change. The last time he and Rebel had pulled into the Dervish's parking lot, his palms had been sweaty with nervous excitement. But this time he was reluctant.

He wasn't sure whether he could follow Reb's advice, wasn't sure if he even *liked* the idea of owning anyone, especially Alice. But he certainly didn't want to lose her either. Those three hours he'd spent with her in a darkened movie theater, the way she had scooted closer to him in the backseat of Reb's car—it had been the best night of his life. He wanted to relive it over and over, and he couldn't do that if Alice packed up her stuff and left Dahlia behind. Maybe if he went with her. But they were practically strangers. There was no way she would ask him to go with her, but if she stayed here . . .

"Here." Reb arched his back to lift his butt off the seat, fished his wallet out of his back pocket, and handed Michael a ten-dollar bill.

Michael peered at the money, then gave his brother a quizzical glance. "What's this for?"

"Show her a good time," Reb advised.

Except Michael had no idea what a "good time" was, not when it came to a girl like Alice. "How?"

"Hell, I don't know," Reb muttered, pushing the car door open. "Figure somethin' out."

Michael watched Rebel stalk across the parking lot. He took a breath and shoved open the passenger door, his thoughts momentarily derailed by the temperature. It was getting hotter by the day, the trees wavy and distorted like some psychedelic trip. The air felt thick, hard to breathe. And while Michael would have been content standing out in the parking lot for hours, contemplating his next move, the heat forced him forward.

The little bell above his head jingled, the cool air of the place hit him head on, and like déjà vu, Alice looked up from the counter and smiled. A couple of customers milled around, flipping through records, their heads bobbing to the music pumping through the speakers. It was stuff Michael actually recognized this time. He'd heard it on one of Misty's stations. She always laughed at the lyrics. Something about boogying with a suitcase and doing the milk shake.

Rebel and Lucy were near the back of the store. She was giggling, and he was leaning against the wall with his ankles crossed, looking slick. Michael sucked in a breath and stepped across the front of the building. His eyes swept the place, snagging on the golden arches through the window—an oasis just across the street. He caught Alice's eyes wandering the front of his shirt, but Michael was too distracted by his thoughts to give her a chance to react. If he didn't act fast, Lucy and Reb would disappear into the storeroom and Alice would be stuck working the front. He watched her mouth quirk up into an amused grin—lips parted, words balanced on the tip of her tongue—but he cut her off.

"You wanna get somethin' to eat?"

She looked surprised, as though it was the last thing she had expected him to ask. Shooting a look toward the back of the store and the customers that were there, she gave Michael a playful glance. "You buying?"

"Sure," he said, his fingers crumpling the ten in his pocket. If anything, she'd accept the invitation just to get out from behind that counter. After all, she hated her job, right?

"Hey, Luce," Alice called toward her friend. "You're in charge."

"Where're you going?" Lucy asked.

"I'm going on my lunch break. Michael's taking me to a five-star restaurant."

Lucy and Reb exchanged looks before Lucy replied with an easy "Cool." Reb gave Michael a subtle nod, then turned back to the girl beside him, leaning into Lucy like a vampire, ready to bite.

• • •

Michael held open the door for Alice, then followed her inside the McDonald's. His mouth watered at the scent of grilled meat—*two all-beef patties, special sauce, lettuce, cheese*—and salty fries. Alice chuckled as they stood in line, both of them staring up at the menu board. "Okay, now *this* is classy," she joked. "Did you call ahead for a reservation?"

Michael didn't reply; he only smiled down at the scuffed-up tips of his boots. Alice pressed her arm against his as they waited to be helped, a slender finger looping around his thumb.

Michael got a Big Mac and Alice ordered a Happy Meal, which the cashier refused to sell her because Happy Meals were for kids, not adults.

"You've got to be kidding me," Alice scoffed at the girl behind the counter.

"Sorry, it's the rules," the cashier said with a shrug.

"But it's not even for *me*," Alice explained. "It's for our baby." She wrapped herself around Michael's arms and flashed the girl a smile. "Right, Mikey?"

Michael's mouth went dry, but he wasn't about to let anything stand between him and his Big Mac. "Yeah," he confirmed. "We gotta feed our kid."

"It only eats hamburgers," Alice said.

"*It?*" The cashier asked, peering at them both through narrowed eyes.

Alice grimaced at her slipup but recovered fast. "Look, I'm pregnant, all right? Just sell us the dang Happy Meal and we'll be on our way."

Five minutes later, Alice and Michael sat at a table, Michael relishing his Big Mac while Alice ate her hamburger and fries and wore her prize—a pair of canary-yellow McDonaldland sunglasses, Ronald McDonald's creepy clown face staring out from above her nose. Michael couldn't look at her without cracking up. A few older patrons gave them curious glances as they passed by with trays of food. The looks didn't seem to bother her. She refused to take the sunglasses off, her cheek full of fries, the tip of her combat boot kicking at the leg of Michael's chair.

"We really should go see that movie again," she said. "I keep thinking about it, and I'm pretty sure I missed parts, like, important stuff, you know?"

Michael nodded, taking a bite of his burger. Squares of chopped lettuce fell onto the wrapper between his elbows. It was even better than he remembered. Maybe because, this time, Reb wasn't there to ruin the taste.

"Sometimes things only make sense in retrospect," she mused. "You don't know what you're looking at until you know what happens next, and then you have to go back to the beginning to see the signs. They call it foreshadowing. Comic-book writers use it all the time."

She was smart, possibly smarter than Reb. Michael loved that. He loved the fact that she wasn't afraid to act silly or look dumb, or to tell him about her dead dad and her depressed mom, as though they'd been friends their entire lives. He wished he could be just as open, spill everything about himself and get it off his chest. He wanted to tell her about his family—about Misty Dawn and how she liked to dance to old hokey records and cheesy pop music, about Rebel and how Michael was afraid of him but they were still best friends. He wanted to tell her about his first time down in the basement at the age of ten, how Wade had locked him in there with a dead girl and wouldn't let Michael out until he field dressed her the way he would have any other kill. But he knew he couldn't tell her any of those things, and it made it hard to look her in the eye. Alice was perfect, and he was nothing but secrets. Dark ones. Darker than the basement after all the lights went out.

"Michael?"

When her fingers brushed his forearm, he almost jerked away. He expected to see the fear he knew was coming—the look in her eyes that assured him that she had figured it all out. Alice knew what he was because she'd read his mind, his poisonous thoughts. But she wore a look he hardly recognized at all—concern.

"Are you okay?" she asked, pulling the funny glasses from her face.

"You ain't really pregnant, are ya?" he asked. It was the first thing that came to mind.

Alice burst into laughter. "No, stupid." She leaned back in her seat and grinned. It was the most beautiful smile Michael had ever seen. "Anything else you want to ask me?" She batted her eyelashes, though he wasn't sure what she was getting at. So he asked her the question that he'd been wanting to ask for days.

"Are you really gonna leave Dahlia?" He knew it was intrusive, but he couldn't help himself. He needed to know. For the first time in his life, he felt like he was connecting with someone. It was the kind of link that he hadn't experienced before. But the possibility of losing her continued to loom in the back of his mind. He had to know whether she was leaving so he could make her stay.

Her smile faded a notch. "I don't know, I mean . . ." She hesitated. "I guess I should be flattered you're asking."

Michael stared down at the plastic tray full of empty, ketchup-smeared wrappers. His stomach twisted around his burger, and he was suddenly sorry for having eaten so much so fast.

"*Should* I be flattered?" she asked, reaching out to touch his arm for a second time, to pull him back from the wasteland of his own thoughts.

"Maybe I can come with you," he told her. But that was *not* supposed to be the deal. If Rebel had been there to overhear him, he would have pummeled Michael in front of the entire restaurant. Michael cast a quick glance her way, just to see if she was still wearing the same expression—a delving, inquisitive smile. She wasn't.

She shook her head at him, not in a response to his suggestion, but in some sort of acknowledgment, like she finally understood. He waited for the terror, the disgust, but her eyes lit up instead, sparkling with something he couldn't explain. Mischief? Fascination?

"Michael Morrow, you're the strangest boy I've ever met." She leaned back in her seat, her head cocked to the side. Her eyes wandered across the front of his T-shirt and her mouth twisted upward at a single corner. "Do you even know who that is?" She nodded at the portrait across his chest. Michael looked down and felt stupid for wearing the secondhand shirt. If anyone knew who the guy was, it was Alice. He should have known, should have seen it coming, and maybe subconsciously he had, but the realization of it made him feel foolish now.

"Naw."

Alice's easy smile bloomed into another grin. "It's actually appropriate," she said. "David Bowie. He wrote a song called 'Space Oddity' . . . about a spaceman, y'know? Maybe he was writing about you."

"Why do you say that?"

"Cause I already told you, you're the strangest boy I've ever met. It's like you're from a different planet." She shifted her weight in her seat, her gaze fixed on David Bowie's face. "I thought you said you'd miss this place if you left. But now you want to leave?"

Michael didn't know how to explain his sudden change of heart. When he had uttered it days before, he'd believed it. But that had been before the woman. Before Rebel's faraway smile. Before he had leaned down and kissed the dead in the hopes of having it feel like real life. He remembered the way Reb had made him toss his most favorite things into a hole in the ground. The way he had made him bury them as if to remind Michael that, without Reb's permission, he wasn't allowed to love or dream or *be* anything.

It was rule number one.

"I . . . guess I just wanna see what else is out there," he said softly. "It wouldn't be so bad seein' it if I wasn't alone."

Alice leaned forward, their table of wrappers and ketchup packets between them. She brushed her fingers along his jaw-line. His heart sputtered beneath muscle and bone, and for a moment, he was sure he'd never breathe again. She was only inches away, her hazel eyes drifting across the curve of his bottom lip. It was then that he realized their eyes matched in color almost perfectly. Somehow that small detail gave him the courage to tip his head forward and press his mouth against hers.

The world stopped.

For one perfect moment, every person who had ever existed in his life vanished from the earth, leaving only her.

Their kiss lasted two seconds, three at most, but it felt as though they had sealed Michael's fate.

He knew then that he could be happy, if only he could make Alice a part of his life. If he stayed with the Morrows that could never happen, not without twisting her into something unrecognizable. Into someone like him.

Alice leaned back and slid the Ronald McDonald glasses back onto her face. "A little birdie told me it's almost your birthday," she said. "Is that true?"

"Yeah, it's true," he said, and he suddenly knew what to wish for—something impossible, something he doubted he could ever have. He pictured them both climbing into the Oldsmobile and driving out of West Virginia; him barreling down the road without a license; heading toward the ocean, toward golden yellow sand and a pink hotel.

"I'll have to get you something, then," she said. "Maybe a David Bowie record to go along with that shirt. How old are you going to be, anyway?"

"Twenty."

The number gave her pause. She pulled the glasses from her eyes and searched his face, as if looking for an answer to a question she hadn't asked.

"What?" he said.

"Nothing," she said, a veil of uncertainty blurring her features. She continued to stare at him for a while longer before clearing her throat. "We should probably get back. My break's been over for ten minutes now." When she rose from the table to leave, a rush of panic overwhelmed him. He hadn't asked her to keep what they had discussed a secret. If she told Lucy, if Reb found out . . .

He dumped their tray of wrappers into the trash bin and followed her outside, trailing her back to the store.

Michael followed her into the Dervish and took a deep breath, the cool air redolent of exotic smoke. The customers that had been inside the store were gone, replaced by a lone girl perusing the new arrivals. But Lucy didn't seem to care that the Dervish had a customer. She was perched on top of the counter with Rebel between each of her jeaned knees, as though she was in her own bedroom rather than at her place of employment. They were both grinning as Michael and Alice approached, their amusement clear. "Well, well," Reb chimed in. "If it ain't the lovebirds."

Alice rolled her eyes, but she was smiling despite herself. "You shouldn't be canoodling like that, especially not with . . ." She tipped her chin toward their customer. "If Jason comes in and sees you that way, he's liable to fire us both."

"Oh *please*," Lucy scoffed, but she gave Reb a little push and dropped down from the counter with a pout. "Like he ever comes in here, right? That's what he's got us for." She turned her attention to Michael, changing the subject. "Hey,

I heard it's almost your birthday. That's fun. Gonna have a party?"

Michael ducked his head into his shoulders and gave the group an embarrassed shrug.

"Well, we *call* it his birthday," Reb clarified, "except that we ain't actually sure it is."

"What do you mean?" Alice gave Michael a curious look, and for a moment he caught a flash of reluctance in her eyes.

"I think we should go," Michael murmured. He wanted to tell Alice about himself in his own way, at his own pace. He didn't need Rebel laying out the details as though they were his to give. Except that, according to Reb, they *were* his to give. His brother had given Michael a taste of freedom, and now he was going to sour it with a grim reminder—freedom was nothing but an illusion. Any autonomy Michael felt was a privilege, not a right.

"He didn't tell you?" Reb feigned surprise. "Michael was adopted."

Alice blinked at the news.

Lucy shifted her weight from one foot to the other, her arms crossed protectively over her chest.

Michael frowned at the floor. He didn't want to talk about it, not like this, not in front of Reb and Lucy. He suddenly felt like he was perched on a tightrope, Reb threatening to push him off balance, threatening to clue Alice in to the fact that this tattered curtain of normalcy was nothing but a ruse, that the spaceman was from a planet of hard-hearted brutality.

"I'm gonna wait in the car," Michael said beneath his breath. He could hardly hear the conversation over the thud of his heart. One wrong word, one weird look, and Reb could ruin everything.

. . .

Rebel remained inside the Dervish for an unnerving amount of time. Michael paced around the Oldsmobile as the sun beat onto his shoulders, imagining the worst possible things—Reb telling the girls about the woman from the night before, describing the way Michael had dragged her down into the basement. He was sure he had been alone, but what if Reb had seen Michael touch the dead woman's breast? What if he'd seen Michael press his mouth to her dead, blue lips? What if, somehow, he knew Michael had been wishing it had been Alice?

When Reb finally came out of the record store, he was smiling with a sort of self-satisfaction. Something about it pushed Michael to the edge of his patience. He couldn't help himself. His willpower to keep silent withered and the words came tumbling out.

"Why did you *do* that?" he demanded, staring across the plane of the Oldsmobile's brown roof at his brother. "You say you want me to be happy, and then you turn around and butt in."

"*Hey.*" Reb gave him a stern look. "Don't forget who you're talkin' to, shithead."

"Oh, I remember who I'm talkin' to, Reb. I'm talkin' to a guy who tells me to do one thing and then tries to screw it up!"

"How am I screwin' it up?" Reb asked, suddenly casual about the whole argument, as if it was of no consequence at all. "I just said you were adopted. Like you weren't gonna tell her anyway."

"Except I wasn't."

"How's that? You just weren't gonna talk about yourself at all?"

"About the family?" Michael shook his head, incredulous. "Why would I talk about the family? Why would I, Reb? That don't make any sense."

"You want to be with her?" Reb asked, nodding toward the Dervish. Michael failed to respond, and Reb narrowed his gaze at his brother's silence. "I asked you a fuckin' question," he snapped. "You best answer before I get pissed."

"Yes!" Michael spit out.

"You like her, then. That's good. I'm happy for you, brother. But you remember what I told you a while back, when we were talkin' about wives and killers and how they live with the lies?"

Michael clamped his teeth together, glaring down at the roof.

"You want her, you gotta bring her into the fold."

He swallowed, felt his mouth go dry. "And Lucy?" he asked, almost afraid to hear the answer. "You gonna bring her into the fold too?"

Reb laughed, and when Michael looked back up, Rebel was looking at the tie-dye colors of the store, as though contemplating going back inside. "Lucy?" Reb shook his head and gave Michael a menacing smile. "You notice Lucy's hair? Claudine's favorite."

The whole world shrunk in on itself.

Michael shot a frantic look back at the record store. He wanted to rush back in, scream for both Lucy and Alice to get the hell out of there, to run to wherever they could, as long as they didn't tell Reb where they were going.

Reb slid into the car. The engine roared to life. Michael watched Alice step in front of the plate-glass window, her figure faint and milky behind the glare of the sun. But he could see her well enough to watch her raise a hand in a silent good-bye, as if it were forever instead of just for now.

The heat hit him hard.

He felt like he was going to be sick.

"Get in the car," Reb barked from the driver's seat. "I was just kiddin', you idiot. Take a fuckin' joke."

Michael ducked down to look through the open window. Rebel sighed dramatically and slumped in his seat. "I swear," he said, holding up his hands. "I like Lucy. I shouldn't, but I *like* her."

For a second, Reb actually looked uncomfortable, a look that nudged Michael away from panic and toward belief.

"You swear?" Michael asked. He knew he sounded pathetic, but he didn't care. This was bigger than the both of them, bigger than Momma and her urges or keeping Misty safe.

"I pinkie swear." Reb snorted. "Faggy enough for you? Now get in, for God's sake. I'm meltin' out of my fuckin' skin."

Michael shot a look back toward the shop. Alice was still standing there, watching their exchange from behind the glass. He forced a smile and lifted his right hand in the same silent good-bye she had moments before. But even with Reb's assurance, it still felt like the farewell was permanent.

. . .

That evening, the Morrow house was heady with the scent of a rich beef stew. Momma had sliced up carrots and potatoes and simmered the entire concoction down until it was thick and delicious. But it was so hot, both outside and in the house, that it was difficult to enjoy. Reb, Wade, and Michael sat around the table in nothing but their stained white undershirts and pants while Misty fanned herself with a folded up *Seventeen* magazine. She hummed an Elton John tune beneath her breath. Momma didn't seem to notice the heat, eating her dinner with her head bowed, her eyes fixed on the scarred tabletop. Rebel cleaned his bowl, wiping it down with a piece of white bread. When he rose from his seat, Michael followed him across the kitchen with his eyes. Reb's joke about Lucy was still sitting heavy in his chest. Michael wanted to believe Reb didn't mean her any harm, but the longer he thought about it, the more uncomfortable he felt. The fact that the Dervish had become a regular spot for them was problematic, because before the Dervish, regular spots had always been jobs.

"This is good stew," Reb said, complimenting the chef. "Real tasty. We should have this more often." He came around the table and grabbed Michael's empty bowl. When Michael made like he was about to rise, Reb shook his head. "Take a load off," he said.

He slid one bowl onto the kitchen counter while taking the

other to the large pot on the stove. He dipped the ladle into the stew and spooned out a fresh helping, then pivoted on the soles of his shoes and returned to the table, sliding a second serving in front of Michael with a smile.

"I'm goin' out," Reb announced.

Michael stared down at the steaming bowl before him, nausea tightening around his neck like a noose.

"Goin' out where?" Wade asked.

"It's a secret." Reb fished the car keys from his front pocket, the eight-ball keychain catching Michael's eye. There was something there, along with the keys . . . a square of paper that Reb was quick to tuck back into his pocket.

"You need me to come?" Michael asked, standing from his seat, but Reb placed a hand on his shoulder and pushed him back down. "Eat up. Relax. Listen to records with Misty."

Michael gave Misty a questioning look. She shrugged and continued to fan herself, sweat glistening on her forehead.

"I told you," he said. "It's a *secret*. You can't come." Rebel stepped out onto the back porch without another word.

"Maybe it's for your birthday," Misty said after a moment.

Michael stared down at his bowl and willed himself to stay in his seat. He listened to the Delta's engine roar outside, thought about long walks and shovels and wolves. And then he took another bite of stew, not because he was hungry, but because it was the only thing to do.

19

ONLY DAYS AFTER Lauralynn's disappearance, seven-year-old Michael wobbled into his and Ray's shared bedroom, dragging a weatherworn Pearl Lager cardboard box behind him. Ray watched his little brother in silence as Michael piled what little possessions he had into the crate, stripped his bed of its dirty sheets, and hugged his pillow to his chest before stalking down the hall. Tailing him out of curiosity, Ray found Wade and Misty in Lauralynn's old room. Misty had her own box and was filling it with items from Lauralynn's closet—dolls and books and clothes. Ray couldn't help but sneer at the fact that the boy responsible for his sister's death would now be sleeping on her mattress and drawing pictures at her old desk. Lauralynn was being erased and neither Misty nor Michael seemed to care.

Ray tried to comfort himself with the fact that at least now, with Michael down the hall, he'd finally have some privacy, but loneliness came on fast. Before long, Ray started sneaking downstairs in the middle of the night to steal Wade's bottles. He figured if whiskey numbed the pain of a broken arm, it could probably dull the ache of a broken heart. He was right, and two years later, Wade presented Ray with a case of cheap gin for his thirteenth birthday. He had tied a shoddy bow around the box and muttered, "Now you can stop stealin' my stuff," as he pushed it toward his son with the toe of his boot.

By fourteen, Ray had changed his name to Rebel, though nobody except Michael cared. Reb and his parents would square off every other day. Sometimes he'd think about outing them to Michael and Misty. He'd tell his siblings about what he had seen that night years ago, explain that they couldn't go visit Lauralynn, not because Claudine hated her own parents, but because Lauralynn had never set foot in North Carolina at all. But Reb continued to hold his tongue. Because, when it came down to it, it hadn't been Claudine or Wade who had sealed Lauralynn's fate. It had been Michael, and Reb wanted vengeance.

Rebel began to stalk the woods with Michael during his hunts. It gave him the opportunity to push his now-ten-year-old brother around without Wade glaring from across the yard or Misty protecting him with her pleas and sheltering hugs. But Reb soon acquired a taste for killing, and it wasn't just watching Michael shoot at birds with that old kiddie rifle.

With leaves and twigs crunching beneath their feet, Michael spotted a family of pheasants, took to a knee, aimed, and pulled the trigger. Reb scoffed when they flew away. He was ready to ball his hand up into a fist and sock Michael in the shoulder for being such a lousy shot, but the bird Michael had been aiming for wavered in the air. The bullet had grazed it. It did a weird death roll in mid-flight and dropped.

"You're lucky," Reb told him. "'Cept that thing ain't dead, so it hardly counts as a shot."

Both boys rushed toward the spot where the bird had fallen. Rebel was right. The bird lay wounded on a bed of autumn leaves, its wings frantically flapping about its body as it struggled at their feet. Michael took a few backward steps and looked at it through his rifle scope, but Reb grabbed the barrel of the gun and shoved it away.

"Whatcha doin'?" Michael asked. He was still too young to read into the predatory glint that flashed in Rebel's pale green eyes.

"I'm gonna help it," Reb explained, his words empty of emotion. He squatted in front of the pheasant, picked it up by its wings, and yanked in opposite directions. Michael yelped and stumbled backward when one of the wings came free of its body. The gray-spotted bird didn't make a sound. It only thrashed against the ground as blood spouted from where the wing had once been. The other beat wildly, as if, by some miracle, the struggle would allow the bird to somehow fly away.

Rebel snorted out a laugh as it flopped around, spraying his sneakers and jeans red. He laughed even harder when he saw the horrified look on Michael's face. That night, Reb feasted on roasted pheasant while his little brother stared at his plate, green in the face.

Reb's bloodlust solidified something unspoken between him and Claudine. He still hated her guts, but he liked the sudden attention. And he loved the fact that Michael's hunting trips were almost completely phased out after Reb had proven he was a far more ruthless hunter.

"I like it when they squirm," he told Claudine one evening. "I like hurtin' 'em."

Claudine looked up from her knitting and stared at her son for a long moment, as if considering his words. And then she smiled.

The next afternoon, Wade and Rebel parked along the highway in Wade's beat-up pickup truck. An hour later, a girl walking the soft shoulder came into view. Wade leaned into the steering wheel and pointed her out through the cracked windshield.

"She lives down the road," Wade explained. "What we call an Appalachian ghost."

"What's that?" Reb asked.

"Means she ain't really alive anymore," Wade told him. "She's doped up. Doesn't even know where she is half the time. A good for nothin' junkie. Nobody's gonna miss that when it's gone."

Reb licked his lips and nervously waited for her to come closer.

"That's the trick you gotta remember," Wade said. "Nobody can know 'em, and if somebody does, nobody can care." When she was less than a few yards away, Wade stuck his head out the window of the truck and smiled. "Need a ride?"

She didn't think twice, didn't even answer or check who was offering. She simply crawled into the bed of the pickup and lay down, as though all she wanted to do was sleep.

Rebel didn't get it. Even as he helped Wade pull her out of the back and drag her across the yard, he didn't see the point. There was no fear in this girl, which meant there was no fun. Claudine took one look at her and muttered for Wade to tie her up in the basement.

"Let her sober up," she said. "She won't care she's dyin' unless she knows what's goin' on."

When Wade got her out of the cellar two days later, the girl's eyes were as wild as any animal's Rebel had ever seen. Dry vomit crusted the front of her T-shirt. The crotch of her bell-bottomed jeans was damp. Reb stared at her in disgust, unable to pull his gaze away from the circle of stained denim between her legs. Claudine gave her water, and after drinking it, the girl looked a little more alert. Reb watched his mother like a kid would watch a magician at a birthday party, trying to figure out the trick before she did it. Claudine met her son's eyes, and for a moment she wore nothing but a blank stare, as if there was nothing behind her gaze but a long stretch of darkness. After a moment she gave him a maternal smile. *Don't worry, son,* it said. *Watch and learn.* That was when she pulled the glass from the girl's grasp, placed it on the railing of the back porch, and nodded at her husband. Wade stepped behind the girl without a sound. Reb could tell the girl hadn't noticed him from the way she was staring at Claudine with question marks for eyes.

"You're probably wonderin' why you're here," Claudine told her, wiping her hands on the front of her apron. "You ever wanted to be a teacher?"

At first, the girl didn't respond. Her skin was a weird yellow color. She looked sleepy and sick. But eventually she spoke. "You're crazy. I ain't no teacher."

"Well, you are today, honey," Claudine said.

Wade's hands clamped down on the girl's biceps.

The girl started in surprise, but her shock soon shifted to realization. And with that realization came the widened eyes, the quickening of breath, the struggle for freedom.

"Go ahead, darlin'," Claudine nodded, urging her on. "Fight 'im."

Reb ran his tongue along the inside of his mouth, dry like the Sahara. The girl let out a yell, desperate to jerk her arms clear of Wade's hands. She began to scream, and something stirred in the pit of Reb's stomach. It was dark and delicious, the same dirty feeling he got when he snuck old *Playboys* out of Wade's army footlocker when nobody was looking.

"Nobody's gonna hear ya," Reb whispered to himself, his eyes fixed on the struggling girl. "Nobody's gonna save ya. Nobody's gonna remember. I'm gonna wipe ya out."

She screamed harder—terror meshing with desperation. The strained sound of her fear gave Rebel goose bumps. His pulse quickened. His pants were suddenly uncomfortable. When he reached down to tug at the fabric, he felt a hard lump behind his zipper. His eyes jumped to Claudine to see if she had noticed. Her dark look of satisfaction assured him that she had indeed.

Claudine drew a roll of silver duct tape from the pocket of her apron and held it out to her son.

"Go play," she told him.

The sight of the tape made the girl scream even louder. She thrashed wildly, her cries a hysterical aria tearing itself from her throat. The closer Rebel got, the easier it was to make out the peppering of infected dots along the inside of her left arm. Claudine held the girl by one of her ankles while Reb wrapped tape just above her crummy old sneaker and then pulled it toward her other leg. As the girl screeched above them, Reb felt a pang of what must have been love swell up in his heart for his mother. She was giving him a gift. This was her apology.

Wade jabbed the back of the girl's knees with his own and she folded up like an accordion, falling to the ground. Wade stepped away from the girl and his son, but not before dropping a switchblade next to Reb's feet. Wade had a lot of stories about that knife. In one, he stole it off of a dink during his leave in Saigon. In another, he found it on a *mama-san* who had come wandering into their camp. Rebel didn't know which story was true, but the letters etched into the handle proved that it came from Vietnam. Something about the feel of the knife assured Reb that the blade had tasted blood; his quiet, pensive father had a darker past than Reb had ever considered.

Rebel kept her tied up in the yard for two days. Wade would have preferred the basement, but Reb liked being able to see her from his window, and Claudine liked seeing her too. Sometimes the girl cried, other times she begged. She shrieked when he carved his name into her belly, bucked and prayed and implored him to kill her when he tried to cut off the pointer finger of her right hand. The blade of the knife was too dull to do the job, and she passed out shortly after he made his attempt.

He caught Michael staring out onto the yard from Lauralynn's window only once. Misty Dawn was at his side. They held on to each other, their eyes wide and glassy as Reb looked up at them from his crouch above the girl. When he met their stares, Misty turned away, but Michael's gaze was fixed. It felt like a challenge, one Reb decided to call him out on when he grew bored with the half-dead girl at his feet.

Claudine finished her off while Rebel locked himself in his room. He touched himself as the girl gave a final scream, replacing the junkie's sallow face with Lauralynn's inside his head. After he was done, he went back downstairs and made an announcement.

"I think Michael should finish the job. He knows how."

Wade dragged Michael across the yard toward the basement as the boy carried on and tried to pull away. And for a moment Wade hesitated, as if thinking about sparing his youngest son.

Claudine eventually lost her patience—probably because Michael was hollering as loudly as the girls did. Or maybe it was because she hated seeing Wade vacillate between doing what needed to be done and what he thought was "right." Abandoning her post at the kitchen window, she shoved Michael down the stairs after the dead girl who had Reb's name etched into her skin.

Rebel sat outside the locked cellar door for hours, grinning to himself. He stabbed at the dirt with Wade's old knife, listening to Michael pleading to be let out in short, gasping wails. Knowing that nobody *would* let him out until he did what he had to do. Thinking about how, if it was up to him, he wouldn't ever let Michael out at all.

20

AFTER REBEL LEFT the house, Michael and Misty Dawn listened to records in Misty's room. Misty played everything from Nancy Sinatra to the Monkees. When she spun the Beach Boys, Alice's sly smile crept into the corners of Michael's mind. But rather than taking pleasure in the memory of her saying the band was "for shark bait," he felt his stomach pitch. He was unable to stop picturing that nefarious grin crawling across his brother's mouth.

He excused himself while the Beach Boys sang "Good Vibrations," ducked into his room, and slid onto his bed. Lying there, he tried to put himself in the worst possible scenario—Reb showing up in the middle of the night with a screaming, terrified Lucy. Or maybe she wouldn't be terrified at all. Maybe Rebel would show her up to his room, close the door behind them, and Michael would listen to lustful moans until Reb had had enough. *Then* the screaming would start, because no matter how stupid Reb thought Michael was, he knew one thing for sure: a visit to the Morrow farmhouse was a one-way trip.

He rolled over and pulled his blanket up to his chin despite the heat. Staring at the peeling wallpaper through the moonlit darkness that filtered in through his dirty window, he squeezed his eyes shut and tried to sleep. Just as he began to drift off, his eyes darted open at the sound of something simultaneously strange and familiar. It was the soft thump of bass, the accompaniment of a weird, watery guitar, the odd warble of melancholy vocals muffled by the wall between Misty's room and his own.

Misty was playing Alice's Cure record, low, but still audible. The sound of it made his stomach churn.

He considered getting up, and asking her to either turn it down or off completely—he was trying to sleep so that his mind *wouldn't* be wandering in circles around the Dervish. He didn't want to think about the girls, about Dahlia, about where Reb might have gone. But before Michael worked up the energy, his door creaked open. A slash of hallway light illuminated the wall for a beat, then was gone. He glanced over his shoulder, and for the briefest of moments, he swore he was seeing a ghost. A nightgowned figure swayed in the shadows to the dampened music that slithered through the wall.

"Miss?" He squinted, propped himself up with an elbow, and brushed away strands of long unruly hair so that he could see her better. Misty scampered barefoot across the hardwood floor. She crawled onto his mattress, her knee-length nightgown skittering up her legs, revealing the tops of her thighs.

It all came back to him in a flash. The record. Misty dancing. Rebel in the doorway. Misty hitting the wall. Reb's fist smashing into Michael's face. His tongue drifted across the healing cut along his bottom lip, and he remembered Reb's most recent warning, the one his brother swore was the last Michael would ever receive. If he screwed up again, Reb would dump his worthless carcass deep in the mountains, where no one would find him.

"What are you doin'?" Michael asked, reflexively scooting away from her, pressing himself flush against the wall.

"Makin' sure you're okay. Why'd you leave?"

"I'm tired."

Misty went quiet for a moment. Her head was on his pillow. A finger of moonlight played across her neck. She sighed, tilted her chin up enough so that he could see her face despite the darkness of the room. "Tell me about this girl," she said.

"What girl?"

"Oh please." She waved a hand over her head, dismissing his feigned confusion. "Ray told me all about her." Her nightgown pulled up at the bottom hem by an inch. Michael's eyes darted to her legs. They were almost ethereal in the moon's glow, so pale they could have belonged to Alice—Snow White personified. "You went to the movies, took her out to eat and everythin'." Her bottom lip formed a childlike pout.

"Reb's gonna be back any minute," Michael croaked.

"He ain't gonna be back for *hours*," Misty said, still frowning. "And besides, I thought we were friends."

"We *are* friends," he insisted, "but you can't be in here. You know what'll happen."

She rolled onto her side to face him, so close that he could feel her breath lingering across his lips. She placed a palm against his chest while he remained glued to the wall, willing the house to make him disappear. "You protect me, don't you? Because you love me."

He swallowed.

"Tell me," she urged. "Because you love me."

"Because I love you," Michael repeated, tensing when Misty's bare leg drifted atop his own.

"So how come you don't treat me that way?" she asked. "There somethin' wrong with me? I ain't as good as she is? I ain't as pretty? How come she gets to go to the movies and I don't? I ain't never been to the movies before. Ray never offers."

"It was my first time." His throat was dry. His words brittle. "I didn't know we were goin' until we were goin'."

"But when you knew you were goin', you coulda told him to come back and pick me up . . . but you didn't because you didn't want me there. You wanted to be alone with that girl. What's her name, anyway?"

He hesitated. Something about saying Alice's name aloud inside that house felt wrong, as though a piece of her would be trapped inside those walls forever if he did.

"You ain't gonna tell me?"

"I don't wanna talk about her," he said. "I just wanna go to sleep."

Misty rolled away from him. He waited for her to get up, to leave his room before someone discovered her. But she spoke up to the ceiling instead. "I ain't really your sister, you know." She turned over to look at him again. "Not by blood anyway, and that's all that matters. If you wanted to try things . . ." She paused, considering her words. "Just to see if *she'd* like 'em, it wouldn't be no sin." She gave his hand a forward tug, placing it on her breast. Michael yanked it away as though she were made of fire. Hurt flashed in her eyes. She narrowed them, spinning pain into anger. "You and Ray run off every other day, goin' with girls so pretty I'd just about vanish next to 'em, and I'm left here by myself. You say you'll never let Momma hurt me, but you're so busy runnin' around with Ray that you wouldn't be able to stop somethin' bad from happenin' even if you wanted to. Because I'm always here, and you ain't. You already forgot me. I'm nothin' to you."

He stared down at the crumpled sheets between them, guilt weighing down his heart. She was right—he hardly wondered what was going on back home when he was with Alice. Momma could lose her temper and lock Misty in the basement, or worse. All while Michael was busy fighting the butterflies in his stomach, his heart swelling every time Alice touched his hand.

"You sorry about it?" she asked.

Michael nodded, not looking at her.

Before he knew what was happening, Misty Dawn's mouth was against his. He drew in a sharp intake of air, instinctively pushed her away, and skittered off the bed.

Misty sat up stick straight as Michael darted across the room, needing to put distance between them. She stared at him through the darkness, her green eyes wide and wounded. Michael knew she was lonely—she had it worse than him. Misty was allowed to go into town only a few times a year, and that was under strict surveillance. For some reason or another, Momma was convinced that the moment she let Misty off her leash, she'd pull up her skirt and invite any passing guy to give her the love she was so desperate to feel. Michael had never believed Misty would act that way. But now, standing with his back against the wall, he wondered if Momma had been right all along. Maybe all that romance stuff Misty was so fond of reading had gone to her head, had twisted her up somehow.

"I know you two are breakin' the rules."

The acknowledgment made him tense. A flash of heat burned his cheeks, making the already hot room spike by a few hundred degrees.

"But I ain't said nothin' because I love you. I want you to be happy, but what about *me*?" She pressed a hand to her chest, imploring him for an answer. "Sometimes I think you like Ray better. You two have secrets, adventures, and what do I got?" Staring down at the mattress, she shoved a few tangled strands of hair behind her ears. "I just want it to be like it used to be. You remember?"

Michael remembered.

After Lauralynn had gone off to North Carlolina, he and Misty huddled together for companionship. That huddle had lasted more than a decade, but age tore them apart. Misty retreated into her Harlequin novels; Michael's stakeouts got longer, the girls more frequent. Momma got hungrier, Reb got more demanding, Wade became more ambivalent. Michael had always lived with the threat of abandonment hanging over his head, lived in constant fear of it happening. It became one of Rebel's mantras: *Do what I tell you or I'll leave you for dead.* Misty was right—Michael *said* he would protect her, but he had been preoccupied with his own survival for years.

And now there was Alice, a girl who had Michael fantasizing about taking off to faraway places, living some other person's life. It was a life he knew he'd never fit into, but one that he wanted anyway. In the back of his mind, Misty was always there with him, but that was just it—she was in the back of his mind, not the forefront where she ought to be, where she had been for so long. Michael had the luxury of riding around in the Delta, staring out the window and daydreaming, but what did Misty have beyond this house? What would she have if he disappeared and never returned?

Michael turned to his desk and pulled out the drawer. He shifted pens and markers around until his fingers found what they were looking for and held the gold chain with the cursive *M* pendant up to the moonlight. Misty gaped at it as he stepped across the room, unclasped the chain, and draped it around her neck.

Taking a seat next to her, the mattress creaked beneath his weight. Misty plucked the pendant from the hollow of her throat and inspected it in the darkness.

"It stands for 'Misty,'" he told her. "See? I didn't forget."

She gave him a sad smile.

"I think it stands for 'Michael,'" she said, then got up, drifting into the shadows at the far end of the room. Slipping through the door, she left him alone in the dark.

• • •

It was well past four in the morning when Michael heard the Delta pull up to the house. He had hardly slept, his thoughts bounding from Alice to Lucy to Rebel to the responsibilities Misty had reminded him of. As he crawled out of bed to see whether Reb was alone or whether he had brought someone home, he still couldn't shake the dread he would feel at seeing Lucy slide out of the passenger's seat. He supposed it would have been better for Misty if Lucy were dragged to the cockeyed, weatherworn monstrosity that was the Morrow farmhouse. It would have given Momma something to do, distracting her from the daughter she didn't seem to want. But Michael pushed the notion from his head. No, Lucy couldn't come anywhere near this place, no matter how much it would placate Momma's appetite. But that thought only confirmed Misty Dawn's accusation that she was fading from his thoughts. He was forgetting about her, when he was the only person she had.

But, as it turned out, all that worry was for nothing. Because Reb was alone.

. . .

Michael woke to a stern knock on his bedroom door. Shielding his eyes from the sun, he squinted as Rebel filled the doorway. "Get up," he said. "We're going to town."

That was when Michael realized just how difficult keeping Misty safe and happy would be. These endless excursions were pulling him from what was important. They were forcing him to break his promise. He dressed quickly, and by the time he got his boots on, he knew what he had to do.

Misty was still sleeping when Michael ducked into her room. He pulled Alice's record off the turntable and slipped it into its sleeve, then snuck out of the room like a thief. When he finally made his way across the backyard to the car, Reb already had the engine idling. Michael slid into his seat, secured his seat belt, and lay the record across his knees. Reb gave the record a momentary stare before shifting into reverse. They didn't speak until they were a few minutes shy of town. Reb was the one to break the silence.

"What're you bringin' that for?"

Michael looked down at the picture of the forest in his lap.

"Ain't we goin' to the Dervish?" he asked.

"Yeah, so?"

"It's a loan," Michael reminded him. "I told Alice I'd bring it back."

"You gonna get another one?"

Michael didn't bother considering the idea, shaking his head in response as soon as Reb posed the question. Rebel didn't like the reply. He kept pulling his eyes from the road, casting glances at Michael and the record as if mulling something over. At first he held his silence—it wasn't Reb's style to give much of a damn about anything—but he lost his patience sooner than expected.

"What do you mean *no?*" he asked, sounding aggravated. It was strange hearing that tone come out of him—so close to a whine that, for a brief moment, it transported Michael back to their childhood. There was ten-year-old Ray, exasperated by something Michael had said or done.

"I'm just not gonna get another one," Michael murmured, not sure why this was any of Reb's business anyhow. What did his brother care if Alice let him borrow another record? Reb hated it when Michael sat in Misty's room, so what was the point of encouraging him to pick up more music that he could only listen to with his sister anyway?

"Well, *why not*?" Reb prodded. "Not like you gotta pay for it. You just bring it back later."

"It ain't a library, Reb," he said. "I don't wanna bring it back later, and I don't wanna get Alice in trouble." His chest felt constricted, and the heat inside the car wasn't helping. He was trying to keep his intentions hidden. But Reb had a knack for picking up on things that were out of place. It was strange for a man like Rebel to have a flair for empathy. Of course, he was only observant when he had something to lose.

"What the hell is wrong with you today?" Reb asked, his gaze still bouncing between the windshield and Michael's face. "You sick or somethin'?"

Michael *felt* sick, but the sensation wasn't related to any illness. He imagined anyone would have felt the same in his position. He was minutes away from giving up something he genuinely wanted but couldn't have.

"I'm okay," he said, hoping it would be enough to make Reb drop it.

"Bunch of bullshit," Reb grumbled. "You look like hell, and you're actin' weird."

Michael shut his eyes and took a deep, nerve-soothing breath. He tried not to think about the inevitable—the way the little bell would ring over his head, the scent of sweet smoke, the way Alice would raise her hand and smile. He had no idea what he would say to her, whether he'd offer any explanation at all. Maybe he'd just slide the record across the counter and walk out. Maybe he'd hand it to her and say *I changed my mind— I hate it after all.*

He opened his eyes when the Delta slowed, rocks popping beneath the tires. Reb guided the car off the highway and onto the shoulder. He shoved the gearshift into park and stared intently at the steering wheel. After a while, he shot a look at his passenger and posed a question.

"Why don't you stop playin' games and tell me what's goin' on before I bust your head in?"

Michael swallowed, his nerves roiling up his windpipe like a swarm of wasps. Alice, he could handle. She'd smile and say *Hey* and he'd just turn away and leave; but Rebel was a whole other matter. Reb always got what he wanted. And even though Michael couldn't figure out why he was so hell-bent on Michael and Alice being together, he knew enough to see the storm coming.

"I don't wanna go to the Dervish anymore," he said.

The words felt disembodied, as though they hadn't come from him at all. He felt the hairs on his arms, his neck, even the ones on top of his head, stand on end—a cat in a corner, back arched, fur electrified. He hoped Reb wouldn't push this time, afraid that if he did, Michael would finally lose his composure and lash out.

This was about Misty Dawn.

Things had to change.

Michael had promised her she wouldn't be so alone anymore. He was determined to keep his word this time.

"What the hell are you talkin' about?" Reb asked. "What happened?"

"Nothin'." Michael stared down at the record in his lap, then looked out the window, tired of those spooky, neon-white trees on the cover. "I guess I'm just"—he searched for a word that would be at least halfway convincing—"bored."

"*Bored?*"

It was the wrong word.

Reb pushed himself against the driver's seat and emitted an exasperated laugh.

"This was always *your* idea," Michael reminded him. "I don't know why you care. Either way, I'm done. I'd rather stay home."

They sat in a silence so heavy that Michael was sure they'd both suffocate if they sat there long enough. It didn't matter that the windows were rolled down. He wiped a hand across his face. The cicadas buzzed in the trees along the sides of the highway, growing louder by the second. It took all his effort not to clasp his hands over his ears and scream for them to shut the hell up.

"You'd rather stay home," Reb said flatly, still trying to digest it. "You find a girl you like—a girl who likes you back—and you're done." He shrugged like it was nothing. "Just like that. I guess we just gotta chalk it up to you bein' pathetic. That's why you're turnin' your back on the only girl out there who gives a shit about you, right?"

Michael gritted his teeth.

"The only chick who gives half a damn about you, and you're gonna turn around and tell her to screw off, 'cause you're better than her."

Reb's eyes darted to the record again.

"Hey, Alice," Reb said, raising his voice as if calling out to the Dervish miles away. "Michael fuckin' Morrow is better than you. You ain't got shit on *this* hillbilly. He's got big plans. He's gonna see the world!"

Suddenly, words were tumbling out of Michael's mouth.

"Misty gives a shit about me."

It was reflexive—an involuntary spasm that had come in the form of a sentence rather than the jerk of a knee or the twitch of a muscle. Michael watched Rebel's expression shift from belligerent to deadly with understanding, and he immediately regretted saying anything.

"Misty." Their sister's name slithered through Reb's teeth. "She the one who packed your bags and took you on this guilt trip? Made you feel bad 'cause she's cooped up in the house and"—Reb gasped dramatically, pressed a hand to his chest and batted his eyelashes—"oh *no*, she's *lonely*. What else did she say? Or, maybe I should ask—what else did she *do*?"

"Nothin'." Michael shook his head, insisting.

"Like what she did when I had to pull her offa you? That sort of nothin'? Like what she did when I had to shove her across the room and smash your stupid *face* in?" Reb leered at him. "You know that's why Claudine hates her, don't you? She's sick, Michael. That girl's a whore."

"She didn't do nothin', Reb, I just—"

"You're just lovin' on Alice one day and want nothin' to do with her the next." Reb nodded, satisfied with his conclusion. "Oh, I get it. Now I *get* it. You're just tryin' to protect your sister. That's real sweet."

Michael nearly recoiled when Rebel patted him on the arm.

"*Real* sweet, you watchin' out for the family and all. But like I said—Misty? She's sick. And when you're sick you need some medicine. Who better to give you medicine than your own sweet momma?"

The air left Michael's lungs.

He opened his mouth to speak, to scream, to beg Reb not to do this, but all that came out was, "I need to talk to Alice."

Reb gave him a sad sort of smile and shifted into drive.

"Yeah, you do," he agreed. "And you *will*. But not today. We gotta get back home. Somethin' just came up. Somethin' I gotta take care of right about now."

21

MICHAEL LEAPT OUT of the Delta before it came to a stop, ran across the backyard, and took the stairs three at a time. Misty Dawn's bedroom door swung wide and slammed against the inside wall. It vibrated in its frame, the doorknob knocking a crescent-shaped hole in the old wallpaper. A few paperbacks toppled over with the impact, spilling to the floor from the two-by-four Wade had nailed to the wall as a make-shift shelf. Misty yelped when Michael grabbed her by the arm and pulled her out of bed. She'd still been asleep despite the hour and her hair was wild and matted.

"Get up," he said, but he hardly looked at her as she found her footing. He was too busy shooting glances over his shoulder, sure that Rebel wasn't far behind. "We gotta get out of here," he said, but he had no idea how they were going to escape the house or where they would go once they did.

Better to hide in the woods than die inside those rooms.

"Michael, what . . . ?" Misty's words trailed off when a bang sounded from downstairs, like someone upending a table. Reb yelled from one floor down, a bellow that made Michael's blood run cold.

"Here's *Johnny!*"

Michael spun around and looked into his sister's confused face. She was toeing the edge of fear, trying to keep it together, because she didn't have the facts, had no idea what was happening. He could see her fighting against an onslaught of panic. The muscles of her face twitched. Her face flickered through expressions like a cheap TV: apprehension, anxiety, cowardice, dissent.

"What—is that Ray? Who's Johnny? What's goin' on?" But there was no time to explain. Michael grabbed her by the hand and rushed into the hall. Other than taking the stairs straight down into Reb's arms, the second-floor windows were their only option. Michael's window was above the back porch. If they hopped on the roof, they could shimmy down one of the gutters and book it into the trees.

There were footsteps on the stairs, but Michael could hardly hear them over the pounding of his heart. He dragged Misty behind him as he bolted for his bedroom door.

"They're coming to get you, Barbara!" Reb yelled from down the hall. Michael didn't know who Barbara was, but he wasn't going to stick around to find out. He lunged for the window and struggled with the latch, but it was rusted in place. Michael hadn't opened the window in years despite the heat. None of the windows had screens, and Michael didn't like the bugs. He spun around, searching for something he could use to smash the glass—his desk chair. He let go of Misty's hand to grab it, hefted it up in his arms, ready to swing.

"Michael?!" Misty's eyes were wide. She was waiting for

direction, pleading with him for some means of flight. Before Michael could smash the glass, Rebel filled the doorway and gave them both a strangely upbeat smile.

"Oh, *hey* guys," he said.

Then he lunged.

Misty twisted in place, her hair flying out around her in a pale yellow-red halo. She tried to duck around Reb, but he grabbed her by the arm and gave her a vicious pull. Misty cried out. Her right arm flopped at her side. She stared at it with disbelief, her mouth a large *O* of surprise, tiny gasps escaping her throat like the chirps of a bird. Her arm hung limp, unmoving. Reb grinned at her shock, as if amused that she couldn't catch her breath to scream.

Michael seized the opportunity. He swung the chair at his brother rather than the window, but Reb saw it coming. He grabbed the chair in mid-air, and with the piece of furniture held aloft between them, he reeled back and planted the heel of his foot hard against Michael's chest. Michael fell back against the wall, the wind knocked out of him, the chair clattering to the floor.

Reb turned back to Misty, and when she finally sucked in enough air to cry out again, he buried his fist just beneath her rib cage. She doubled over with a groan but wasn't allowed to writhe for long. Reb jerked her up to her feet by her good arm and pushed her out the door, then stopped short to shoot Michael a look. It was a challenge: *Well, come on, protect her.* Then he gave Misty a brutal shove toward the stairs.

Michael stood frozen against the wall, his chest heaving,

his eyes burning, his world spinning out of control. He could hear Reb barking commands at their sister while Misty made horrible retching sounds that echoed up the stairwell. He felt something loosen inside of him, snap out of place and tumble from the center of his chest to his feet.

Rebel was leading her to the slaughter. He was going to drop her at Momma's feet, a woman who was only waiting for an excuse. The time had come.

Downstairs, Misty screamed.

Michael forced himself to move.

He ran down the hall and caught them at the base of the stairs. Misty was on the floor, holding her uninjured arm out as if to ward off evil—the devout lacking a cross to shake at the devil. Rebel loomed above her, waiting for something.

Michael descended the stairs, hating how slowly his feet were moving, how reluctant he felt, when he should have been leaping to Misty's aid. But a lifetime of being afraid couldn't be cast off like a worthless hand-me-down. He was no superhero. His fear was too ingrained, as much a part of him as a fingerprint.

When he finally came to a stop on the third riser from the floor, he saw what Reb was waiting for. Momma crossed the room with a dirty dish towel in her hands, the faint scent of raw onions trailing her like an aura. Her face twisted up in a strange brand of scorn. "What's this?" she asked, giving Reb an expectant look.

"It's a whore," he told her. "Just like you always said."

Momma's gaze drifted from Rebel to where Michael stood

on the stairs, lingered there for a moment, then moved to the weeping girl at her feet. Wade appeared at the opposite end of the foyer, the dining room to his back. He kept his distance, looking more annoyed by the unfolding events than worried. For whatever reason, Michael caught himself wondering whether this was what Vietnam had been like—Reb, a soldier, standing over a sniveling woman; others waiting to see what was going to happen, whether the soldier would have mercy on her or pull out his weapon and silence her cries, nobody truly caring either way.

"Misty Dawn is gone," Reb announced. "This ain't my sister. She's diseased, contagious. Michael might already be sick."

Michael blinked. He looked to Misty for explanation, but she had her forehead pressed to the floor. A pool of saliva had collected beneath her nose and mouth. She continued to cry into it like a leper waiting for death.

"She tried to seduce Michael a few days ago, but I caught her."

Momma's gaze snapped up from Misty Dawn to Michael.

"I warned her," Reb explained, "but she tried it again, last night when I was gone. And she'll only keep tryin' until she gets away with it."

"How do you know?" Momma asked flatly.

"Because *he* told me." Reb motioned to his brother.

Michael's mouth fell open. "What? I . . . no." He shook his head in denial. Reb was *lying*. If Michael had said anything, he had insisted that Misty hadn't done anything at all. Yes, she had come into his room, but it was only because she was hurt

and lonely and desperate for affection. Anyone else would have
done the same thing.

Misty turned her head enough to look up the stairs at him,
and despite her desperation and haze of pain, Michael spotted
a look of betrayal in her eyes.

How could you?

He shook his head again.

You told?

"I swear, I didn't say nothin'," he promised, his gaze fixed on
his sister's anguished face.

"So it's true," Momma concluded.

"No!"

Michael rushed down the remaining stairs and crouched
beside Misty. She turned her face away from him, glaring down
at the floorboards, making him hate himself for being so stupid.
Rebel was right, always right—Michael was an idiot; he always
messed things up.

"Well, which is it?" Momma asked, her tone unnervingly
steady. "Either Misty Dawn tried to seduce you, or Ray is lyin'.
Either way, someone's sinnin'."

Michael looked up at his mother. The floral pattern of her
dress made her look alien-thin. From his vantage point on
the floor, her cheeks looked hollow, almost sunken, and the
circles beneath her eyes were so dark they were nearly black.
She looked like a monster—a praying mantis with a taste for
blood.

"Falsely accusin' a family member of lyin' is lyin' too,"
Momma said. "And you know what lyin' will get you."

Exile.

The woods.

Michael's gaze darted to his father, searching for help. Wade stood motionless for a long while, as though considering the situation. But he eventually bowed his head in a solemn way, as if to say that Momma was right: lying was unforgivable. Rebel was turning Misty in out of loyalty to the family. He was betraying one for the good of all.

A sob wrenched out of Michael's throat. He folded himself over Misty's crumpled frame, his cheek pressed against her ear, and whispered, "I'll go to the woods for you, Misty. If you want it, I'll go."

Misty found a second wind. She pushed him away and sat up, her face slathered with tears and spit. Her hair was plastered across her cheeks and forehead in wet, matted strips. She looked at her mother, narrowed her eyes, and hissed, "It's true. Misty Dawn is gone. I've come for Michael. I'm a no-good filthy whore. Now kill me, you stupid bitch."

Michael stared at her.

Terror choking on its own heartbeat.

Reb teetered between what looked like surprise and glee.

Momma's face twisted into a mask of furious disgust so all-encompassing that Michael half-expected fire to burst from her eyes, her mouth, her fingertips. He waited for Momma to reach down, grab Misty by the hair, and yank so hard that Misty's head tore from her body, as though it had been precariously balanced atop her shoulders all her life. And maybe it had been.

Momma sneered. "Take her to the kitchen."

Reb grabbed Misty by her good arm and began to drag her across the floor. Michael's hands shot out, clutching the hem of his sister's nightgown. His eyes glittered with terror. His breath hitched in his throat.

"No!" he cried out, so strained that it was a wonder it had made it out of his throat at all.

Misty turned her head to look at him as Reb pulled her along. When their eyes met, she began to weep—huge, gasping wails, like a girl headed to the gallows. She could see into the future as clearly as he could. It was over. This was the end.

"*No!*" he screamed again, wanting to grab Misty by her other arm. But he was afraid to hurt her. That collapsed shoulder looking so wrong. If he tried to pull her back, her arm may have come clean off in his hands—like Reb jerking the wing off a pheasant, dooming the animal to a slow and painful death.

By the time the three of them reached the kitchen—Rebel dragging Misty, Michael behind him—Momma was standing next to the table with something tucked away in a dish towel. A wooden handle jutted out of the fabric, held tight in her right hand. Michael skittered across the floor and wrapped his arms around his sister. He tried to envelop her completely, desperate to make her disappear, but a hand fell against the back of his head. Fingers tangled in his hair. Rebel yanked Michael back, peeling him away from Misty's huddled form, and for half a second Michael was sure his own life was over too. Momma loomed above him, the blade of a butcher's knife glinting in the light. Her mouth was a hard, straight line, her eyes drawn into slits. But she didn't pull the blade across Michael's throat. Instead, she mimicked Reb's move, grabbed Misty's hair and pulled back. Misty's head came up, her face puffy and red from crying.

Before Michael could react, the razor edge of the blade sliced across the base of his sister's neck. Michael's eyes widened as gore fanned out across his face and arms. Misty's blood splashed hot against his skin.

Wrenching himself free of Rebel's hold, he lunged for Misty's crumpled body and tried to stop the bleeding. He frantically pressed his palms against her neck, but it was no use. Within seconds, they were both covered in iron-scented red. Blood soaked Misty's once-white nightgown, staining it a deep burgundy. The ends of Michael's hair dripped like wet paintbrushes waiting for a canvas.

Momma threw the knife onto the floor. It clanked against the boards next to Michael's knees. He didn't acknowledge the weapon, didn't look up to see what he was sure was written across her face: this was Misty's own fault. And as a parting gift, Michael would be the one to sop up her blood.

Michael sat with Misty in his embrace, rocking her back and forth as he stared across the kitchen into nowhere. By the time he finally gathered the strength to look up, the room was empty and the house was eerily quiet.

And for the first time in his life, he truly understood.

This was not his family.

This was not supposed to be his life.

22

WHEN REB STEPPED inside the green-shuttered house through the unlocked sliding-glass door, Bonnie was sitting on the couch watching some sappy made-for-TV movie. She turned away from the television and blinked in surprise. But rather than panic at the stranger standing in her home, she smiled.

"Michael," she cooed, rising up from where she sat, giving Reb a kiss on both cheeks. "What are you doing here? You should have called. I'd have made something to eat."

Reb returned her smile. "That's why I didn't call. Didn't wanna put you out."

Bonnie tsk-tsked at that, pulled her long, box-dyed hair back into a ponytail, and blushed with embarrassment when she realized what she was wearing.

"Well, you could have at least called so I could have gotten *decent*, you know. I'm a mess."

Bonnie Rasmussen wasn't exactly stylish. Reb took in her loose-fitting sweatpants and pale-blue tank top with a cartoon sheep in the middle. He was convinced the woman owned nothing but shirts with some sort of animal printed on them—cats or dogs or cartoon owls. Judging by the photographs on the wall, she hadn't always dressed that way. A hallway photo that must have been taken in the 1950s or '60s had Bonnie looking like a wind-chafed starlet. Her hair was big and bouncy like Brigitte Bardot's. A wide-legged jumpsuit had been cinched at the waist with a thick, woven belt. Time had not been kind to Bonnie. She had lost her looks and fashion sense. All that was left was a depressed widow whose interests stopped at birds, books, and bad TV.

But her limited hobbies were exactly what Reb had been hoping for. It left her free of distraction and wide open to making a new friend. She had been reluctant at first, nearly not letting Reb inside to use her phone when he'd pulled the oldest trick in the book.

Sorry, ma'am, but I think I've run outta gas and I ain't got no way of gettin' home. Mind if I use your phone?

Bonnie had been dubious. No matter. Reb had given her a megawatt smile. Two minutes later, he was standing dead center in her kitchen while Bonnie offered him a glass of iced tea.

Their second meeting had been less awkward. Reb had arrived on her doorstep with a bunch of cheap carnations from the nearest gas station—red and white, a few of them dyed a garish blue in celebration of the Fourth of July. When Bonnie answered the door, she looked about ready to cry at the sight of him. She invited him in for lemonade and they watched a Pirates game together. She asked him questions about himself, which he answered with quaint-sounding lies. He told her he was four years younger than he was, that his father was a miner, and that he had a younger sister who was a senior in high school—she was a creative type, the kind of girl who could really make something of herself if she could just get out of West Virginia.

By the time Reb stepped uninvited into Bonnie's house while Michael waited outside, he had visited her every week for nearly a year.

He had bought her a greeting card for her birthday. Had given her chocolates on Valentine's Day. Had sat with her at the kitchen table and gorged himself on mashed potatoes and turkey a few days before Thanksgiving. At Christmas, he had presented her with a small heart locket he'd torn from a screaming girl's neck. He could tell Bonnie looked forward to their visits by the way her face lit up, knew that he'd thoroughly wormed his way into her heart when, rather than scolding him for not knocking, she smiled when he appeared unannounced.

"Let me at least put on something decent," Bonnie insisted. She tugged down on her blue tank top as though trying to hide the ugliness of her sweats. "I have a cheesecake in the fridge. Just picked it up at the store this afternoon. I even got a can of whipped cream, just the way you like."

"You shouldn't have," Reb told her, but she waved her hand at him, dismissing his niceties, and sidestepped him on her way to the master bedroom. Reb took the opportunity to sidle up to the main window, hook a finger around the curtains, and peek out at the Delta in the driveway. Michael's shadow shifted somewhere in the front yard. It was too far to be discernible, but he was definitely there, counting down the minutes before following Reb inside.

He cleared his throat, pulled his attention from the TaB commercial playing on TV—*the beautiful drink for beautiful people*—and moved through the living room to the darkened hallway. Bonnie had closed the door to the master bedroom behind her. Reb opened it without a knock. Standing in nothing but her underwear and her cartoon-sheep tank top, Bonnie gasped when the door swung open. She yanked the shiny satin bedspread toward herself in an attempt to cover up.

"What are you doing?" she squealed. "Michael, get out!"

He smiled, and while he couldn't see himself, he hoped he looked like a wolf—the big bad boy who had spent a year planning on blowing Bonnie's house down.

"Don't be shy," he told her, stepping further into the room. Bonnie gaped at him, still clutching the duvet despite it hardly covering her at all. He paused at a chest of drawers and drew his hand across its top in an almost coy sort of way, like a little boy about to make an attempt at his first kiss. "You know, over our last year together, I've grown pretty, um"—he shrugged, gave her a bashful look—"*fond* of you."

Bonnie blinked at him. The weird mix of fascination and confusion she wore made him want to snap her neck. Something about it made her look so stupid, something about it reminded him of Michael.

"Come on," he murmured, "don't look so surprised. I mean, we've spent a lot of time with each other."

"But *never* with the intent of . . . of . . ." Bonnie stammered. "My God, Michael, I thought you knew."

"Knew what?" he asked, inching closer. "That you ain't interested?" He raised an eyebrow at her, challenging her to admit it. "That you and me were just *friends*?" He lifted his hands, made air quotes around the word to emphasize his point. "Come on, Bonnie. You're breakin' my heart."

"I . . . I had no idea . . ." She shook her head. "If I had known, I would have made it clear, I would have told you, I . . ."

"You . . ." Reb stopped at the foot of the bed, not more than five feet from where Bonnie stood.

"I would have called the whole thing off!" She spit out the words. "Now I think you should leave."

"You think I should leave," He echoed, frowning at the carpet. "After a year of bein' friends, you're gonna kick me out like some stray? You know how much that hurts?" He grabbed a handful of comforter and gave it a firm pull, yanking it from her fingers. She gasped and stepped back, stretching her blue tank top over her hips, still trying to be decent despite her growing fear. "I don't like it when people hurt my feelin's, Bonnie. You can understand that, can't you?"

"You're crazy," she whispered, seeing her young companion for what he truly was. "Please, get out. Leave me alone, before I call the police."

Reb held up his hands as if in surrender. "Okay," he said. "I'm sorry." He saw her relax. *As if it could be that easy,* he thought, and he lunged at her before she had a chance to think. He threw her on the bed and pinned her to the mattress. And while he worked the top button of his jeans, he was fascinated by how simultaneously turned on and revolted he was. She was lying about how she felt about him—she had dyed her hair strawberry blond after *he* had told her how good she would look as one. *She* had invited him over time and again, cooking for him, sitting a little too close to him on the couch, her hand occasionally brushing his. Cheesecake. Oh, and that canned whipped cream he liked so damn much. If Bonnie had been anyone else, Reb would have dragged her outside and tossed her in the trunk without laying a finger on her. But Bonnie wasn't anyone else. She was his project, a yearlong effort, his magnum opus of patience and planning.

He pushed her panties aside and hissed into her ear. "You have no idea how long I've been waitin' for this. You're my masterpiece, Bonnie."

He nearly laughed when she uttered his fake given name into the bedroom just as Michael filled the doorframe.

Nearly laughed at how damn perfect it all was.

23

W HEN MICHAEL FINISHED scrubbing the blood from between the grooves in the kitchen floor, it was dark outside. His knees were raw, his head was throbbing, and he could hardly see past his own weariness. But Misty was still waiting, wrapped in a blanket on the back porch—the blanket he'd slept with since he was a boy.

He walked around the side of the house and stared at the storm doors that led down to the basement. It was what Momma expected, but this time it wasn't what she'd get. Rather than pulling Misty down those rickety stairs, he retrieved the old, splintered shovel Rebel had made him drag into the woods and tucked it into the blanket like the dead girl's bedfellow. And then he carried his sister, bare feet bobbing, into the trees, the porch light shining at his back.

He walked in stops and starts for nearly an hour before laying Misty on the crest of their favorite hill. It was high enough to overlook the surrounding peaks and valleys. During the times Michael had been convinced his own days were numbered, he imagined himself being buried in this very spot. It was a peaceful place, far enough from the farmhouse to be free.

He sank the spade into the soft earth, barely holding it together as he went through the motions of digging his sister's grave. It was only when he realized just how perfect the spot was that he broke down, sobbing against the pain in his shoulders and back, in his hands and his heart.

The sunrise would peek over that valley only a few hours after Misty was in the ground, burning away the hazy purple mist of the night.

It would be what she'd see every morning until the end of time.

. . .

Michael didn't return home. Instead he spread the blood-soaked blanket over a bed of leaves, lay down, and pulled the corners over his legs and torso like a poor man's sleeping bag. With one arm outstretched, he buried his fingers in the dirt of Misty's grave.

When he woke, the sun was high and the heat was stifling. He squinted through the shivering leaves above his head and scowled at the cloudless sky before his eyes stopped on the lump of soil that bulged from the ground beside him. But despite the viselike tightening in his chest, he didn't cry. If there was a limit to how many tears a human could shed, Michael felt as though he'd reached it.

Standing there, staring down at Misty's grave, he wondered how old Lauralynn was now. Close to twenty-five, he guessed. Once upon a time, he used to think that she would rush back to their farmhouse in the West Virginian hills as soon as she had the chance. Now he understood why she never had. Lauralynn must have seen it in Momma's eyes so many years before, the true depth of that frightening hollowness.

Pulling in a breath, he tried to steady himself. It was only after he turned in search of a few downed branches to fashion a cross that he realized he was covered in Misty's blood. Had it been anyone else's, he would have pulled off his shirt and buried it. But the rust-colored stain that stretched from the top of his chest to the knees of his jeans made him feel closer to her. It was the last piece of her that he'd ever have.

He plucked a couple of average-size branches from the ground and stripped them of their bark, exposing clean, white wood beneath. Lashing the cross together with those same strips, he pushed the poor-man's cross into the soil at the head of the grave. He'd make a more permanent marker in the basement later, one that wouldn't break apart in the wind or get washed away in the rain. But for now, this would do.

Michael started to make his way down the hill, back to the farmhouse that stood lonely and secluded in the distance. And as he dragged his feet along the ground, he was struck by the fact that he didn't feel the hate or anger he knew should have been there. All he felt was guilt, because he had failed at the only job he truly had—nobody had assigned it to him, but it was one he had taken on himself. He had spent years satiating Momma's thirst, had gone through his entire life doing what Reb told him. All to be a good brother and son. To avoid abandonment in the woods. To keep Misty safe.

Except Misty had never really been safe. Not until now.

. . .

When the farmhouse finally came into view, Michael could see Wade and Momma sitting on the back porch. Neither one of them spoke as he shuffled through the backyard and up the steps. It was as though they were unaware of where he'd been and what he'd been doing, as though they were blind to the blood that covered him from his head to his knees. They simply let him duck inside the house, go upstairs, and close his bedroom door behind him.

The day wore on into night, Michael drowning the memory of the previous day's events in a dreamless sleep. His hands clung to the stiff fabric of his blood-soaked shirt as he tossed around on his squalid mattress. Three words rolled through his head on a loop: *Misty is gone.*

When Michael woke, Rebel was leaning against the jamb of the bedroom door, cleaning his nails with his switchblade. Seeing Michael stir, Reb looked up from his hands and smirked.

"You look like an axe murderer, brother," he said. "Like a goddamn *horror* movie, them elevators bleedin' into the hotel lobby. Why don't you get yourself cleaned up?"

Michael looked down at himself. Dried blood crusted his arms, some of which had come off in patchy dandruff-like flakes. It blotted his mattress like burgundy snow. His hair was clumped together at the ends, the dried tips so hard that they were needle-sharp.

"Hurry up," Reb said. "I don't wanna wait around all day."

Michael blinked up at him, understanding what Rebel was

saying yet not wanting to process the words. Reb intended to drag Michael into town. Despite what had happened, Reb was still going to force him into the Delta. Michael was going to be made to ride alongside his brother all the way to the Dervish, as though nothing had happened.

"You gotta be kiddin'." He heard the words leave his mouth, but they felt detached, as though they were coming from another Michael just behind him. A more rebellious doppelganger that hadn't existed before now.

Ray cocked an eyebrow, then went back to his manicure. "Do I look like I'm kiddin'?"

Michael shook his head, not in reply to Reb's question, but in response to the whole situation. It was as though Rebel hadn't been the slightest bit affected by Misty's death. Of course not.

A rush of anger spiked Michael's blood. What did Reb expect was going to happen—that they were going to run off to the Dervish so he could screw Lucy, so that Michael could pretend everything was all right?

"Don't you even care?" His fingers shook as they took hold of the lumpy mattress beneath him.

Reb glanced up from his nails and gave an easy shrug. "Sure I do," he said. "Because who's gonna finish readin' *Winnie the Pooh*?"

Michael stared at his last remaining sibling, not understanding. He was ready to tell Rebel where to put his stupid plans and his weird riddles when a single thought stopped him short: Alice. If Michael played along, he could at least warn her.

Then Alice would have a fighting chance. But if Michael blew up and told Rebel to go fuck himself, Reb would get aggressive. In Reb's eyes, Alice was Michael's girl, and what better way to get even than to hurt her? Michael couldn't let that happen. He *wouldn't*.

Michael got to his feet, but he didn't have the strength to feign ambivalence. "You're a goddamn psycho," he said, brushing past him on the way to the bathroom.

"You and me both, brother," Reb murmured beneath his breath. Surprisingly, that was all he said.

. . .

The car ride into town felt like the longest Michael had ever taken. He sat in the Olds with his hands in his lap, his T-shirt sopping up the water that dripped from his wet hair. He didn't speak or look out the window. He only stared at the now-clean skin of his hands and arms, replaying the way Misty's blood had fanned out across the kitchen floor.

"She wasn't your sister anymore," Reb explained. "It wasn't her. She was, like, possessed, you know? Like that movie about that kid where her head spun around and she floated up to the ceilin' and all." He paused, as if contemplating the ridiculousness of his own statement, before continuing on. "You didn't see that flick, did ya? Good movie. Real cool. Anyway, look at the bright side. Now there ain't nobody to make you feel guilty about gettin' with another girl."

Michael glared down at his hands and held his tongue. It was safer that way. Not responding meant not running the risk of saying something wrong, which would send Reb over the edge.

"And you didn't bring the record," Reb noticed. Michael had left it in Rebel's car after their last ride, but Reb had brought it upstairs to him to make sure Alice was still on Michael's mind. "Either you've changed your mind about breakin' it off or it's somethin' else," he said. Out of the corner of his eye, Michael saw Reb peering at the road. Reb looked more thoughtful than Michael remembered seeing him before. Finally, Rebel looked back at his brother, and Michael consciously avoided his gaze. "Nah," Reb said. "It's somethin' else. You're distracted. Boohooing about Misty. You just forgot it at home."

"Then maybe we should go back and get it," Michael suggested, unable to help himself.

Ray considered it, then shook his head with a look of indifference. "It don't matter," he said.

"Why?"

"For you, nothin' matters," Reb explained. "You gotta have free will or some guts for shit to matter, and you don't got neither. *I'm* the one who decides what matters and what don't . . . and Alice, she matters. She matters a *lot*."

Michael pulled into himself, not wanting to talk anymore.

Free will—he supposed he had it, but Reb was right: you had to have guts to use it. Despite his anger, there was still that underlying fear of being alone in the woods. Of not knowing whether to go right or left. Of listening to the birds settling in for the night and the whisper of crickets rising up around him. A constant chirp so loud and repetitive it could drive a man crazy if he wasn't already mad. But Michael's fear of being driven into the wilderness wasn't enough to keep him in check. Not anymore. If he hadn't ever met Alice, he would have nothing to lose. But Alice was there, bright and vivid in Michael's mind, as though Rebel had known all along that he'd need an extra angle, another way to play the situation to his advantage. Michael pressed his palms together as if in prayer, squeezing them between his knees.

"You got somethin' to say?" Reb asked.

Michael sucked his lips in and bit down, holding fast to his silence.

"I get it—you miss your precious sister. But at least now we've got somethin' in common." He turned his head to give Michael a hard look. The emotion that glinted in his eyes was completely alien—empty yet so full of rage that Michael couldn't grasp exactly what it was he was seeing. A body without a soul. A husk that used to be a person but was now nothing but a vessel of hate.

But losing a sister to distance wasn't the same as losing a sister to death. If Rebel wanted to, he could pack up his things and drive out to North Carolina, he could go see . . .

Michael blinked. It was the perfect solution, a perfect way to get Reb as far away from Alice as possible.

"Let's go see Lauralynn," he said, giving his brother a hopeful look. "Let's drive out to North Carolina, right now, the both of us."

Reb gave a bitter laugh. "Yeah? You wanna see the old-as-shit spinster and the crazy fuckin' army vet?"

Michael frowned at Reb's response. For once, he had hoped to see a spark of something other than anger in his sibling's eyes, but the mention of Lauralynn only made Rebel look all the more resentful.

"You know that old fucker used to rape Claudine when she was a kid, right? Remember when they came to visit and brought Lauralynn and Misty them ugly dresses? The time Grandma Jean smacked me in the mouth and chipped my front tooth with her ugly old ring?"

Michael nodded.

"I saw the old bastard sittin' out on the porch with LL; had his hand up her skirt, and it wasn't coming back down anytime soon either. Shit like that's generational, born into the family like them diseases they talk about on the TV. Like cancer." Reb went quiet for a moment, then took a breath before muttering a few more words to himself. "Probably better the way it happened for her."

Michael didn't understand what Rebel meant by that last part, but he was too distracted by the insightfulness to question it. He finally looked out the window, wondering if it could be true—he knew Momma had lived through her own personal hell as a girl, but *that*? Was that why she was so angry, so hungry for blood? The similarities between the girls and Misty had struck him more than a few times—pale skin, strawberry-blond hair. If they appeared to be like Misty . . . maybe that's what Momma had looked like when she was younger too? Maybe Momma wasn't picking those girls because they looked like her daughter, but because she saw something of *herself* in them.

Perhaps killing them was the only way she knew how to quench her anger, how to sequester her pain.

Rebel eased the Delta into the Dervish parking lot and pulled the brake. Michael's eyes snapped to the sherbet-colored record store ahead of them. His stomach pitched at the sight of it, and for a second he was sure he was going to be sick. He thought about rushing inside and pulling Alice into the storeroom. He'd reveal just enough to wind her up, get her good and scared. He'd tell her to get as far away from Dahlia as she could possibly go. It would have been the perfect excuse to finally start her life in a place that was deserving of such a girl. But rather than shoving open his door and bolting across the sizzling pavement, Michael was overwhelmed with conflicting emotions, not knowing whether he should laugh or scream.

Because it suddenly all made sense. *Momma* was the victim, and in his mind that bound him to her just as it had bound him to Misty. The Morrows had taken him in, had fed him and given him a place to live. They had saved him when his real parents had abandoned him. Momma had killed Misty to protect him.

Michael's breath caught in his throat. His head spun, and he squeezed his eyes shut. Everything that the Morrows had done had been born of pain, nothing but festering wounds, people trying to set the world right. His conscience wouldn't let him abandon them. His mind wouldn't ever let him disconnect.

"Are you comin' or what?" Reb asked, but he didn't bother

waiting for an answer. Waving his hand at Michael in dismissal, he murmured a "Whatever" and climbed out of the car.

Michael was trapped.

He could have run after what happened to Misty—before Rebel had told him about Momma, before he could process the fact that her death was for *him*. But there was Alice to think about.

He could have told Alice everything, but it was too risky. If Reb found out, he'd have to kill her to protect the family. Because despite the twisted darkness that made them who they were, as far as Reb was concerned, the Morrows stuck together. Everything they did was for each other.

Which was why they would never let him go. No matter what opportunity arose, there would always be something . . . either guilt or fear, something to trap him, to keep him in his place.

He jumped at the sudden tap on the passenger door. Alice stood in the glaring sun, bent at the waist, looking through the open window.

"Hey," she said with a smile, but it faded fast. She held something in her hands—a folded sheet of paper. Sliding a pair of sunglasses down her nose to get a better look at him, she plucked them from her face when she caught sight of his dismay. "What's wrong? Are you okay?"

"Yeah, I'm all right, I just . . ." He shielded his eyes from the sun, hoping it would also hide some of the emotion on his face. "It's been a bad few days."

Alice frowned and crouched next to the car, her arms

folding across the ledge of the open window. "I'm sorry," she said. "I know how that can be. You want to come in?" She motioned to the Dervish behind her. "We've got the air cranked. It's like Antarctica in there. I'll let you borrow my sweater, and maybe a towel for that hair." She tried at a smile but came up short when Michael declined the invitation with a faint shake of his head. "You sure?" she asked. "I don't want to leave you out here by yourself."

"It's okay," he assured her, but Alice wasn't convinced. Her spearmint scent mingled with the smell of old car and worn leather.

"It's not okay," she countered. "What happened?"

He couldn't bring himself to look her in the eyes, didn't want to catch her gaze if all he was going to do was lie. "Just trouble at home," he murmured. "I've been thinkin' . . . you should do it."

"Do what?" she asked, giving him a curious glance.

"Get out of Dahlia, do somethin' better."

Alice rolled her eyes a little, as though the suggestion was ridiculous, but a faint grin graced her lips. "Yeah? Just pack up and go?"

Michael nodded. "Just go. I *want* you to go. You can't stay here, not anymore."

"Wish it were that easy," she said, casting a reproachful glance at the store behind her.

"What's so hard about it?" Michael asked. "If you can find a job here, you can find one anywhere. A better job. At the newspaper, like you want. Drawin' comics . . . not wastin' away."

"Yeah, but what about Lucy?"

Michael shrugged, not getting what Lucy had to do with anything.

"We've got an apartment together," Alice explained. "I can't just bail on her. We've got rent to split."

"Take her with you."

She laughed, as though the simplicity of the suggestion struck her as particularly funny. "Just like that, huh? Forget the lease. Forget that we pretty much single-handedly run the Dervish."

"But what about the future?" Michael glowered at the frayed denim stretched tight across his knees. "You're better than this."

"And you're going to come with me?"

He glanced up at her. When she rested her cheek against her forearm and gazed up at him with those eyes, he felt like he could just about explode. He wanted a life with her, wanted to see the world while holding her hand, even if that world only extended as far as Pittsburgh. Something about the way she was looking at him sent a bolt of courage through his heart. Before he knew what he was doing he leaned in and kissed her. It wasn't like the one they had shared in the McDonald's, shy and nervous and unsure. This was a *real* kiss like in the movies, so real that she slid halfway through the window and coiled her arms around his neck, the tips of his wet hair tracing trails of moisture along her arms. When she pulled away, her eyes were sparkling. She brushed a few strands of his hair behind his ears and let her hands cup his face before unleashing a gorgeous smile.

"Spaceman," she whispered. "Take me to the moon."

"What's that mean?" he whispered back, feeling so close to tears he was afraid she'd see them welling up in his eyes. But she burst into a fit of airy laughter instead.

"It means I'll think about it," she said. "But until then, the future can wait."

Michael's heart sank. He made a move to grab her, to pull her back inside the car and tell her everything—*You have to get out of here*—but stopped short when she glanced over her shoulder. Rebel was making his way back to the car. Alice ducked down and handed Michael the paper she had in her hand—a few sheets stapled together at the fold to make a little book.

"Birthday present," she said. "Don't read it in front of Rebel . . . or Ray, or Casanova. Whatever you want to call him. See you later." She gave him a wink.

Michael watched her step away from the Olds. She gave Reb a wave and a cheerful "Hey" on her way back across the parking lot.

Reb slid into his seat and leaned back, watching Alice with a disconcerting amount of interest. When he finally turned his attention to Michael, he smirked.

"I saw that," he announced. "Both of us did." He pointed to the shop. "Windows all across the front, see? You can see a whole bunch of things through glass, like your baby brother makin' out with the girl he said bores him. What's that?" He nodded at the paper in Michael's lap, but he made no move to grab it.

"Dunno. Birthday present. I'm not supposed to read it yet."

Reb gave him a weird smile. "I got you somethin' too. You're gonna like it. It'll cheer you right up. I can hardly wait to see your face."

.   .   .

Sliding out of the car, Michael bypassed the house and went to visit Misty Dawn instead. Sitting beside her grave, he faced the valley below and smoothed the pages of his birthday present in his hands. The cover was plain, save for a tiny hand-drawn gift box in the center of the page. Inside was a drawing that looked just like the one he had seen in Alice's sketchbook. A short-haired girl sat at the Dervish's counter, looking bored and forlorn, a thought bubble above her head reading: I SHOULD REALLY QUIT MY JOB. The next panel showed the same girl perking up and putting on a smile, greeting a long-haired boy at the door, his face hardly visible, his body language lost and melancholy. A man's face, bisected by a large lightning bolt, was drawn across his chest. It was a surprisingly accurate representation of the David Bowie shirt Michael had worn on his last visit to the shop. Page after page, the little book told the story of a girl and boy growing closer until, in the final three panels, the boy leaves the record shop with a smile and a wave. The girl is left behind the counter once more. But rather than looking listless, she looks blissful. And rather than thinking about quitting her job, the thought bubble above her head holds no words, just a tiny heart filled in with ink. Small but undeniable.

Michael stared at that heart for what felt like an eternity, his mind reeling, his own heart squeezing tight and relaxing beat after beat. His gaze wavered away from the page, paused on the pile of soil beside him, and for a moment he could swear he heard Misty's turntable playing faintly through the trees. He pictured the *M* of her necklace glinting in the sun, imagined her smiling at him before fading into the woods. *M for Michael*, she whispered. Not *M* for *Momma*, for *mourning* or *misery* or even *Misty Dawn*. It was *M* for *Michael*.

And though he wasn't sure he could ever have it, he wanted to earn Alice's tiny inked-in heart.

24

REBEL MORROW DIDN'T possess the usual interest in girls. His were fantasies of a darker sort—the kind of stuff that involved plastic sheeting and electrical tape. But it was all for the cause, and so he put on his best civilian smile and approached Lucy Liddle in the cereal aisle of the local grocery store.

Lucy wasn't a drifter; she wasn't the type of girl who could vanish off the face of the earth without a trace. She was tall and slender, with glossy reddish-gold hair that swept across the middle of her back. Her appearance was remarkable—the kind of face boys fantasized about seeing gaze up at them from a bed of rumpled sheets. She was the kind of girl who got "discovered" at a Midwestern shopping mall and went on to do modeling or TV commercials. Lucy Liddle was beautiful. She had a lot of friends and close family that lived in town. She held a regular job where she'd most certainly be missed. She was the last person in West Virginia that should have been a mark. And yet she became just that from the moment she turned her head, glanced over her shoulder, and gave Reb a mischievous smile.

The day Reb and Lucy met, they smoked a joint in the Delta while watching the sunset. A week later, she invited him to the Dervish to listen to records after hours. She liked Paul McCartney and Billy Joel—guys Reb wouldn't have been caught dead listening to otherwise. But he bobbed his head and pretended to be enjoying himself. Had it not been for Michael, Reb would have twisted her head off her shoulders as she sang along to "You May Be Right."

Rebel met Alice for the first time a few days after the listening party. Lucy pulled him into the Dervish during a lunch break, shrugged her shoulders in a bashful sort of way, and introduced him to her best friend as *the guy I told you about.* Reb could see it in Lucy's eyes: despite their short time together, he was more than just a guy—he was a boyfriend. That was fine by him. It was just another step toward the ultimate goal.

Before long, Rebel claimed his work schedule had changed. He could only spend time with Lucy while she was working at the record store. It was an inconvenience, but doable when both she and Alice were sharing a shift. Standing at the counter while Lucy was in the restroom, Reb rolled his neck and gave Alice a look.

"You seein' anyone?" he asked, unabashed by the directness of his inquiry.

Alice, however, was caught off guard. She laughed a little and shook her head as if to say *You're something else*, but he didn't take it that way. He read it as a *no*, because Reb had been watching Alice more closely than he had been watching Lucy. That was the thing about people who didn't know they were in danger: they didn't hide much.

"I've got a brother," he told her. "Younger. How old are you, eighteen?"

Alice blushed and nodded, busying herself with sorting a handful of new arrivals. "Good guess," she murmured.

"You'll like him," he assured her. "He's . . . different."

"Different how?" she asked, finally taking the bait.

"Quiet. He sure as hell ain't like *me*, if that's what you're askin'."

Alice smirked.

"It's okay," he said, "I know you ain't crazy about me. Watchin' out for your friend and all. Lucy's lucky to have someone like you."

Alice smiled at the records in front of her. "Yeah?" She peeked up at him before looking down again.

"I'll bring him around," Reb said. "He could use a friend."

That was all it took.

The seed had been so easy to plant, he chuckled all the way home.

Despite Lucy's fondness of him, Rebel kept his distance from her and Alice's apartment. He liked toying with her, giving her what she wanted in the back room, but never everything. He knew how girls like Lucy worked. They met a nice person, fell hard, and were eager to pull the guy into their life. First, an invitation back to the apartment. Then, a visit to meet Mom and Dad. The more reluctant the guy appeared, the harder the girl tried.

"I wish you'd finally have time to come over," Lucy whined, sitting on the counter with Reb nestled between her knees. "That room is starting to make me feel dirty." She nodded toward the storeroom with a frown. "Cheap, you know?"

"You couldn't be cheap if you tried," he said. "Tell you what: why don't you come over to *my* place? Meet the parents, make it official."

Lucy's eyes lit up. "Really? I mean, are you sure? I don't want to, like, rush you into anything."

"You broke me," he confessed. "We're gonna have a surprise party for Michael anyway. It would blow his mind if Alice was there."

Lucy laughed and threw her arms around his neck, then pressed a kiss to his mouth. "Oh, I'll *make* her go," she said with a grin. Before she could unwind her arms from around his neck, the little bell above the door rang. Michael and Alice stepped inside. Alice was wearing a pair of ridiculous yellow sunglasses. They both smelled of greasy french fries from the McDonald's across the street.

• • •

Rebel stared through the windshield at the girls' apartment complex. The trees that lined the front of the building glowed in soft yellow hues beneath the parking lights. He soaked in the moment, thinking that this was the way God felt before dropping a church roof on a gathering of parishioners or wiping out an entire town by way of a tornado. The power was invigorating, sensual. He rubbed his sweaty palms against the thighs of his jeans, stepped out of the car, and climbed the stairs up to apartment 2A. He nearly laughed when he realized his mouth was dry. After so many kills and so many screaming girls, so many thrashing bodies and terrified stares, he was actually nervous.

Lucy answered the door with a wide smile, her hair pulled into a high ponytail. She had on a pair of high-waisted blue jeans with the kind of flowy, satiny halter top Misty Dawn would have worn. "Ray, hi! Alice is almost ready," she said. "We aren't going to be late, are we?" She gave a clock on the wall an unsure glance. "I don't want to ruin the surprise."

"Nah," Reb said. "It'll be fine."

She stepped aside, inviting him in. The apartment was sparse—nothing but an ugly gold-and-brown floral-print couch in front of a black-and-white Zenith TV. He expected it to look more like the *Three's Company* apartment but was glad there was no Jack Tripper to deal with.

"Do I look okay?" She held her arms out to the side, spun around, and smoothed the front of her shirt down with anxious hands. Save for the ties at her waist and the nape of her neck, her entire back was bare. "This isn't too modern, is it? Your mom wouldn't like something else better?" The way her muscles tensed and relaxed beneath the smooth surface of her skin made him hungry.

"You look great," he told her. "She's gonna love you."

Lucy bit her bottom lip, but was cut off by the opening of Alice's bedroom door. The short-haired girl was wearing a black V-neck shirt, a pair of dark jeans, and a riveted leather belt. Her combat boots flopped around her ankles, the top eyelets left unlaced. She was the polar opposite of her roommate. Reb had seen pictures of girls like her before—weird chicks with giant mohawks walking down the streets of London. Alice was on the fringes of punk, toeing the line as closely as she could without becoming the pariah of Dahlia, West Virginia.

Lucy cleared her throat, looking somewhat concerned as Alice came into view. "Umm . . ." She hesitated, looking to Reb for help. "Hey, Al? You sure you want to wear that?"

Alice paused in the center of the room, looked down at her choice of clothing, then blinked at Lucy, perplexed. "What? Too much?"

Lucy shrugged, looking a little uncomfortable. "It's just that . . . I'm kind of trying to make an impression, you know?"

Alice cocked a hip to the side and tipped her head in a mischievous sort of way, and for half a second she was the hottest chick Reb had ever seen—not his type, but undeniably sexy.

"No, it's perfect," Reb said. "Michael's style."

Lucy still looked unsure, but Alice gave them both a smile, pulled the riveted belt from her hips, and dropped it to the floor. "There," she said, pushing her fingers through her hair. "It takes the edge off. I'm kind of nervous, anyway." She laughed a little.

"Nervous about what?" Lucy asked, but Alice just shook her

head, as if to forget she had said anything. Instead, she stepped across the small living room, ducked into the kitchen, and held up a bottle of red wine.

"We aren't old enough to *officially* bring this, but Ray is. . . ."

Rebel raised an eyebrow in approval. "Good idea," he said. "A party ain't a party without a splash of red."

25

S TILL OUT IN the woods with Misty Dawn, Michael considered spending another night there with her, but decided against it. The bugs were eating him alive. That, and it still seemed important for him to go back home. His return felt heavy with something; maybe promise, maybe ruin. He didn't know, but his gut told him he'd find out if only he would follow his instinct. Michael had heard of that before—someone taking a different way home only to discover they'd avoided a terrible accident, a person missing a flight only to learn later that the plane had crashed upon landing. He had never experienced such a magical incident himself, but he believed it was possible. And so, with that instinct souring his stomach, he drew his hand across the crest of Misty's grave and rose to his feet.

He took his time getting back, weaving in and out of the trees, plucking handfuls of leaves off of branches as he went. The sky shone pale purple, delicate shades of grapefruit-pink streaking the horizon as the sun settled to the west. By the time the lights of the farmhouse sparkled through the few remaining yards of forest, the sky had lost its cotton-candy coloring and had settled into a deep, velvety blue.

Michael hovered along the perimeter of trees just shy of the backyard. Alice's hand-drawn comic book was folded into his back pocket for safekeeping. The fresh mosquito bites up and down his arms were starting to itch. He squinted at the Delta parked alongside the house, but the view was different. Tonight, Wade was bent over his rusty old pickup parked next to Reb's Oldsmobile. Michael crossed the wild grass of the yard with slow, even steps, pausing next to his father's truck. Wade glanced up from beneath the hood, then swiped at his cheek with a greasy palm. The caged work light sitting on the engine block cast strange shadows along the angles of his face. Michael was struck by how old his father suddenly looked. Maybe it was that he hadn't been paying attention, but Wade's hair looked grayer than it did the last time he saw him. A couple of liver spots dotted the skin around his temples. His eyes crinkled at the corners when he turned his face up to give his adopted son a look.

"Damn carburetor's dead," he grumbled. A mundane problem for an ordinary life. For a split second Michael forgot it all—Momma's girls and Misty's grave. For the briefest moment, they were nothing but father and son casting twin scowls at a machine that refused to work, bound by a common goal.

"Might have parts in the shed," Michael announced. "Want me to go look?"

"Already did," Wade said. "Didn't see what I was lookin' for. Probably need to drive out to the yard."

"Shouldn't go while they're open, though. I'll go tell Reb

to get ready. We should probably take some meat for that dog they've got watchin' the place."

"Nah, forget it," Wade told him. "We'll go later. Go on inside. Momma's been waitin' on you."

Michael frowned at that, the mention of Momma a staunch reminder that life was far more complicated than car trouble, that the Morrows were more than a standard gang of yokels. Momma made them special. She made them what they were.

"Did I do somethin' wrong?"

"Dunno. Best go in and find out."

Michael reluctantly turned away from the truck. He would have much rather stayed outside with his dad and worked all night on that truck, so long as he didn't have to go back inside. It would have been a welcome reprieve from knowing that he wasn't normal, that none of them were. Perhaps a conventional task here and there would magically transform them from monsters to people.

Climbing the steps of the back porch, Michael hesitated. The kitchen was dark, which was unusual. The kitchen light burned longer than any other inside the farmhouse. Sometimes it clicked on before the sun rose and glowed bright long after dark. The kitchen was where Michael would forever place his mother in his memory. He'd remember her standing at the stove or peeling potatoes at the counter, her apron strings tied tight around her waist.

He pulled open the screen door and stepped inside the house.

"Momma?"

Scanning the darkness, his vision strained to see through the shadows that had settled like dust bunnies in the corners of the room. He frowned at the bare bulb that hung overhead. He reached up as he passed it. It radiated heat, as though someone had flipped it off only moments before. Michael thought he had seen it burning when he had come through the trees, but he couldn't be sure.

That was when he spotted a flicker of light coming from just down the hall, a warm dancing glow, like firelight. The soft yellow light made the dingy old wallpaper look solemnly pretty—the kind of haunting appeal that only ancient things possessed.

Following the glow, Michael slowly crossed the kitchen and stepped into the hall.

He turned the corner and sucked in a breath of surprise. Golden sparklers burned like stars as they jutted out of a birthday cake sitting on the dining room table. Rebel sat in Misty's old seat, that strange smile of his pulled tight across his lips. Momma stood behind him, her fingers wrapped around the top of the wooden-backed chair. And for the briefest of moments, Michael swore he could see Misty Dawn sitting at the far end of the table, where the shadows were darkest. Her ghost was attending the party, not daring to miss his birthday, even in death.

"Surprise," Reb said. He rose from his seat and met Michael at the head of the table, then patted him on the back as if to wish him well. "We were worried you wouldn't make it. Woulda been a waste of perfectly good cake."

Michael smiled at the sparkling confection despite himself. It shone like a supernova, and again he swore he saw Misty thrown into relief. He blinked, his smile wavering as he did a double take.

"What? You see somethin'?" Reb raised an eyebrow at the darkness on the opposite side of the room.

Michael was ready to shake his head and deny he'd seen anything. It was just a trick of the light, his imagination bringing his sister back for a special occasion. It was easy to forget that she was gone for good. That she wouldn't be playing her records upstairs or dancing in the hallway or beaming at him when he gave her a new piece of pilfered jewelry. But before he had a chance to dismiss it all, a muffled cry came from the far side of the table.

Michael's head snapped to the side.

His heart stopped dead as Rebel's smile morphed into a serpentine leer.

"So, I know you've been havin' doubts," he said. "Stuff about leavin' us, about wantin' to run off in search of somethin' better, whatever that means. So I got to wonderin', why does my baby brother want to go lookin' for somethin' better than what he's already got? What's he missin' that he thinks he can find somewhere else? And then I realized . . . shit, it's probably *my own* damn fault."

Michael was only half-listening over the thud of his heart. His eyes were fixed on the dark side of the room, trying to see past the glare of sparklers and into the shadows there. Reb, however, was a fan of undivided attention. He slapped his hand onto Michael's shoulder and gave it a rough squeeze, drawing his brother back to him.

"I mean, I kind of rub it in your face, huh? The whole adopted thing? That can't feel good. Shit, of *course* you want to leave." Reb almost looked solemn in the flickering glow, but Michael assured himself it was only a trick of the light. Rebel never looked solemn. It was as if he was physically incapable of it. "And now with Misty gone, you're lonely. I admit, I ain't the best big brother I could be."

Michael swallowed, his mouth dry. He couldn't help looking back to the shadows. There was something terrible in that darkness, and he was terrified to know what it was.

"So, to be a better brother, I got you two presents instead of one," Reb announced. With that, he stepped over to the cake and gave it a shove across the tabletop.

Michael watched the plate skitter across the wood, the blinding brightness of the sparklers decaying the gloom.

For a moment, he was sure it was Misty come back from the dead—a miracle, like Jesus resurrected. But then the girl shook her head, trying to cry out past the silver duct tape that covered her mouth. Her hair tumbled across her shoulders as she attempted to wriggle free, but it was no use. She was bound to the chair by loops of tape—wrists to armrests, ankles to chair legs.

"Lucy was supposed to be for me," Rebel explained, "but this is better."

Michael couldn't speak.

His pulse thudded in his ears.

The flare of sparklers hurt his eyes, like looking into the sun.

He turned to face his brother, shook his head in silent refusal.

No, he wouldn't do this.

No, he wouldn't go along with it.

No. He wouldn't.

Not this time.

No way.

His eyes searched the room. Momma remained where she
had been all along, gripping the chair, but Wade was nowhere
to be seen.

"I had a feelin' you'd get overwhelmed. It happens," Reb
said. "You know that rifle you used to hunt with when we were
kids? I got that thing for Christmas one year, and I was so surprised to get it that I ran upstairs and cried all faggy like a girl.
I guess I couldn't get over the fact that it was for me, or maybe I
felt guilty that I was the only one who got somethin' great while
everyone else got shit." He shrugged. "Hell, I don't know, but I
got all goddamn weepy about it and nearly told Wade to take it
back. I guess you could say I was a sensitive little fucker, just like
you." He smacked Michael on the back. "Consider this my way
of sayin' sorry for being such an ass for so long. I think them
fancy folks up in New York City would call it divine inspiration;
a little push in the right direction, since you've been so damn
confused . . ."

When Wade stepped into the dining room, Michael's gaze
darted to him for help, but Wade wasn't alone.

A scream clambered up Michael's throat.

Alice twisted against Wade's grasp, taped up like Lucy,

mascara running down her cheeks. He swore he could hear her yelling his name deep in her throat—desperate pleas for help. Suddenly it all became clear. Wade had been waiting outside, bent over his truck, staking Michael out the way he and Reb scoped out marks. Wade had been waiting for Michael to come home as part of the surprise.

Michael made a sudden move for his father, ready to tear Alice from his grasp, but Rebel intercepted him. He pressed his palms firmly against Michael's shoulders to hold him back, his cold smile dancing in the light.

"Whoa whoa whoa, take it easy, Mikey. Nobody's gonna hurt Alice."

Michael stared wild-eyed at Reb's grinning face.

The room fell into a sickening spin.

His breath came in ragged gasps.

"Calm the fuck down, huh? I worked a long time on this. Don't ruin the fun."

Wade pushed Alice further into the dining room, and she cried harder when she saw Lucy at the far end of the table. The tears in her eyes flashed like wildfire. Her head whipped around to look at Michael for a second time, and despite the tape that covered her mouth from cheek to cheek, her terror was unmistakable.

Reb's fingers dug into Michael's shoulders to keep him in place. "You wanna be a Morrow, don't you? Bound by blood and all that shit? Only problem is, your blood ain't ours. But Lucy's will do."

Momma placed a gingham-checked tea towel onto the table,

unfolding it flap by flap to reveal the same knife she had used on Misty Dawn. The blade winked with a warm orange glow. Both Alice and Lucy released a communal moan of fear and disbelief, but there was no doubt as to what the Morrows expected to happen here. Alice tried to jerk out of Wade's grasp again but she hardly gained an inch. Lucy thrashed against the chair, her face twisted with animalistic fear. But she couldn't move, couldn't so much as make the chair legs rattle against the hardwood floor.

"No," Michael whispered, his gaze frozen on the knife.

Rebel drew in a breath and plucked the blade off of the table with a disappointed look. "Refusin' gifts is rude, Mikey," he murmured. "And, see, I wouldn't mind so much if this whole thing hadn't taken so much effort to put together. It's not easy keepin' somethin' like this a secret when you've got someone shadowin' your every move." He slapped the knife against Michael's chest, the tip pointing up toward his chin, the wooden handle crushed against his sternum. "I guess you could say this gift is nonrefundable."

Reb gave Michael a push toward Lucy, who screeched when they both inched toward her. She fought against her restraints, her face puffy with tears, her hair glued to her wet cheeks.

Michael kept his distance, but Reb continued forward. He stepped behind Lucy, then placed his hands on her shoulders with a thoughtful expression. She shrank away from his touch, but Reb either didn't notice or care. He leaned down, pressed his cheek against hers, and flashed Michael a smile as though the two were posing for a gruesome photograph. Lucy gagged and wept while Rebel waited for Michael to take it all in.

"I told Momma about your plans to leave us, and she got real upset," he explained. "She almost got teary-eyed thinkin' about her baby boy runnin' off into the big bad world. It's dangerous out there, you know." His dour expression grew into wicked amusement. "She got worried, Michael, that maybe you wanted to find your *real* momma, and if you did, you'd forget all about us—forget all about *her*."

Michael's eyes darted to Momma, but Momma's face was blank. It was that same hollow-eyed emptiness he'd seen just before she dragged the knife across Misty's throat.

"That's a common fear of parents who adopt kids, you know," Reb continued. "Losin' the kid they raised as their own to the assholes who dumped 'em like a bag of trash along the side of the road. You were too young to remember, but *I* remember. You, sittin' out there with a sign, sellin' rocks, like you were tryin' to prove you were worth somethin' . . ."

"I don't wanna leave." Michael spoke the words into the room, imploring for her to believe him. "Momma, I don't . . . I swear, I don't." He did, but he wouldn't. Not if it cost Alice and Lucy their lives. He'd let that dream go. He'd forget the postcards. Forget Times Square. Forget that bright-pink hotel on the beach.

"Except you're lyin'." Rebel looked disappointed. He stepped away from Lucy and returned to Michael's side, looping his arm around his shoulders. "We all know you're lyin', and that's against the rules. Now you gotta make it up to us. Time to prove you really are worth somethin' after all."

The room tilted on its axis.

Had Reb not been close, Michael would have toppled against the table, his knees suddenly refusing to serve their purpose.

Reb tapped his finger against the blade of the knife that Michael hugged against his chest, then leaned over to speak quietly into his ear. "You take that and you show Momma she raised you right. Or forget all about it and tell us that you don't wanna be part of this family after all."

"And if I do that . . . ?" Michael asked, his words parched, cracking beneath the strain of his own fear. He already knew the answer, but he had to hear it to know it was true. He needed to be reassured that this wasn't some terrible nightmare, that he hadn't fallen asleep next to Misty's grave, that this wasn't his worst fear realized, conjured by an overactive imagination, by grief and anger and stifled hate.

"Well, if you do that, it ain't gonna be such a happy birthday," Reb murmured. "If you do that, you and Alice are gonna be together forever, but not in the way you want. And Lucy's gonna stay right here." He winked at her. "After all, there ain't no use in wastin' a perfectly good strawberry blonde."

Sick with the thud of his own heartbeat, Michael shot a look over at Alice. As soon as their eyes met, she shook her head frantically as if to say no—whatever Reb had told him, he didn't have to do it. There were other options. But that was wrong and Michael knew it. There was no choice. It was down to Lucy or to the three of them together. Alice still had a chance. She would hate him, but he could still save her, offer her some shred of salvation.

"Do it, brother." Any shade of amusement was now gone from Rebel's voice. He was all business, and his patience was waning. "Prove yourself and we'll keep Alice in the basement for you. She'll probably hate you for a while . . . but if she don't love you yet, I'm sure she'll learn."

Michael took a single step forward.

Alice screamed behind her gag in protest.

Lucy thrashed and wept, desperate to get away, but the chair didn't budge.

Michael hesitated as she fought to loosen her restraints, hoping that the tape would give, that somehow she'd jump up and make a mad dash for an exit without someone tackling her to the ground.

Reb slapped an encouraging hand between Michael's shoulder blades. "You've seen 'em struggle before. She ain't any different."

But she *was* different. She was Alice's best friend. If Michael killed her, Alice's life would be spared—at least for the moment. And that was all he needed, a moment; just enough time to figure out how to get her out of there, how to get her free. But it also meant that Alice would hate him. She'd never look at him the same way again.

"I'm gettin' bored here," Reb complained.

Michael swallowed, his fingers tightening around the hilt of the blade. He considered spinning around and slicing where Reb's leg met his torso, cutting right through his femoral artery and watching him drop like a wet rag. But it would have been no good. As soon as he did it, Wade would be on him. And

Momma wouldn't spare any of them. Even if by some miracle he managed to get away, he'd be running from that farmhouse alone. Alice and Lucy would be dead.

But if he killed Lucy, maybe he and Alice could live.

"Do it," Reb growled behind him. He gave Michael a forward shove.

Michael stumbled toward Lucy, who was now staring at him with impossibly wide, imploring eyes.

No choice.

"Do it."

No way around it.

"Fucking *do it*."

It had to be done.

Michael lifted the knife with a shaky hand.

Alice exhaled a muffled cry.

Lucy stared up at the blade, her face a mask of desperation.

Michael squeezed his eyes shut.

"Do it or Alice is dead," Reb said. "But not before I bury myself inside her."

Michael's arm began to wobble. His fingers began to loosen, ready to drop the knife.

An involuntary act of defiance.

A revolt.

"Fine," Rebel hissed. He was suddenly moving across the dining room toward Alice and Wade. Alice gave a shriek when she saw him coming. Michael shot a look to his side, watching Reb approach the pair with impatient steps. Reb reached into his pocket and drew out his switchblade.

"No," Michael said, but there was no volume in his voice. "No!" he repeated, but it was nothing but a whisper, nothing but Reb upon Alice.

Alice weeping.

The blade popping out of its handle.

Michael turned back to Lucy.

Every sound in the room was muffled.

Every move elongated like a slow-motion movie reel.

Lucy shook her head, her hair fiery in the muted light, her eyes squeezed shut as the butcher knife cut through the air.

Her eyes darted open.

The blade slid into her stomach.

Shock replaced fear.

She stared at him, wordless.

You killed me. You . . .

He drew the knife out of her flesh, deep burgundy blossoming beneath her billowy top, weighing down the silken fabric with its heavy, sopping wetness.

He pulled back.

Stabbed again.

Lucy threw her head back, a cry ripping from inside her throat.

He thrust the knife into her again. A third time. A fourth. A sixth and a tenth. Until her moans fell silent.

He stabbed until he was sure she was dead.

Until the suffering was through.

Only then did the knife fall from his grasp and clang against the floor.

Michael stumbled backward. His eyes were fixed on the dead girl taped to the dining room chair. A pool of blood bloomed around her feet. It dripped down the wooden chair legs and crawled between the floorboard cracks. His attention only wavered when Alice released a sound so desperate that he was sure Rebel had killed her anyway. But Reb was standing a few feet away, his switchblade clean, his eyes fixed on Michael, that leering grin having returned.

Wade shoved Alice out of the room. Michael urged himself to follow, but he couldn't move. Momma silently drifted out as well, mostly likely to help Wade with the storm door, with the chains beneath the house, with securing Alice to the wall down there.

They left Rebel and Michael staring at one another, a dead girl between them. Finally, Reb reached into his pocket and slid a folded scrap of paper onto the table along with the keys to the Delta, the eight-ball keychain smacking the tabletop.

"Your *real* present, from me to you," he said. "Happy birthday, baby brother."

Reb stepped out of the dining room, and Michael was left staring at the keys. It was only after he swept the folded scrap of paper off the table that he realized the Delta was merely a means to get to his gift.

On the paper, a crude map: a sketched drawing of where Michael was headed.

A lopsided little house, green shutters flanking the windows.

26

M ICHAEL HAD DRIVEN a few times in his life, but despite the foreignness of Rebel's car, he didn't have time to be nervous. He climbed into the driver's seat, shoved the key into the ignition, and threw the car into reverse. The Delta peeled down the dirt road toward the highway that would take him to the address scribbled across the top of the paper. The idea of that house he had gazed upon from atop a peaceful hill tied his stomach into knots. The thought of running down to the basement to check on Alice had crossed his mind, but he hardly considered it. The key to Alice's safety was in that cottage ten miles away. He understood now that everything was happening by careful design; this was Rebel's master plan. If Michael wavered, Reb was liable to call the whole thing off and carve Alice a brand-new smile.

But by the time he reached the intersection where the dirt road met a lonely West Virginia highway, he leaned back in the driver's seat, shifted into park, and fell apart. The sobs tore out of him, one after the other, coming so quick he couldn't catch his breath. He pressed his forehead against the steering wheel and cried into his blood-streaked hands. For Alice and how scared she must have been. For Lucy and that final pleading look she had given him, knowing that he was the only one in the world who could have spared her life . . . and yet he hadn't. He wept for all the girls, from his present to his past, each one unique in their own way. Their smiles turning into screams. Their wrists and ankles bound. Their faces turned up to the sky in search of God—as if he could possibly exist in a world where men like Rebel and Michael Morrow were allowed to live.

He grabbed the steering wheel with tear-streaked palms and squeezed it tight, his knuckles turning white. He tried to shake it free of the dashboard, as if that momentary flare of aggression could somehow subdue the pain he felt.

Thoughts of Alice shook him out of his temporary state of turmoil. As if summoning another magic trick, she managed to reach out to him from her prison beneath the farmhouse and lull him into a strange state of emotionally wrecked calm. If he followed the steps, he could help her. If he placated Reb by doing what he said, he could save her, and maybe himself.

When he arrived at his destination, he pulled into the gravel driveway and stopped a good distance away. He stared at a house he recognized yet couldn't believe he was seeing again. The place had once given him a strange sort of peace, but now only filled him with dread. He sat motionless for what felt like forever, trying to convince himself that he had the wrong place, even though there was no question that it was the right one.

Lights burned inside, as though someone was home, but Michael knew it couldn't be. The same lights had been on the night they abducted the woman who lived there. They'd been on for days, as if in memorial to the house's former owner. He imagined the woman coming home, covered in blood, dragging her feet. Perhaps she was just inside, sitting in front of the TV, a scorned ghost waiting for her murderers to return.

Michael cut the engine but left the keys in the ignition. He pushed open the door and rose from the car. And for whatever reason—whether his senses were heightened or it really was warmer than usual—the evening heat hit him head on. It was heavy and oppressive, trying to push him down into the earth, to pin him where he stood. Something was trying to keep him from moving forward with whatever plan Rebel had set in motion. If it hadn't been for Alice, he would have stood there for the rest of his life, staring at the lights that seemed so melancholy in the way they shone through closed curtains. He stared at the front door they had left open days before, undisturbed by a single visitor.

He left the car door open and the dome light glowing in his wake, as though doing so would somehow help him get back to where he had come from. Gravel popped beneath the soles of his boots as he passed the small bistro table and chair beneath the bowed branches of a pine. Birdhouses swung from jute rope slung across the tree's branches, its leaves shivering in the breeze. Stopping near the front entrance, Michael stared at the slash of light that shone through the open space between the door and the jamb. He remembered how the woman had fought. How she had thrashed in Reb's arms. How she had breathed Michael's name into the quiet of the bedroom.

Please, Michael, don't . . .

He was afraid to go inside, but he pushed open the door enough to slip in anyway. His heart leapt into his throat when a man's voice swam into his ears. It was professional-sounding, like a cop's or an FBI agent's. The voice spoke in low, gruff tones. At first he was sure he'd walked in at the worst possible moment. The police were scoping out the place. Someone had reported the woman as missing. They were there, investigating, looking for clues, and there was Michael, stepping right into their arms. He twisted where he stood, ready to bolt out the door. But he stopped when the voice was cut off by a commercial. A Dr Pepper jingle played into the room.

Michael peeked around the corner of the foyer and into the living room. The place was empty. The television was on.

He inhaled slowly and stepped further inside, his arms at his sides, his hands balled into anxious fists. He didn't understand what he was doing there, had no idea what he was looking for. Rebel had left no instruction, only an address, as though whatever Michael was supposed to find was so obvious that clueing him in would have spoiled the game.

The interior was quaint—a perfect match to the exterior that had given him a fleeting sense of peace. The living room was simple. A couch and an armchair faced an entertainment center. An open can of soda sat on a coaster next to a bookmarked paperback novel. The NBC peacock flashed on the screen before some sort of made-for-TV movie took its place. Michael's gaze drifted to the fireplace and the mantel above it, drawn to a framed photo that sat there. He approached slowly, careful not to upset anything, and stopped in front of a family photo. A mother and father smiled at the camera. A little girl in a pink dress was balanced on the mom's hip. A little boy threw a peace sign at the camera.

Lights burned bright in the kitchen. He left the fireplace behind and entered a simple room with Formica countertops and linoleum floors. A pot rack hung from the ceiling above a small kitchen island. It housed a collection of cookbooks as well as another framed photograph. A glass-encased pillar candle sat next to it. This time the little boy was front and center. He was hugging the leg of a man who looked as though he'd just crawled out from the furthest depths of the earth. A mole person. The man mugged for the camera while the boy wore his father's orange hard hat, a light attached to the front. The frame was engraved: FOREVER WITH YOU.

Michael rubbed the back of his neck as he turned away, a slow-growing panic burgeoning at the base of his guts. What if he didn't figure out the puzzle? What if there was no puzzle at all? What if all this had been a trick to get Michael out of the house? What if Rebel never intended to let Alice live?

He turned in a circle, struggling to see the clues, to find anything of significance that would lead him to an answer.

That was when he saw a stark blot of white against the hall-way's wood-paneled wall. A folded sheet of paper was tucked beneath the edge of a picture frame.

Stepping into the hallway, Michael hesitated. His fingers hovered mere centimeters from the paper, stalling, knowing that whatever the note revealed would somehow change his life. And then, as if that very thought spurred him on, he snatched it from the wall and unfolded it.

Reb's sharp, angular handwriting was scrawled across the page: WELCOME HOME.

The photo it had been tucked beneath was of the same small family—Mom, Dad, and two young kids posing in front of that very same green-shuttered house. Dad had hoisted the little boy onto his shoulder. The boy's arms jutted out like a superhero about to take flight. Mom was laughing as though Dad had just told a particularly funny joke. Dad wore a charming half-smile as the toddler in Mom's arms reached out to her father, wanting to join her brother higher up. Michael looked down the length of the hall. The walls were covered in similar framed photographs, offering to tell the family's story, much like Alice's comic-strip panels.

The next photo was of the two kids, chocolate Easter bunnies clutched in their hands, their smiling faces smeared with melted confection. They were small—the boy maybe three or four, the little girl younger than that. But before the boy could grow into his sneakers, he vanished from the pictures like a ghost.

Mom and Dad now smiled for the camera with only the little girl between them, a Christmas tree blazing behind them. But Mom's smile was distant, and Dad looked like he was faking it. Eventually, as though succumbing to their sorrow, neither parent appeared in the pictures at all. The photos only featured a dark-haired girl. A shot of her on the swings at school. Another of her at a birthday party at a pizza place. Each one showed her age in succession until, coming to one where the girl was maybe ten or eleven, Michael could no longer pull his gaze away. There was something terrifyingly familiar about the girl's face, about her smile.

The master bedroom was nothing special—a chest of drawers, a few bedside tables, and a bed that was halfway undone. The comforter rested half on and half off the mattress. Michael looked away from the bed, the woman's panicked expression flashing through his head. A photograph of the little boy occupied one of the bedside tables. Another glass-housed pillar candle sat beside it, almost completely burned away.

Michael stalked across the hallway to another door—this one closed—and peeked his head inside. The room was dark, illuminated only by moonlight, yet he could see right away that it belonged to a girl—the one in the photos, all grown up. Various band posters covered the walls. A white, black, and red striped comforter was pulled across the bed, and pillows of varying sizes were propped up against the headboard. A dresser with a large mirror sat against one of the walls. Its top was littered with small trinkets, a stack of eight-track tapes, a few hardcover novels, a jewelry box, another photo.

It was this picture that made him lose his breath. His fingers crumpled the note in his hand as the world faded in on itself. Everything but that photo blurred.

Alice and Lucy smiled into the camera, their arms around each other's shoulders. Alice's hair was chopped into a pixie cut. She beamed at him through the glass of the picture frame.

Michael didn't get it. He couldn't put it together. His mind reeled around the details, refusing to put them in the right order, shielding him from the truth beneath a haze of confusion. But clarity eventually moved in, burning the haze away, leaving Michael gaping at the photograph in front of him.

He stumbled out of the room, his gaze now snagging on a picture in the hall—Mom again, a golden *M* shining in the hollow of her throat.

The woman they had abducted.

Screaming in the backyard, struggling for life.

Michael dragging her down the basement steps.

Hanging her upside down.

Cutting her throat.

Bleeding her dry.

He pressed a hand to the wall, steadying himself, sending a few pictures of a younger Alice to the floor. He tottered down the hall and back into the living room. Stopping to grab hold of the back of the couch, he shot a look to the open front door, noticing the entryway table he had missed upon entering the house. There, upon that long, skinny table, was nothing short of a shrine to the little boy who had disappeared from under this roof. The table was packed full of framed photographs—some of just the boy, others of him and his parents. A carefully arranged candle garden sat upon a metal plate in the center of the display. The largest pillar was stamped with a scripted *M* in gold relief—a perfect match to the necklace Mom had worn.

M for Michael, Misty whispered into his ear.

We don't talk much, Alice reminded him.

Welcome home, Ray told him.

Michael stared at the photograph, at the golden *M* he had buried with Misty Dawn upon that hill. He tore away from the candles and spun around to look at the living room, suddenly hit by a sense of something he didn't understand. A memory he couldn't place. The scent of something sweet, like maple syrup and pine. The vague recollection of that fireplace decked in evergreen and Christmas lights. The television playing Saturday morning cartoons. The earthy smell of soot.

When he looked back to the picture, the little boy's face didn't belong to a stranger, but to the person he knew best.

He fled the house and into the front yard, his heart hammering, nausea taking over. The heat punched him in the chest. He had to squat in the grass, his fingers digging into the soil.

This had been his house.

She had been his mother.

The woman he had taped up and forced into the trunk of Ray's car had been *his mother*.

Please, Michael, don't . . .

A flash of the basement.

Of latching the delicate gold chain around Misty's neck.

Of Rebel's leper grin as he refilled Michael's bowl with a second helping of . . .

Oh God.

Hot vomit spewed from his throat, splashing across the grass and the tips of his boots. His stomach cramped, doubling him over. He threw up again as tears ran down his face, streaking his cheeks.

He cried out into the night, his yell a wounded animal's wail.

Alice . . . she was his sister—a relation that Rebel had purposefully sought out and twisted in his favor. The girl who had finally made Michael wish for more was someone he could never have.

He vomited a third time, his body wracked with bone-creaking tenseness. Overcome with a sudden bout of chills, he shuddered so violently that he was sure he was in the beginning throes of a seizure. Epileptic shock.

He kneeled in the darkness, long strands of hair framing his sweat- and tear-drenched face. Staring across the yard, his vision drifted along the ground until it settled upon the roots of a cut-down tree. The axe handle jutted up at an angle, winking in the moonlight. It was a weapon that had been unwittingly left for him by his birth mother. An instrument of destruction to set all wrong things right.

Michael's fingers touched the dirt, the sick still burning at the back of his throat. His eyes blurred behind incredulous tears. Gathering himself as best he could, he hefted himself into an upright position. His stomach spasmed with another wave of queasiness, but he forced the feeling to the back of his mind as he pressed forward. Reaching the stump, he grabbed the axe with both hands and pulled. It came free without a fight, which was exactly how he expected the Morrows to fall.

They'd never see him coming.

He was immune to them now.

Cleansed by his own hate.

27

MICHAEL PULLED THE Oldsmobile onto the side of the dirt road a quarter mile away from the farmhouse. Sliding out of the car, he put the keys into his pocket and opened the trunk. He stared down into the small chamber that had housed so many squirming, frantic women, a trunk that smelled of urine and fear. It was empty now, save for two things: a roll of silver duct tape that represented his past, and his mother's axe, which represented an inevitable future.

He grabbed the axe, slammed the trunk shut, and began to walk the rutted road that would lead him to his false home one final time.

The farmhouse looked almost silvery in the moonlight. There was something grotesque about it. Every angle was slightly skewed, as though the place belonged in a particularly dark fairy tale. Its odious appearance was fitting, seeing as to how it held Snow White captive in its bowels. Michael increased his grip on the axe handle as he approached. He skimmed the side of the house, passed Wade's truck, with its still-raised hood and its carburetor removed, and climbed the back porch steps with silent feet.

The house was dark. No flicker of firelight from the dining room. No sound of a phantom record playing from behind his dead sister's door. The only disturbance was the momentary creaking of stairs as Michael climbed, one step after the other, stalking upward to the second-story hallway. He nudged his bedroom door open and peeked inside. Empty.

He proceeded to Misty's room. His heart twisted at the memory of her lounging in its threshold, tying her macramé knots while she played album after album. He'd have done just about anything to hear some ABBA or Neil Diamond right then. Even Simon & Garfunkel would do. He turned the knob and let the door swing open. It too stood vacant in the dark.

Michael checked the bathroom before stopping in front of the final door at the far end of the hall—Rebel's bedroom. Hefting the axe up to rest on his shoulder, he readied himself to use it, then reached for the doorknob. He didn't understand what had driven his brother to such madness. What terrible evil had Michael committed to turn Reb into such a demon? Despite the fact that they had both grown up in a house of horrors with a monster as a mother, Rebel's attack was personal. Somehow, Michael was to blame.

His room was empty, just like the others—nothing but an unmade bed and an old night table littered with empties and crumpled cigarette packs. He turned away from the room, half-expecting to find Reb standing at the opposite side of the hall, but there was no one. Michael was alone.

He narrowed his eyes, steeled his nerves, and stalked down

its length before descending the stairs. His next destination would yield results. Downstairs, at the opposite end of the house, Momma and Wade were tucked into bed. He silently unlatched the door and pushed it open with the blade of the axe. The all-encompassing darkness assured him that Wade was standing in the shadows somewhere on the opposite side of the room, a shotgun pointed squarely at Michael's chest. But his eyes adjusted quickly, the moonlight making the room glow blue. He made out the silhouettes of two people on a sleigh bed as old as the house itself. There, in the dark luster of night, Wade and Claudine Morrow appeared as nothing more than a serenely sleeping couple. Michael wondered if their eyes needed to be open to be what they were; was a killer still a killer while asleep? Did Momma see blood and hear the screaming in her dreams?

Michael hesitated, a sudden pang of guilt turning the axe heavy in his hands. He was starting to see how he could separate himself from the responsibility of the things he'd done in his life. The fear. The manipulation. The sense of duty that had been beaten into him. Without the Morrows, he would have died in the Appalachian hills, cold and alone. But the newfound ability to disconnect was burdened with a question: If Michael was allowed to slough the wrongs from his shoulders because he was never a Morrow at all, did that mean Momma could blame the abuse she had suffered for turning her into what she had become?

Sometimes things only make sense in retrospect, Alice reminded him.

Alice. Smart. Beautiful. The only real family he had left.

He detached his doubts from his thoughts and his thoughts from his body and moved to the foot of the bed. Wade lay on his back, breathing through an open mouth. Michael raised the axe high. Its heaviness vanished, as though he was being helped by an invisible hand. Adjusting his grip on the wooden handle—a baseball player ready to swing—he took a defensive stance, one that promised no chance of him losing his balance should Wade spring out of bed like a jack-in-the-box.

The head of the axe pulled his grip back behind his shoulder. And then he swung.

A pang of sorrow hit him as the axe flew through the air. It was a momentary jab of self-reproach reminding him that, of the three Morrows that remained, Wade was the lesser of evils. He had always been tender with Michael, teaching him how to hunt. But now, in split-second hindsight, Michael made the connection—the reason *why* Wade had taught him how to field dress the animals he caught as a kid.

Every kindness, no matter how small, was anchored in blood.

Wade was as guilty as the rest of them. By association. By silence. By ambivalence.

The axe blade connected with Wade's chest.

The crack of fracturing bone sliced through the silence.

Wade sat up, his mouth agape, a loud *hehhhh* rushing from his throat as air flew from his lungs. Michael gave the axe a firm backward pull to loosen the blade. As soon as the cutting edge was freed from Wade's chest, a geyser of glistening, moonlit blood poured down his stained tank top. His mouth worked like a fish's—silent, opening and closing. Their eyes connected in the pale darkness as Wade waited for the next blow, but Michael stepped away from the bed.

Momma had bolted upright, startled by the sound of her husband's chest caving in.

"Wade?"

She strained to see in the dark for a moment, not noticing Michael, who was making his way to her side of the bed.

"Wade?!"

The emotion in her voice caught him off guard. There was more feeling in it than he'd ever heard before. Her hands flew to Wade's chest and shoulders as her husband fell back onto his pillow with a gurgling sound. Blood bubbled up from between his lips. His eyes stared blankly up at the ceiling. Momma gasped, her blood-smeared hands pressing over her mouth to silence a scream. Michael couldn't help but watch her with baffled interest. It was strange to see a woman who had been so cold finally have a human response.

"Momma."

Michael spoke the word from the shadows of the room.

She jumped at the sound, reeled around, and stared wide-eyed into the darkness, but she said nothing.

Michael stepped closer to the bed, showing himself, the dull metal of the axe blade catching the moonlight.

Her face pulled into a taut look of surprise. She was expecting someone else. Since their numbers were low, Michael could only assume her suspicion had immediately landed on Rebel's shoulders. He wished he was more like his phony brother just then. He wanted to manage a cold, emotionless smile, but he couldn't pull it off. This was the part where Michael was supposed to say something witty that would terrify her even more, quips that Reb could deliver like a seasoned actor.

Here's Johnny!

But Michael hadn't ever been as witty as Reb, and his silence appeared to be frightening enough.

Momma leapt from the bed. Michael was sure she was half-blind—her eyes hadn't had time to adjust to the night. But she managed to grab the bedside lamp off the stand and tear the plug from the wall. She held it out in front of her, as though trying to invoke the spirit of Thomas Edison, but she called a different name.

"Ray!"

The syllable left her throat in an ear-splitting screech, but Michael knew Rebel wouldn't come. This too was part of Reb's design.

A part of him wanted to revolt, to let Momma live just to screw up his brother's plans, but he couldn't do it. Letting Momma go raised too many what-ifs, and Alice needed a guarantee.

"Michael," she gasped, "what are you doin'?" She shot a desperate glance back at Wade, her face twisting with emotion. "What have you done?" she whispered. "What have you done?" She shook her head, as if coming to a realization. "It's okay. Michael, it's okay. We'll take care of this. Don't worry, Momma will make it right."

The question slipped.

"Like you did with Misty?"

"Is that what this is about?" Momma lowered the lamp an inch, as if finally able to see him more clearly now. She furrowed her eyebrows at the boy she'd stolen and called her own. "Misty Dawn got what she had comin'."

"I'd ask if she was even yours," Michael murmured, "but she looked too much like you to belong to anyone else."

Momma's eyes went hard. The pain of losing Wade only moments before drained from her face. The monster he knew to be his mother stared out at him from inside its human disguise. Michael tightened his grip on the axe, his mouth going dry at seeing the switch flip from distress to volatile madness.

"We saved your life," she hissed. "You best remember that, boy."

"Did you even know?" he asked, the axe pulled back over his shoulder, the blade hovering inches from the ceiling. "That woman from a few nights back, did you know who she was?"

Momma narrowed her eyes, but it wasn't a glare as much as it was her fending off confusion.

"And Alice," he said.

"Put it down," she told him, the lamp held high, her free hand stretched out ahead of her, ready to ward off any oncoming blows. "You wouldn't hurt your own momma, now would you?"

Michael's heart knotted, squelching a few beats before starting up again.

He stared at the woman he had considered his mother for

the entirety of his memory and shook his head—a response that seemed to give Claudine a glimmer of hope.

She lowered the lamp a little, taking a backward step toward the wall, waiting for Michael to do the same. But instead of re-examining his intent, he murmured a response—"Not if I had known it, no"—and brought the axe down in a wide, swift curve.

The blade caught Momma's shoulder, embedding itself an inch deep in flesh and bone. A scream tore from her, guttural and wailing, but that didn't sway him. He'd heard those types of sounds all his life. She had taught him to ignore any pleas for mercy, and he didn't intend on letting her down now.

He swung again, but she ducked out of the way. The blade struck the back wall with a splintering crack. The lamp caught him on the side of the head, its heavy ceramic base thudding against his temple, but Momma didn't have the strength to hit him hard enough. The lamp crashed to the floor, shattering at her bare feet. Michael crushed ceramic shards beneath the heavy soles of his boots and reeled back once more. The razor edge of his weapon lodged itself in the soft tissue of her side. Blood sprayed across the room in a sideways fan. It spattered the walls and the bedsheets, glittering in the pale light that filtered through the dirty window. She caught herself on the bedpost and cried out in agony, her nightgown blooming red. For a moment, Michael saw her not as his false mother, but as the girl Rebel had suggested she'd once been: terrified, abused, cowering in her own hell.

As if reading his mind, she struggled to gasp a handful of words past her pain, pleading for mercy.

"It ain't my fault, Michael."

He wanted to feel sorry for her as she wept, wanted to be big enough to say that he understood. But he was done with lying.

As he pulled the axe back, she raised her hands to protect herself, her sobs coming freely now.

"Please," she begged. "I never meant to hurt no one."

Michael squeezed his eyes shut.

And then he choked out "I'm sorry," and brought the axe down for a third and final time.

Her cries came to an abrupt stop. Michael blinked against the back spray of blood that misted his arms, his T-shirt, his face. He wiped at his cheek with his forearm, then pulled at the axe handle to retrieve his weapon. When it wouldn't come loose, he placed a booted foot against Momma's chest, readjusted his grip, and gave it another tug, loosening it from her skull.

.   .   .

Michael stumbled out onto the back porch, the night's heat mingling with the scent of blood and iron. He had to get down to the storm cellar, but he stopped to lean against the porch balustrade. The nausea steamrolled him. His chest heaved, the air so smotheringly hot that, for a moment, he was sure it was too thick to breathe. And now, with adrenaline at a momentary lull, his head started to hurt. Momma hadn't knocked him out with that lamp, but a goose egg was already growing above his left temple, like an ingrown devil's horn finally trying to break free.

He forced himself down the porch steps and into the grass, stepped around the side of the house, and stopped in front of the cellar's storm door. His queasiness intensified as he stared at the weatherworn wood and the rusted hinges. The deadbolt was unfastened, which meant Rebel was down there. He wouldn't have left it unlocked had he been anywhere else.

A sense of foreboding washed over him, one Michael had become all too familiar with after a lifetime of threats of abandonment. But this feeling was stronger. More urgent. Almost paralyzing in its severity. So savagely intense it threatened to double him over again. The axe nearly slipped from his fingers as he stared at that door. He imagined Alice naked. Upside down. Half-skinned but still alive. That room, once a cold, dank gray, would now be a vibrant, living red. The walls and the floor would be painted in her blood while Rebel grinned up the staircase like a hyena.

Another round of vomit roiled in his stomach, threatening to come up. He crouched in the grass and tried to steady his breathing. He reminded himself that those sinister images were nothing but a reflection of his own terror. They were his fears brought to life by a vivid imagination. "She's alive," he whispered, trying to convince himself that, after all this planning, Reb wouldn't just kill her, not without an audience. Not if Michael wasn't there to see it.

He shifted the axe from his right hand to his left and hefted himself up to his feet, using the weapon like a cane. Wrapping his free hand around the rusted door pull, he was overcome by another wave of hesitation. If Alice was still alive, she'd have had time to process what had happened to Lucy. She'd been down there long enough to look around, to see the hooks, the chains, the knives, and put it all together. As soon as she laid eyes on Michael, fear would warp her features. He'd never see her smile again. If they both survived this, he would be the nightmare that would haunt her dreams.

With his hand still thrust through the storm-door handle, he reconsidered going down there. He could walk away from all the madness—a move Reb would never see coming. Perhaps, in time, Michael could forget the way the axe blade had sunk into Wade's chest and how Momma had begged for her life before she had died. Maybe, somehow, he could dull those memories with the knowledge that he'd done the world a favor, saving countless lives by wiping those murderers from the face of the earth. But that would still leave Rebel to prowl the streets, a man who would forever be a killer. And of course, it would still leave Alice—a girl he would never forget, no matter how much time passed or how far he ran. His taking off would still leave her in that basement, locked in with a monster, abandoned by Michael, who, for the first time in his life, had a shot at being the hero.

He pulled open the door and let it slip from his hand. It fell back against the ground with a dry crack, the old hinges groaning against the shudder of wood. The light was on down there—a weak and sickly yellow burn of an old, bare bulb. Michael shifted the axe from his left hand to his right and began his descent.

Halfway down, he spotted Alice cowering in the corner of

the room. Her wrists were still taped together, but they were also bound by a length of rope that had been knotted to a metal O-ring screwed into the wall. She was covered in grime, as though Wade had pushed her into the dirt outside before dragging her down the stairs. Her jeans were ripped beneath her right knee. A gash winked in the muted light from behind dark denim, but otherwise she looked uninjured. Intact.

Michael's gaze darted from one end of the room to the other, searching for signs of Rebel, but his brother was nowhere to be found. His absence made the hairs on the back of Michael's neck bristle. The last thing he had expected was one final chance to be alone with her. He hadn't anticipated an opportunity to explain himself. To tell her how sorry he was.

"Alice . . ." His voice was weak, but it easily breached the silence of the cellar.

She jerked her head up from between her arms and stared at him with wide, disbelieving eyes. Because how dare he show his face after what he'd done to Lucy? How dare he approach her ever again? Michael moved down the remaining risers, hesitating before stepping onto the concrete floor. She looked away, curling into herself as much as she could.

"I'm not gonna hurt you," he said, only to realize how ridiculous it sounded. He was covered in blood and carrying an axe. She would have been crazy to believe him, but he was still compelled to convince her. He let the weapon slip from his fingers and moved to the wooden bench where he stored his tools. Once there, he pulled open a drawer and retrieved a knife. Alice peeked up from behind her arms again. But this time, with

Michael so much closer and the axe replaced by an even more frightening nine-inch blade, she began to struggle. A whimper escaped from behind the tape that still covered her mouth.

Michael approached her with slow, deliberate steps. He squatted next to her and shot a look over his shoulder, checking to see if Rebel had finally arrived, knowing it was only a matter of time before he appeared. When Michael's hand brushed her arm, Alice began to screech. Desperate to get him away from her, she kicked at him with her combat boots, the laces flying wildly as they whipped through the air.

"Stop," he said, trying to catch her feet with his free hand, but Alice kicked even harder, straight into the knife he had brought to free her from her bonds. The edge of the blade slashed across a denim-wrapped calf, immediately drawing blood.

"Stop it!" he hissed beneath his breath, dropping the knife to restrain her legs with both hands.

Unable to kick at him any longer, Alice threw her head back and sobbed.

"You just did that yourself," he told her. The cut to her leg was deep, bleeding fast into the dark fabric. "That wasn't me."

He went back to the workbench, digging through one of the drawers until he found a dirty rag. Tearing it in half, he closed in on her again. He tied it tight around her leg, and when he looked up at her again, her expression had gone placid. He swallowed, reached out his hand, and pulled the duct tape from her mouth.

Screaming would have done her no good, but Michael hoped she wouldn't yell regardless.

"I told you," he said quietly, "I'm not gonna hurt you."

Alice said nothing. She turned her head away from him and began to cry instead.

"I'm so sorry," he murmured, the sound of her tears twisting him up. "I never meant for any of this to happen. I didn't know. It was Rebel, he . . ."

If she was listening, Michael couldn't tell. His excuses made him feel stupid. They felt like hollow half-truths. Of course he hadn't meant for Alice to get hurt, but claiming that he hadn't known? That was nothing short of a lie. Reb and Michael had broken the rules together. And Michael had gone along with it because his emotions had blinded him. Alice had infected him with hope.

"I'm gonna cut you free," he said, picking the knife up from the floor. "But you gotta promise me you won't run."

Alice shot him an incredulous look, as though he was nuts for asking her to stay put.

"This isn't my idea," he explained. "But I don't know where Reb is, and if you go out there . . ." He clenched the muscles of his jaw, his gaze meeting hers. "Just, please don't run out there, okay? I don't know where he is. We're gonna get out of here together, but you gotta trust me. Okay?"

She watched him with terrified eyes as he worked the tip of the knife beneath the rope and cut it free. Her still-taped hands dropped to the floor and she immediately skittered away from him, frightened, an animal in need of escape.

"You killed Lucy."

The accusation tore out of her in a sob so raw it stung.

"You killed my best friend, you son of a bitch!"

She threw her weight against him, tried to barrel through him like a runaway semi through a chain-link fence. Still crouched, he wasn't prepared for the sudden shift of weight. He had to catch himself to keep from tumbling backward. His momentary loss of footing gave her the opportunity to make a break for the staircase. For a split second, Michael was paralyzed by indecision. Was he supposed to stop her so that he could protect her, or let her run so she could get as far away from that house as she could?

Alice's boots thumped against the splintered risers. She was nearly at the top when a breathless gasp escaped her throat, and a single-word greeting made Michael's blood run cold.

"Howdy."

Rebel's tone was weirdly jovial.

Michael scrambled to his feet, the knife still clamped in his right hand. He looked at it as if seeing it for the first time, then shot a look across the room to the axe he had abandoned close to the stairs. That was a better bet. It would let him keep his distance. One good hit and Reb would be down for the count.

The muscles in his legs tensed as he let the knife fall to the floor with a *clang*. He bounded toward the axe and the stairs simultaneously, ready to finish this once and for all. But he stalled out when Alice screamed. His eyes darted upward just in time to see Reb's arms piston away from him.

Alice cried out as she fell back.

Michael flashed back to her mother, *their* mother—how her

corpse had slipped and tumbled down to the concrete floor, her neck cracking in the silent gloom.

Distracted by Alice's yell, the tip of Michael's boot connected with the axe handle and it went spiraling across the floor like a faulty boomerang. He jutted out his arms as Alice pinwheeled through the air, her bound hands offering no hope of purchase. For a moment, he was sure he'd miss her. She'd hit the ground and snap her neck—like mother, like daughter—and then everyone Michael had ever cared about would be gone.

But he caught her. A momentary flush of victory swelled up his chest, but Alice cut his triumph short when she recoiled from his touch.

"Oh, goddamnit," Rebel muttered with a roll of the eyes. "My brother, the big hero."

"I know what you did." Michael backed away from the staircase as Reb descended into the basement. His gaze skimmed the ground, searching for the axe. He caught sight of the handle peeping out from beneath his workbench.

"Oh yeah?" Reb looked self-satisfied. "Ain't it just *brutal*? Did you get a chance to tell Alice about it yet, or do I get to tell her the story myself?"

Alice had run back to her original spot against the wall, as though repositioning herself where Reb had left her would somehow spare her punishment.

"I heard you yelling at him," Reb told her. "*You killed Lucy!*" He squeaked out the words, mocking Alice's grief, then snickered. "But *son of a bitch*?" He cocked his head to the side, giving them a thoughtful look. "How 'bout that. Interestin' choice of words, don't you think?"

Michael shot Alice a look, but he didn't dare turn away from Rebel for long. Alice's terror had faded a notch, just enough to make way for an ounce of confusion.

"You don't get it, do you?" Reb asked her. "Because it's fuckin' *complicated*, that's why. You know how long this thing took to put together? Or maybe you're as stupid as your big brother, here." He nodded to Michael with a snort. "Your momma wasn't all that bright either, so maybe dumb runs in the goddamn family."

"Don't," Michael said, holding up a hand to keep Reb from coming any closer, from saying any more. "You wanna kill me, drive me out to the woods? Okay. Just leave her alone."

"Into the woods?" Reb scoffed. "We're so far out of the woods it's, like, epic. Fuckin' *epic*. Now, what did you do up there?" He nodded up at the ceiling, signifying the house that sat above them. "Did you kill 'em? Chop 'em up like that crazy Lizzie Borden chick, forty whacks and all that?"

Michael swallowed against the thump of his heartbeat, backing up with every forward step Rebel took.

"I hope you did," he said. "I *know* you did. Revenge is hard to resist. I got personal experience with that."

"How?" Michael asked, unable to stop the question from slipping past his lips.

"*How?*" Ray almost sneered at that. "Shit, I don't know, maybe because you killed Lauralynn? You don't remember how it happened? You, sneakin' around, stealin' one of her rabbits, skinnin' that thing in the forest and feedin' it to her for dinner?

Gotta say, that was dark. Hell, maybe you were the one who taught me everythin' I know, not the other way around."

Michael stared at Reb for a long while, not able to process what he was hearing. He remembered the rabbit. Even though it was years ago, he was never able to shake that memory. The remorse that surrounded it kept it from fading like the others. But he had eventually been able to push it to the back of his mind, because at least Lauralynn had gotten out of the house.

"Lauralynn's in North Carolina," he said softly, as though reminding Rebel of what really happened to their big sister.

"Oh, she ain't in fuckin' North Carolina, you stupid shit," Reb snapped, his eyes going black with resentment. "I watched Wade carry her into the woods that night, and the next mornin' she was gone."

Michael opened his mouth to speak, but he didn't know what to say. There had been a moment when he had feared the worst for Lauralynn. But he always managed to convince himself that Grandma Jean and Grandpa Eugene were a better, safer option than home could ever be.

"Though I guess it was better that Claudine bashed her brains in rather than sending her to live with them two psychopaths, to get raped by that dirty old fucker over and over again."

"I . . . I didn't know," Michael croaked, his hands still held out in front of him. He was nearly backed into the corner now. Alice was less than three feet behind him, her breaths coming in quick, terrified hitches. But Rebel refused to stall his steps.

"Don't matter," Reb murmured. "It don't change the fact that you did what you did. You took my sister from me, Mikey. Yeah, it pissed me off that she paid more attention to you than she did to me, but I could have lived with that. I could have roughed you up now and again and made peace with it. But then you went off and got her killed, and what kind of a lovin' brother could let that slide? At first I thought I could take it all out on the girls, but Claudine . . ." He laughed, shook his head. "No, Claudine insisted on girls that looked like her, like Misty, like goddamn *Lauralynn* . . . and you can see how that could *hurt* a guy like me, can't you?"

"Yes." The word was nothing but a dry grunt. Michael had noted the similarity between Momma's girls and Misty Dawn too, but there was no point in questioning Momma's tastes. Momma got what Momma wanted. If she didn't, Misty was at risk. But during all that time, Rebel had been watching her kill Lauralynn over and over again instead, and it had slowly poisoned his already twisted mind.

"Can't blame me for turnin' my interests to other things," Reb said. "Can't blame me for lookin' away from the thing that hurt me and lookin' toward the thing that would hurt *you* instead."

Michael blinked as his shoulder grazed something behind him. Alice yelped as he stepped into her, Rebel cornering them both.

"Hey, Alice," Reb said, a dark smile crossing his face. "I found your long-lost brother for ya, but I think you two have already met."

Michael couldn't breathe.

Alice's mouth formed a surprised *O*.

She stared at Michael, finally putting it all together. Finally realizing that Rebel calling Michael her brother wasn't a euphemism. It was real.

"Not sure you guys will wanna hang out after this, though." Reb shrugged. "He helped me drag your momma out of the house a few nights ago. You know, outta that cute little place in the hills with the green shutters around the windows? He hung her right here." Reb caught the chain hanging from the ceiling, directly above the drain in the floor. "Cut her throat, drained her blood, gutted her. He did that."

Alice's face twisted with a kind of anguish Michael had never seen before. It was all-encompassing, so consuming that it seemed as though it would swallow her whole, tear her open from the inside out.

"And then we had her for dinner," Reb added casually. "Probably still have leftovers, if you're hungry."

His jackal smile curled up at the corners, forming a devil's grin.

Michael's chest heaved.

Rage. It burned his stomach like battery acid.

He knew he should have been devastated, but those emotions had hit him earlier. All he wanted now was to shut Reb up, to never hear his voice or see that hideous expression again.

"So you see, that's the beauty of all this, brother. I tricked you into killin' your own family . . . and then I tricked you into killin' your adoptive family too. Way better than leavin' you in the woods to die, don't you think? You just abandoned yourself."

A low moan drifted up from behind Michael. It was ugly, mingling with a ravaged sob.

Michael wanted to move, but he was frozen in place. No matter how hard he willed himself into action, he couldn't bring himself to step away from Alice and put her in harm's way. He would derail Rebel's plan by standing there forever, and Reb would be wrong—Michael wouldn't have killed his entire family, because Alice would still be alive.

But then Alice's voice grew into a wail, the full understanding of what Reb had just revealed unspooling inside of her. She pressed her hands to her ears and shook her head so violently that Michael was afraid she'd break her own neck. The suffering poured out of her, her cries startling him into motion toward the axe.

Dashing across the basement, he dropped to his knees and skidded against the smooth concrete. He snatched the handle from beneath the worktable with a quick sweep of the hand. Rebel spun around, momentarily caught off guard, and grabbed the knife that Michael had left on the floor.

Stepping back to the thrashing, hysterical girl, Reb grabbed Alice by her short hair, the knife glinting in his grasp. "Go on. Put her outta her misery, Mikey. You killed her momma and her best friend. You ruined her life, man. You think she's ever gonna forgive you for that? You think she's ever gonna want to see your ugly face again?"

Michael hurried to his feet and hefted the axe over his

shoulder, making a run for them both. Rebel blinked, surprised by his younger brother's sudden volition. His grip shifted to the front of Alice's T-shirt, yanking her away from the wall as the axe came down. Had Reb not moved, the blade would have landed square against his chest, but with him gone, it only sparked against the stone wall.

Michael pulled the axe back again and swung. Ray anticipated it this time and dodged it again—but rather than parrying away, he stepped forward, using Alice as a shield. The strategy immediately derailed Michael's attack.

"You always gotta make shit difficult," Reb complained from behind her shoulder. "Don't you get it? It's too late. The damage is already done."

"Your stupid plan . . ." Michael spoke from between short, quick breaths, his grip readjusting along the axe's handle. "It don't make sense, Reb. For it to work, I gotta kill you too."

Alice whimpered between them when Rebel burst into sudden laughter, as though he was at a good party rather than in a basement standoff. For half a second, the sound of cold amusement threw Michael off. It simply didn't belong, an affront to everything that made sense.

"I guess that would be true if I wanted you to win," he said. "Except *that* would be stupid—me thinkin' a loser like you could win anythin'. You think a sorry sack like you could do somethin' right for once?"

Reb's right arm jerked forward, as if punching Alice in the kidney.

Alice's whimpers went quiet.

Michael took a single backward step, and though he couldn't see it, he imagined his own expression matched hers. Shocked. Terrified.

Her black T-shirt didn't offer any clues, but the blood that pooled around the sole of one of her boots was proof that Rebel had just elevated the nightmare to another level. If Michael refused to finish the game, Reb would finish it for him.

Reb's lips pulled away from his teeth. He shoved Alice toward Michael, and she stumbled forward, her face in agony, her hands pressed to her abdomen in bewildered horror. The knife in Reb's hand was stained red nearly up to the hilt, the wet blade winking in the sickly yellow light. Michael's heart threatened to fail as Alice crumpled to the ground at his feet.

"Shoulda known you'd be too yella to take care of business," Reb said. "But this'll work just as well. After she dies"—he nodded toward Alice with a smirk—"you won't wanna live anyway. Dig a hole big enough for the both of you, brother. Dump her in first, kill yourself after; a regular Romeo and Juliet. It's so fuckin' poetic, Misty woulda loved it if she wasn't already dead."

Rebel expected Michael to drop the axe and help her, and Michael wanted to. Alice's cries were tearing him apart. But he fought the urge harder than anything in his life, and instead of collapsing next to her, a roar ripped from his chest.

He fell into a run, the axe cutting an arc through the air.

Rebel ducked to make himself smaller and rushed forward as well, slamming his shoulder into Michael's stomach, knocking him off balance. The knife slid across the meat of Michael's thigh, cutting deep through denim and flesh, but Michael swung again. He ignored the searing heat of his wound, pushed past the river of hot blood that pumped down the length of his leg and pooled into his boot. The axe made contact this time, catching Rebel on the shoulder. The knife tumbled from Reb's hand, and he would have easily retrieved it had he not spun away to avoid another one of Michael's attacks. And yet despite the red that soaked into his shirt, he was grinning as if savoring the pain.

"It shoulda been like this from the beginnin', you know," Reb said, winded. "The night I saw what you did out there, stealin' that rabbit—you and me, to the death. An eye for an eye."

That was when he pulled something from his back pocket. His switchblade. It slid into place with a smooth *click*. Rebel lunged, the switchblade held at arm's length. The knife caught Michael across the middle, but before Reb could hammer it home, his eyes went wide with surprise. His foot skated out from beneath him on a streak of Alice's freshly spilled blood. The knife flew from his right hand while his left grabbed for the axe in Michael's grasp, either to steal it away or simply break his fall. The handle slid from Michael's hand, the blade hitting the floor next to Reb's prostrate frame.

Michael moved fast.

He dropped to his knees, shoved the switchblade away, and grabbed the kitchen knife Reb had previously dropped with both hands. He whipped around so quickly that he didn't know whether Reb would still be lying there or not, and brought the blade down with such force that he felt the tip of the knife crack hard against concrete. Reb stared up at Michael with a look of surprise, as if stunned that the coward before him had enough guts to go through with one last kill. When Michael finally looked away from his face, he found his hands cupped against his brother's chest. The knife was buried far enough into Rebel's flesh that it was hardly visible from beneath Michael's hands.

Rebel coughed. A faraway grin pulled his face taut. The fingers of his left hand spider-walked across the concrete, searching for the handle of his switchblade or the axe he knew had to be somewhere close. Michael pulled the knife from Reb's chest, ready to stab him again, but there was no need. As soon as the blade came free, a wheezing sound escaped Rebel's chest— like air leaving a balloon. The rush of blood that followed from both sides of the wound left Michael staring in morbid awe. Reb's face went ashen. He looked at Michael with a strange sort of confusion, as if bewildered by the fact that their battle had come to such a quick end. Baffled that Michael had actually won. He opened his mouth to say something, but he coughed again instead. Blood erupted from between his lips and stained his chin. His head dropped to the ground a moment later, his skull thumping against the bare basement floor.

Michael backed away from the body. He swallowed hard, the knife still held fast in his trembling hands. For a moment, he couldn't look away. He couldn't tear his eyes from the man who had been difficult and cruel but who had been one of his only friends in life. What lay before him was falsehood personified. Rebel had never cared, and Michael had never belonged.

But his rage dissipated into the dull ache of sorrow anyway. He couldn't shake the heartsick feeling that overwhelmed him. Regardless of how he had come to be a Morrow, it was impossible to forget his life with them. Despite their insanity, they had still been his family.

Michael crouched down, Reb's blood pooling around his shoes. He reached out to brush his hand across his brother's open eyes. He abandoned the kitchen knife, replacing it with Reb's switchblade. For as long as Michael could remember, that knife was probably the only thing Rebel ever really cared about. But, like Momma, Reb wasn't entirely at fault. He'd been led by the hand by grief, overwhelmed by the sadness he hadn't been allowed to feel, the anguish he hadn't been able to express.

Michael turned his head away, unable to look at Reb's lifeless face any longer. Pushing his heartache aside, he had to focus on the only thing he had left. Alice.

Expecting to see her dead only yards away, his nerves buzzed when he looked to where she had folded in on herself and found that she wasn't there.

There was blood on the steps leading out of the basement. Somewhere overhead in the darkness, Alice was running in the opposite direction of the Morrow farmhouse, slowly bleeding to death.

He bolted up the stairs and careened into the heat of the night. His injured leg tingled, as if half-asleep, red-hot needle pricks biting at the flesh beneath his jeans. The sweltering temperature served up a fresh helping of vertigo. He had to hold onto the side of the house until his head stopped spinning, until the fireworks ceased exploding behind his eyes.

When he finally got moving again, he had no idea which way to go. Alice could have run anywhere. The trees would have given her cover, but the road leading away from the house gave a false promise of salvation. If she had any idea how far they were from the state highway, she would have broken beneath an onslaught of hysterical desperation.

The rutted dirt road was enveloped in shadow, but it wasn't dark enough to conceal the blots of black that dappled the path. She was hard to see—a good eighth of a mile ahead of him on the straightaway. Her black jeans and shirt rendered her nearly invisible, nothing but a pair of pale and disembodied arms floating in the air. She stumbled, her wrists still bound with tape. Catching herself mid-fall, her palms pressed against the hard-packed earth. She tried to get up but only managed to stagger forward a few feet, then ended up on all fours once more.

When she shot a look over her shoulder, Michael slowed his steps. He didn't want to scare her any further, but that didn't seem to matter. Despite his slow approach, Alice began to sob as she rose. Tapping into a reserve of determination, she began to run.

"Alice, wait!"

Michael fell into a jog after her. He pressed his hand against his wounded thigh, his jeans slick and warm with blood. Bleeding to death wasn't only a possibility for her. Footfall after agonizing footfall, Michael started to think it was a reality for him as well.

He gritted his teeth and increased his pace, pushing himself into a flat-out run despite the pain. He had to save her. Had to redeem himself so that she'd know, whether he lived or died, that he had never meant for any of this to happen.

When he caught her by the arm, Alice began to scream. She tore out of his grip, her face a mask of frenzied indignation.

"Wait," he said, his words nearly swallowed whole by her cries. "Alice, please!"

But she wasn't listening. She turned around and around, her eyes impossibly wide, searching the night for some form of defense. Startled by the pool of blood that was gathering at her feet, Michael made another grab for her, but she ran on, her boots clomping against the dirt. She tripped, crashed to the ground. He dropped to his knees beside her as her arms flailed above her head, warbled yelps of refusal tearing from her throat. That was when he realized he was still holding Rebel's switchblade. The knife glistened dark and wet in the moonlight.

Seizing her wrists, he caught the edge of the tape with the tip of the blade and cut through her bonds. Then he dropped his weapon to the road, ashamed that he had been chasing her *with a knife in his hand* all while expecting her to not be afraid.

Her hands flew apart, the strip of tape still clinging to her right wrist. But the fact that he had freed her failed to give her pause. Her hysteria overpowered reason. She continued to fight him off.

"I'm sorry," he said, struggling to catch her flailing hands. "I'm sorry, Alice, I'm sorry."

He wanted her to understand, was desperate for her to say something, anything that would assure him that she understood—this wasn't his plan, it had never been. But she continued to shriek, her hands fluttering above her head in a tangle.

"Please stop," he begged. "Just listen to me. I just wanna tell you—"

"You killed Lucy!"

"I had to," he insisted. "I swear, I never would have if—"

"*You killed my mother!*" she screamed up to the sky. "You *killed her* and you killed my best friend and now I have *no one!*" Her frantic despair shifted in a way Michael had seen before. Her own words sank in deep, and suddenly she was drowning in an ocean of self-realization and defeat. All the fight drained out of her as she crouched in the middle of the road. She pressed her hands to her stomach and wept.

Michael wanted to believe that she was different from the rest, but she looked just like the other girls as she gave up hope.

"I trusted you," she sobbed. "I thought you were special."

He winced at her words. No amount of explanation would ever come close to describing how he felt. He wanted to sweep her up into his arms and hold her for the rest of his life, wanted to apologize a million times in a million different languages, to hopefully strike a chord. And at the same time, he wanted to grab her by the shoulders and shake her until she went quiet. Because why couldn't she understand? Why did she refuse to listen, to see that he wasn't hacking her to pieces but releasing her back into the world? He had killed for her. He had destroyed his own life to make up for annihilating hers.

He stepped away from her to make it clear that he wouldn't touch her, that he meant her no harm. Turning his back to her, Michael lowered himself to the ground and stared at the bank of trees lining the side of the road. His mind drifted a mile away to Misty Dawn. If he was going to die, he wanted it to be on that hilltop next to her, watching the sun rise over the vista of endless tree-covered hills. Of all the people in his life, he had meant to hurt Misty and Alice least—and yet, he had done them the most harm.

"I never meant any of this," he said softly. "I didn't know."

If, on the day he had walked into the Dervish, he had been aware that this was his future, Michael would have let Rebel kill him before he had ever learned Alice's name. He would have killed himself before he would have helped Reb drag Alice's mom, *his* mom, out of her home like a sacrificial lamb. He would have killed Reb long ago if he had seen this coming, be it in a dream, or a nightmare, or a flash of divine telepathy.

Sitting in the middle of the road, he twisted to look back at Alice, three words balanced upon the tip of his tongue. But he faltered when she came into view.

Having gathered herself off the ground, she held the switchblade in her shaking, bloodied hands. He pulled in a shallow breath, his gaze flitting between the blade and her eyes.

"I'm your brother," he whispered.

Something about saying that aloud made him feel at peace.

He hoped it would bring her some comfort, some assurance that he was on her side. But rather than rocking back on her heels and letting the switchblade slip from her hands, she leaned into him—as if to give her long-lost sibling a hug—and buried the knife deep in his gut.

He gave a quiet grunt as a searing pain spread just beneath his ribs, but he didn't jerk away. Rather, he eased into Alice's arms, his own blood-sticky fingers drifting across the slope of her milk-white cheek. Gazing up at her, he admired her beauty, so strong it refused to wither beneath a veil of horror and pain. Her bowed mouth. Her big eyes. The way her skin seemed to glow in the moonlight. She was his Fate, delivering him from a life of horror, saving him from himself.

He tasted copper and winced when she pulled the blade free. She pushed him away and he fell back to sit slouched in the road—nothing but a broken-down Tin Man, wishing he had a heart. The knife fell from Alice's hand with a soft *clink* into the dirt. She lurched to her feet, the palms of her hands pressed over her own wound.

"I was going to run away with you," she said. "Now I'm just running away."

Michael tipped onto his side as she left him behind in the darkness.

Pain metastasized from the center of his torso outward to his limbs like a fast-moving cancer, but he hardly felt it. He was too busy watching Alice limp her way down the road toward the Delta in the distance, leaving him to wonder what it would have been like to have been an older brother. How different things would have been if he had spent mornings around the kitchen table, laughing with his parents and his sister over bowls of Apple Jacks and stacks of pancakes. How it would have felt to watch movies in the living room, lying on the carpet with his chin propped up in his hands and a golden retriever or collie sleeping next to him on the floor. He imagined tearing into Christmas gifts, surrounded by his true family. Imagined how it would have felt to lie on a blanket in the grass and stare up at the fireworks every Fourth of July; a million fractured sparkles drifting back down to earth like falling stars.

But mostly he wondered if, growing up, Alice had been the type of girl to dance and twirl in her room just like Misty Dawn had.

Dancing and twirling despite the madness.

Despite the darkness.

Despite it all.

His eyes momentarily fluttered shut, but he fought the sudden urge to sleep. Opening them again, he saw Alice in the distance. She was only a few hundred feet from the car now, but her steps had slowed. She doubled over, pulling her hands away from her torso to stare at her palms. They shimmered wet and slick in the moonlight.

Michael willed her to keep going. To not give up. To fight.

She had to make it, or it was all for nothing.

She had to get to the car, or Rebel would win, even in death.

The world began to go dark and soft around the edges. For a moment he was sure that the shadows around the trees had come to life, slithering outward to consume them both. The night blossomed into grays and whites, like an overexposed photograph. The trees glowed niveous and pale. Alice's ghostly skin shone ethereal as she desperately lumbered on toward the Oldsmobile, her arms wrapped tight around her waist. He could hear her distant, muffled sobs. He closed his eyes and imagined it was joy instead of sorrow. Him and her. Hand in hand. Laughing like kids.

And just as the world was about to fade, he felt his heart stop. Felt the world collapse. Felt himself dying as the hard bite of an eight-ball dug into his hip.

Because the keys to the Olds were still in his pocket.

They were still in his fucking pocket as Alice's fingers drifted across the handle of the Delta's driver-side door.

ACKNOWLEDGMENTS

My thanks go to all of the people who made this book possible: To my rock-star literary agent, David Hale Smith, who believed enough in this manuscript—and, I suppose, in *me*—to pitch *Brother* to "the big boys." There aren't enough clever T-shirts in the world to express my gratitude. Carpe grillem, good sir. To my fabulous editor, Ed Schlesinger—I'm now absolutely convinced that I'm in the company of a pop-culture expert. To put your mind at ease, I really *do* know the difference between an LP and a twelve-inch single. But details, right? To my husband and partner in crime, Will, thanks for getting frustrated at the powers-that-be when it felt like I was putting in twelve hour days, and for reminding me to stand up for myself (and my sanity) when I was on the edge of the edge. Don't hassle me. I might smash some plates.

To Robert Smith and his incredible band, the Cure, who will absolutely never ever read this tidbit of gratitude . . . thanks for singing me through high school and, as it's becoming quite clear now, continuing to inspire my weirdness with *your* weirdness. I couldn't have picked a better role model for dark and spooky oddity. I mean, seriously, it's pretty perfect. To Jennifer Chambers Lynch, Damian O'Donnell, and the cast of the incredible 2012 film *Chained*—a lot of people will read this and think *The Texas Chain Saw Massacre*, but that's inaccurate. It was *Chained* that inspired me to write this book. And I hope that my mentioning it here will give your fabulous film a little extra exposure. Because, *man* . . . so good, and so underrated.

And of course, there would be no book if it wasn't for you, my readers. I love you, and I will continue to toil away in the dungeon for the sake of your entertainment. Until next time.